Brave the Wild Wind

Also available in Large Print
by Johanna Lindsey:

A Gentle Feuding

Brave the Wild Wind

Johanna Lindsey

G.K. HALL & CO.
Boston, Massachusetts
1985

Copyright © 1984 by Johanna Lindsey

Published in Large Print by arrangement with
Avon Books.

British Commonwealth Rights courtesy of Judy Piatkus
Limited

G. K. Hall Large Print Book Series.

Library of Congress Cataloging in Publication Data

Lindsey, Johanna.
  Brave the wild wind.

  ''Published in large print by arrangement with Avon
Books''—Verso of t.p.
  1. Large type books. I. Title.
[PS3562.I5123B7 1985   813'.54   85–8704
ISBN 0–8161–3909–1 (lg. print)

For my brother Michael, with love

Prologue

1863, Wyoming Territory.

Thomas Blair paused on a hill overlooking the valley where his ranch nestled among juniper and pine, his eyes glowing with pride. The house was only three rooms, and made of logs, but it would stand up to the blizzards of winter. Rachel claimed she didn't mind the harsh home he'd brought her to. After all, they'd started the ranch only two years ago. There would be time to build Rachel a huge house, a place she could be proud of.

How patient she was, his beautiful young wife. And how he worshiped her. She was the epitome of goodness, beauty, and virtue. Because of Rachel and the ranch that Thomas now knew would thrive, he had everything he wanted out of life. Everything. Well . . . Well not quite everything. There was still the matter of a son that one daughter and two miscarriages had robbed him of. He didn't blame Rachel, though. She had tried, uncomplaining at all times. It was Jessica he resented for not being the son he had prayed for, especially so because he had mistaken her for a boy during the whole first week of her life. He'd even had her baptized Kenneth, Kenneth Jesse Blair. The widow Johnson, who had helped with the birthing when the doctor couldn't be found, had been too afraid of Thomas to tell him the truth once he began assuming the baby was a boy. And Rachel, who had nearly died and was so weak she could hardly feed the baby, also assumed she had given him a son.

It was a shock to both of them when Mrs. Johnson could no longer bear the situation and confessed the truth. How bitter he had been! He had never wanted to lay eyes on the baby again. And he never did warm to her, never forgave her for being a female.

That had been eight years before, in St. Louis. Thomas had married Rachel the year before, and she talked him into settling down there. For her he had given up the mountains and the plains of the West, where he had spent most of his life trapping, scouting, and hauling supplies to winderness forts.

St. Louis was too civilized, too confined for a man used to the splendor of the Rocky Mountains, the awesome quiet of the plains. But he stuck it out for six years, running the supply

2

store Rachel's parents had left her. For six years he supplied the settlers who were heading west, to *his* West, *his* wide open spaces. It was not until gold was discovered in Colorado and the Oregon Territory that he got the idea of supplying beef to the mining camps and towns that were spreading over the land he knew so well.

He might have let the idea die, but for Rachel's encouragement. She had never known hardship, never slept on an open plain, but Rachel loved him and knew he was unhappy living in the city. Although she didn't like it, she agreed to sell the store and was willing to wait for Thomas for the year it took him to start the ranch, to gather the wild steers of Texas that were there for the taking, to buy the stockier eastern cattle to crossbreed, to build them a house. At long last, he'd brought Rachel out there to live, letting her name the ranch Rocky Valley.

Rachel's only request before starting a wholly alien life was that their daughter be given the education she would have received if they'd stayed in St. Louis. She wanted Jessica left in the private academy for young ladies she'd been attending since the age of five. Thomas readily agreed to that, not caring particularly if he never saw his daughter again.

His daughter called herself K. Jessica Blair. Jessica, as Rachel had nicknamed her, let anyone who didn't see her name written down assume the *K* was not an initial but the name

Kay. Having the name Kenneth was a dreadful mortification for the doll-like creature she had become. With hair as black as an eagle's wing and eyes the color of turquoise, she was the spitting image of Thomas and therefore a constant reminder of his longing for a son.

But all that was about to change. Rachel was pregnant again, and because the hardest part of starting a new life was over, he could devote more time to her. His cattle had survived two winters and multiplied, and he had met with complete success on the first drive to Virginia City, where he'd sold every head for twice what he could have gotten in St. Louis. Now he was home, much sooner than he had told Rachel to expect him, eager to tell her of his success. So eager, in fact, that he had left his three men behind at Ft. Laramie.

He wanted to surprise Rachel, to delight her with his success, to make love to her for the rest of the day without interruption. He'd been gone for nearly a month. How he'd missed her!

Thomas started down the hill, picturing the look of surprise and joy on Rachel's face when she saw him. No one was outside. Will Phengle and his old friend Jeb Hart, whom Thomas had left behind to look out for things, would be out on the Shoshone range with the herd at this time of day. And the Shoshome half-breed he called Kate would be busy in the kitchen.

The main room of the house was empty. There was a delightful odor of baked apples and cinnamon from the kitchen, and he saw a pie on the kitchen table, but there was no Kate. It was so quiet that he decided Rachel was taking a nap in the big bed they had shipped from St. Louis. He left his guns by the front door so they wouldn't be in the way, and slowly, quietly, Thomas opened the door to his bedroom, hoping not to wake his lovely, golden-haired Rachel just yet.

But she wasn't sleeping. The sight that met Thomas was so utterly incredible that he just stood, frozen, in the doorway. What he saw was the whole of his dream shattering, his wife making love to Will Phengle, her legs beneath him, her arms clasped around him. Thankfully, her face was hidden beneath Will.

"Easy, woman." Will's deep chuckle bounded off the walls as his hips ground into hers. "There's no hurry. God, you're starved for it, ain't you?"

A deep sound started in Thomas, a low rumble that erupted into a savage growl so chilling, it stopped all movement on the bed.

"I'll kill you! I'll kill you both!"

Will Phengle was off the bed in a flash, grabbing his scattered clothes from the floor. Seeing the empty doorway, he knew Thomas Blair had gone for a gun. He was a dead man.

"There is no need to run, Will. He only need see he is —"

"Are you crazy, woman!" Will cried. "That man will shoot first and then look. You stay and explain if you're lookin' to die, but I'm gone!'' Before he even finished he was climbing out of the narrow window.

Through the red haze blinding him, Thomas finally got back to the bedroom. Instantly he fired off two shots from the rifle. When the haze cleared, he saw that the bed was empty. So was the rest of the room. He heard a horse galloping away and ran outside, emptying the rifle at the naked form of Will Phengle riding bareback. The last shot missed along with the others.

"Rachel!" Thomas bellowed as he reloaded the rifle. "You won't be as lucky as he was! Rachel!" He looked around the yard and back at the house, then started running toward the stable. "You can't hide from me, Rachel!"

She was not in the stable, either. And the more he looked, the more enraged he became. Coldly and without the slightest hesitation, he shot the two horses in the stable and then went back to the front of the house and shot his own horse.

"We'll see if you can escape now, Rachel!" he hollered at the sky, his voice echoing through the whole valley. "You'll never get away from here without a horse. Do you hear me, whore? You're going to die by my hand or die on the range, but you're dead to me already!"

Then he went back into the house and proceeded to get roaring drunk. As the rotgut took effect, his rage turned to heartache, then to rage again. Every so often he would get up and look out the windows to see if he could see his wife. As he got more and more drunk, he thought he could finally understand the Indians' drive for vengeance. The Cheyenne and Sioux he had traded with and become friends with had sometimes lived for revenge, died for it, going without rest until it was exacted. He understood that now. Drunk, he understood slowly — but he understood.

When Jeb came in from the range late that afternoon and demanded to know who had killed the horses and where the women were, Thomas wouldn't explain. At gunpoint he insisted Jeb ride for Ft. Laramie to intercept Thomas's men and turn them back for a week or so. Jeb, too, was to stay away. He tossed Jeb the gold he had gotten for the herd, caring about nothing but his privacy.

Jeb wasn't going to argue with a drunken man, especially one with a gun in his hand. He had known Thomas Blair for nearly thirty years, and he never thought the women might be in danger alone with Thomas. So he left.

And Thomas waited, and drank more. At one point he remembered Kate and wondered where she had gone, but he didn't give her much thought. He had never given the Indian girl much thought. She was the daughter of Old Frenchy and a Shoshone squaw, and Frenchy had asked Thomas to look out for her if anything happened to him. It did, and Thomas found the girl at the fort supply depot, whoring for the soldiers there. So he took her in, and it worked out fine, Kate being grateful for a home and Rachel needing the help Kate could give her.

Thomas didn't think about Kate much, and never even saw all the longing, hopeful looks she turned his way. He had never paid attention to what was clearly in her eyes. His eyes had always been only for Rachel, even after all these years.

He waited and waited. Not in vain. She entered the house just as the sun was setting, and Thomas was on her before she could say a word. He hit her and hit her and wouldn't stop, screaming at her, giving her no chance to answer the accusations he heaped on her along with each blow. And after a time she couldn't answer anyway, for her tongue was lacerated and her jaw broken. Two fingers and her left wrist were broken from trying to block his fists. Her eyes were blurred and swelled quickly, and when she crumbled to the floor he began to use his feet on her. A rib broke before he stopped. She didn't know why he stopped, but suddenly he did.

"Get out," she heard after an agoinizing silence. "If you live, I want never to lay eyes on you again. If you don't, I'll bury you decently. But get out now before I finish what I started."

Jeb's curiosity had gotten the best of him, and he returned to the ranch that night, something nagging at the back of his mind. He found Rachel just over the top of the north hill that formed the little valley. That was as far as she'd gotten before losing consciousness. Jeb didn't learn until later what had happened to her and why. At the moment he knew only that if she didn't get help she would die, and the nearest doctor was a good two days' ride.

Chapter 1

1873, Wyoming Territory.

Blue Parker saw her coming a mile away, trotting along on that big-boned Appaloosa she'd come home with last year. A mean-tempered horse if there ever was one. But then, Jessica Blair was pretty feisty, too. Oh, not always. Sometimes she was the sweetest lady, a kind-hearted angel. She had a way of bringing out a man's protective instincts, turning a man's heart clear inside out.

Blue's heart had been lost the very first time she'd smiled at him, flashing her lovely white teeth in a warm grin. Two years ago it'd been, the day he'd come to work for her father, signing on as an extra hand for the fall roundup. He'd stayed on after the roundup, and he'd come to know Jessie well, working alongside her. He'd come to love her — come to hate her at times, too, the times when she'd close up to him and everyone else. Or when she'd fight with her father and take it out on anyone close at hand. She could be cruel then, though Blue doubted it was ever intentional. Her bitterness sometimes made her lash out, that was all. Jessica Blair had not had an easy life. He sure wanted to make it easier for her, but when he'd gotten up the nerve to ask her hand in marriage, she'd thought he was joking.

She was drawing closer, and she spotted Blue and waved. He held his breath, hoping she would stop. He'd seen her so seldom lately. Ever since her father had died she'd stopped working on the range . . . until last week, when *they* had arrived. Blue had never seen her so mad. She'd stormed out of the house and nearly killed her horse riding him so hard.

Jessie stopped, leaning forward in the saddle, resting her arms on the horn. She gave Blue a half-grin. "Jeb spotted some mavericks by the creek south of here yesterday. How about giving me a hand with them, Blue?"

She knew what his answer would be, and as he nodded, his face lighting up with pleasure, her grin widened. She was feeling reckless today. She had passed several other hands but hadn't asked them for help, wanting to find Blue instead.

Full of daring, she challenged, "I'll race you there, and you'll owe me a kiss if I win."

"You're on, gal!"

The creek was only a few miles away. Of course Jessie had won. Even if Blue's sorrel had been as good as Blackstar, Blue wouldn't have let him win.

Jessie had given the race her all, letting out some of the tension coiled inside her in an ever-tightening knot. Winded, she dismounted and fell into the high grass along the creek bed, laughing. Blue was there a moment later to forfeit his kiss, a forfeit that couldn't have made him gladder.

This is what Jessie had wanted all along, this and more she told herself rebelliously. Blue's kissing was nice. But then, she'd known it would be because he'd kissed her once before, in the spring, and she'd liked it. It had been her first kiss. Other men wanted to kiss her, she knew that, but she was the boss's daughter, and they were afraid of both her quick temper and his anger. So none of them dared. But Blue had dared. She hadn't minded at all.

He was a fine-looking man, Blue Parker, with his golden hair and brown eyes, deeply expressive eyes that told her how much he liked her. Most men looked at her the way Blue did, even though her femininity was hidden beneath the male attire her father had insisted she wear.

Her father. Her mood plummeted with thoughts of him.

Just months ago she had been despondent over how alone she was in the world. Yet now she wasn't alone anymore, and she hated that even worse. Whatever had possessed her father to write the letter that had brought *them* to the ranch? She had seen the letter, and she knew her father's handwriting well enough. But why had he done it?

The inconceivability of Thomas Blair asking for help from the person he hated above all others! Hadn't Jessie known that hatred for the last ten years? Hadn't she learned to hate, too, because of his hating?

But her father *had* written that letter. And then he had died, and the letter had been delivered as his will directed. They had come then, and put an end to Jessie's newfound freedom. And she couldn't do anything about it, for her father had arranged it.

It was wholly unjust! Jessie didn't need a guardian. After all, her father had made certain she could take care of herself. She had learned to hunt, to ride — to shoot better than most men! She knew all the aspects of ranching and could, in fact, run the ranch just as well as her father had run it.

Blue was sitting a little ways off, knowing she needed to think. She was remembering the first eight years of her life, before her father took her out of boarding school and brought her to his ranch. He'd forced her to understand the truth about her mother, but she had still loved him even so. Perhaps she had never stopped loving him, even when she hated him. Hadn't she grieved horribly when he died? Hadn't she wanted to kill the man who shot him? But, still, there had been the realization that his death meant her freedom. It was not the way she had hoped to win it, but she had, nonetheless, the chance to be what she really was — not what Thomas Blair had made her into. Now freedom was being denied her *again*.

She had to admit to herself that, suddenly, what she had always wanted was taking second place to her desire to shock them, to show them what Thomas had made of her. She wanted *her* to feel bad, to feel guilty, to believe Jessica wild and immoral. To that end, Jessie had hidden all the beautiful dresses she had only just brought home, all the perfume and ribbons and jewelry she had finally been able to buy for herself. And she had sought out Blue, wanting him to make love to her so that *she* would find out and be shocked.

Thinking about it brought her mind back to Blue. He had crept closer, and as she turned to him he kissed her again, urgently this time. Her blue cotton shirt seemed to open all by itself while they kissed, and she was startled to feel his hand touching her breasts. Should she stop him?

The sound of a man clearing his throat saved Jessie from having to stop Blue. She was grateful, but she realized how this would look to the hired hand who had come upon them. She prayed it was only Jeb, who would understand.

14

Cautiously, she looked over Blue's shoulder, then felt heat rushing to her face. He was a stranger, the man on the beautiful palomino horse. The man was looking down at them with outrageous amusement in every line of his chiseled dark face. He was young and, *damn,* the handsomest man she had ever seen. She was unreasonably mortified. Oh, why wouldn't he stop staring?

Blue started to get up, terribly embarrassed, but Jessie grabbed on to his shirt, giving him a furious look. He had nearly revealed her state of undress to the intruder. Blue's color heightened, and he grinned sheepishly. Jessie continued to glare at him while she pulled her shirt together. Done, she pushed at him to get up, and they both scrambled to their feet. Blue turning to face the man while Jessie hid behind him.

"I'm sorry to interrupt," the man said in a deep voice that clearly indicated he wasn't sorry at all but found the situation highly entertaining. "I could sure use a little help, so I stopped to talk to you."

"What kind of help?" Blue asked.

"I'm looking for the Rocky Valley and a Mrs. Ewing. They told me in Cheyenne I would find the ranch after a day's ride north, but I had no luck yesterday or today. Could you tell me if I'm heading in the right direction?"

"You, ouch —!"

"— are trespassing, mister," Jessie finished

15

for Blue after pinching him into silence. She stepped out from behind him, her embarrassment gone as anger took hold. "And you're a long way from the Rocky Valley."

Chase Summers eyed the girl standing before him so belligerently. He was taken aback by her sudden hostility. After the situation he'd found her in, he hadn't expected her to be quite so young. She looked fourteen or fifteen, just a kid, young enough to get away with wearing pants. An older girl wouldn't dare dress that way. And the man looked to be in his early twenties, too old to be taking advantage of a child.

But it was none of Chase's business. His expression didn't change, not even when the girl's blue-green eyes shot daggers at him. Damn pretty she was, and those unusual eyes were stunning.

"But —" Blue began, but she jumped behind him once more, pinching him again.

"I didn't know I was trespassing," Chase offered. "If you'll just point me in the right direction, I'll move on."

"Just keep riding north, mister," Jessie answered, and warned sharply, "and don't come back this way. We don't like strangers crossing our land."

"I'll remember that," Chase replied. Then he nodded thanks and crossed the creek, riding on.

Jessie stared after him, glaring at his back for some time before she sensed Blue staring at her

16

in the same way. His expression was a mix of confusion and anger, and she quickly looked away. Reaching down for her gun belt, she strapped it on, refusing to look at him.

"Just a minute, gal." Blue caught her arm when she picked up her hat and started for her horse. "What the hell was that all about?"

She tried to shrug it off. "I don't like strangers."

"What's that got to do with lying?" he demanded.

Jessie jerked her arm out of his grasp and faced him, her eyes flashing with all the fury pent up inside her. Blue nearly forgot his anger then, for she was something to behold, her eyes lit up with blue-green fire, breasts heaving, her long braid flung over her shoulder, the braid end touching her narrow hip. Her right hand rested on her gun, and although he doubted she would really shoot him, the threat was there, and he didn't try to grab her again.

"Jessie, I don't understand. If you'll just tell me what's made you so angry?"

"Everything!" she snapped. "You! Him!"

"I know what I did, but —"

"What you did you'd better never try again, Blue Parker!"

He frowned. She didn't mean that. He wasn't about to give her up, anyway. But it would be a good idea to get her mind on something else for a while.

"Well, what'd he do? Why'd you lie to him?"

"You heard who he was looking for."

"So?"

"You think I can't guess why he's looking for her?"

Blue followed her drift. "You don't know anything for sure."

Jessie drew herself up. "Don't I? He was too good-looking. He's got to be one of her lovers, and I'll be damned if I'll let him come to my ranch and carry on with her under my roof!"

And just what're you gonna do when he finds out you lied to him and comes back?"

Jessie was too mad to give it any thought. "Who's to say he'll be back? He's probably from the city, like she is. He probably couldn't find his way out of a hole in the ground," she added contemptuously. "Didn't you see how packed his saddlebags were? He's the type who can't survive without store-bought goods. If he reaches Fort Laramie or gets back to Cheyenne, he won't be eager to venture out on the range again, where the nearest store is days away. He'll go back where he came from and wait for her to come to him — which can't happen soon enough for me."

Blue shook his head. "You sure do hate her."

"Yes, I hate her!"

"It ain't natural, Jessie," he said softly. "She's your mother."

"She's not!" Jessie stepped back as if he had struck her. "She's not! My *mother* wouldn't have deserted me. She wouldn't have let Thomas

Blair turn me into the son he wanted. My mother died here. That woman is nothing but a whore. She never gave a damn about me.''

"Maybe you're just hurting, Jessie," he said kindly.

Jessie wanted to cry. Hurting? How many times had she cried herself to sleep because there was no one there to soften the pain of her life, a life she hated. Hadn't it all been because of her mother? Every single thing her father did was to spite the whore, as he'd called her mother. He had denied Jessie boarding school because her mother had wanted her to be educated. He had denied her anything feminine because her mother had wanted her to be a lady. He had made her what she was because he knew her mother would hate her. Irrationally, he had gone into debt to build a house fit for a queen, done it solely because it was what her mother would have loved and could never have.

"I passed the point of being hurt long ago, Blue," Jessie said in a quiet voice. "I haven't needed her for a long time, and I certainly don't need her now."

Before her tears spilled, Jessie ran to her horse and took off. She didn't mind crying, she just didn't want anyone to see her at it. She rode south, away from the ranch, away from the cause of her tears.

Chapter 2

When Jessie rode into the yard, the sun was setting, the sky to the west streaked with dark reds and violets beyond the mountains. Light streamed onto the porch at the front of the sprawling ranch house, so she rode to the back, where she could enter the house through the kitchen and not be seen. She dismounted and sent Blackstar off to the stable with a soft word and a pat on his backside. He would go directly to his stall and wait for her to come and rub him down. She was famished, had been for hours, and just wanted a little something to take the edge off her hunger before she bedded her horse down for the night.

Blackstar wouldn't mind waiting just a few more minutes. Blackstar never balked at anything Jessie did. He would nip at other people and evey try to get in a few good kicks once in a while, but he was an angel with Jessie. White

Thunder had known he would be gentle with her when he gave the stallion to her. White Thunder had a way with horses that no one could match, and he had raised Blackstar from a colt, raising him just for Jessie. She had never guessed that secret, though. All the time she had thought she was just helping her friend train a horse.

It was such a generous gift. Horses were a sign of wealth among the Indians, and it wasn't as if White Thunder had very many horses. But White Thunder was like that. Blackstar was not the only gift he had given her in the years he had been her friend. He was her closest friend really, next to old Jeb. Blackstar meant the world to her because of their friendship. Just thinking about that, watching the horse trot off toward the stable, she almost forgot about food. But her stomach reminded her, and she stepped into the darkened kitchen and closed the door quietly behind her.

The smells of dinner lingered in the large room, and Jessie looked forward to coming back later and having a big plate of Kate's stew. She scanned the counters for something to pick on quickly, and when she spotted a plate of fresh sourdough bread, she grinned. But then she heard her mother's voice coming from the front room down the hall, and the smile died. She tore off a chunk of bread and started to leave. Then she heard another voice.

She stopped where she was, staring at the

open door leading to the hall. She couldn't have heard right. It wasn't *that* voice, was it? She edged closer to the door, then crept a few feet down the hall, pausing by her bedroom. She could hear the voice distinctly, and her face flamed with color as she recalled the scene. Damn and double damn, to be caught in a lie!

She inched her way closer to the large main room, having to tiptoe because of her riding boots with their two-inch heels. Thank goodness she never wore spurs on Blackstar! She poked her head around the corner until she could see the whole room, the room filled with all the rich things that had put Thomas Blair into debt, debts Jessie had inherited.

Sitting side by side on the thickly padded sofa, their backs to Jessie, were her mother and the stranger. Jessie stared at them for a moment. He had removed his hat, revealing dark chestnut hair that curled on his neck.

"I can't imagine who the girl could be, Chase," Rachel was saying. "But I've only been here a week, and I haven't met any of Jessica's neighbors yet."

"If they're all as hostile as that promiscuous chit, then you would do well not to bother. If I hadn't met up with one of the ranch hands and gotten turned back in the right direction, I'd be sleeping out on the range again. One night of that was enough, thank you."

Rachel laughed. "I take it you've been sticking pretty close to civilization since I last saw you."

"If you can call the cow towns of Kansas civilization." Chase shook his head. "But any hotel room and any hot meal beat a lonely camp fire any day."

"Well, I'm glad you got here. When I sent those telegrams, I wasn't sure they'd get to you. You've always moved around so much. And, anyway, I wasn't sure you would come."

"Didn't I say if you ever needed me just to send word?"

"I know. But neither of us thought I would take you up on it. I didn't anyway."

"You don't like to ask for help." It was a statement.

"How well you know me." Rachel laughed softly, and the sound grated on Jessie's nerves.

"So what's the problem, lady?" Chase asked.

Jessie stiffened. She didn't like the tender way he spoke.

"I'm not really sure, Chase," Rachel was saying hesitantly. "At least . . . it's not any-thing specific yet. What I mean is, I may have asked for your help unnecessarily. I mean . . ."

"Hold on," Chase said abruptly. "It's not like you to beat around the bush, Rachel."

"It's just that I would feel terrible if I'd brought you up here for nothing."

"You can forget that right now. Whether there is anything to what's troubling you or not, I was glad to come. There was nothing holding me in Abilene, and it was time I moved on,

23

anyway. Let's just call this a visit that was long overdue, and if there is anything I *can* do to assist you while I'm here, fine.''

"I can't tell you how much I appreciate this.''

"Never mind about that. Just tell me what the trouble is.''

"It has to do with the man who killed Thomas Blair.''

"Blair was your first husband?''

"Yes.''

"Who killed him?''

"The man is called Laton Bowdre. I met him in Cheyenne a couple of weeks ago, before I came out here to the ranch. I had gone to see Mr. Crawley at the bank, the man who sent Thomas's letter to me. I thought he could explain to me why Thomas had changed his mind after all these years.''

"Didn't the letter explain it?''

"Not really.''

"And did the banker understand?''

"No. He did tell me, though, that Thomas had a considerable debt with the bank.''

"You think that's why he made you Jessica's guardian, because he didn't think she could handle it alone?''

"It's possible,'' Rachel said thoughtfully. "I do know he wouldn't want her to lose this ranch. That's all I'm sure of.''

"Christ,'' Chase growled. "How are you supposed to help her? You don't know anything about ranching.''

"Oh, Thomas didn't expect me to run the ranch, only to see that no harm comes to Jessica before she's twenty, or married, whichever comes first. He felt she wasn't ready to pull her own reins, as he put it, that she would need guidance, a restraining hand, for the next few years. I'm quite sure I wouldn't have gotten that letter if he'd died two years from now. Mr. Crawley said the letter had been at the bank for the last four years. Thomas was worried about Jessica because she's so young. As for the ranch, Jessica runs it — and from what I've seen, she knows what she's doing."

"You're not serious!"

"I only wish I weren't." Rachel's voice held a touch of bitterness. "But Thomas had ten years to work with her, to teach her all there is to ranching. And worse."

"Worse?"

"You'll see what I mean when you meet her. But as I was saying, I met Mr. Bowdre at the bank. Mr. Crawley introduced us. Of course he expressed his regrets — most insincerely, I might add — and explained what had happened. It seems there was a card game in one of the saloons, and Thomas bet a ridiculous amount, sure he had the winning hand. But he didn't, and he accused Bowdre of cheating. Thomas went for his gun, but Bowdre got to his gun first and shot Thomas."

"What does the sheriff say?"

"He says that's the truth. There were a dozen

witnesses, and I talked to several of them. They all say the same thing. It was a fair fight. However, the question of whether Laton Bowdre was cheating was never really answered, and it's too late now. The problem is, he still holds Thomas's marker. A gambling debt is as good as gold in these parts."

"As a dabbler at cards" — he grinned sardonically — "I can't say I'm sorry to hear that."

"Well, that's what's so awful. He wants his money, and Jessica doesn't have it. I really think he would have demanded the ranch if she hadn't confronted him about the marker in front of witnesses, forcing him to give her time to pay the debt."

"How much time?"

"Three months."

"And what does Jessica say about this?"

"She's not concerned. She says she'll take care of Bowdre after the fall roundup. She has contracts for the ranch beef with several of the mining camps up north."

"Then what's the problem, Rachel?"

"It's this Laton Bowdre. Sounds like a sly weasel — at least, that's the impression I got." Rachel worried at her lip, then confessed. "I really don't think he wants the money, Chase. I think he wants this ranch."

"So you think he might do something to stop Jessica from paying him off?"

"Yes. What he could do, I have no idea. And

maybe it's all my imagination. But I would feel so much better if you would check on him, see what kind of impression you get."

"Of course," Chase agreed readily. "But why don't you just take care of the debt and get it out of the way? You can certainly afford to."

"You think I don't want to? I tried to give Jessica the money, but she threw it in my face. She won't accept anything from me."

"Why?"

Rachel laughed bitterly. "Her father hated me, and he taught her to hate me, too. And she does it very well."

There was silence for a moment, and then Chase said, "When do I get to meet this stubborn female?"

Jessie didn't wait to hear the answer. She moved back up the hall and slipped into her bedroom. She grabbed a few things, then went back to the kitchen and took the whole loaf of bread, leaving the house silently.

She was in a seething rage. How dare they talk about her? How dare Rachel call in a stranger to mess in her business? Stubborn female? The bastard! Let him go to Cheyenne and snoop around. Let him come back and report to Rachel. Then let him get the hell out of Jessica's life. But she wouldn't be around to meet him. She wouldn't be back until he was gone.

Chapter 3

Late that night Rachel became anxious over Jessica's absence. She had already asked Chase to check the outbuildings, but he had returned alone, shaking his head. Jessica kept strange hours, but she had never been so late before. Her mother began to imagine all kinds of terrible possibilities.

She went in search of Jeb, Chase following her. He was getting annoyed with this elusive daughter who had, apparently, no concern for anyone's feelings.

They found Jeb in the stable nursing a sick colt. He gave the clear impression of not wanting to be bothered by them. Chase was certain that Rachel was only wasting her time, for he had asked the old man earlier if the girl had returned. Jeb had answered tersely that it was plain to see she wasn't there.

"Jeb, please, if Jessica is here —" Rachel

began.

"She ain't. She came in, saw you had company, and rode off again."

"Rode off? For how long?"

"Can't say."

"Well, when did she leave?"

"Couple hours ago."

"She should be back soon, shouldn't she?" Rachel asked hopefully.

Jeb didn't look up once. "Don't reckon so."

"Why not?"

"She was pretty fired up when she took off — like she used to get when she'd fight with her pa. I don't reckon we'll be seein' the little gal for a week or two, at least."

"What?"

Jeb finally glanced up at Rachel. She seemed so stricken that he relented. "If it were last year, she'd probably be gone only a few days, 'cause she used to go to the Anderson homestead about ten miles from here. She'd go there to spite her pa because he refused to allow her any more schoolin'. Mr. Anderson was a teacher back East."

"Then what's the point in mentioning it, Mr. Hart?" Chase demanded.

Rachel put a hand on his arm to stop him, having learned that Jeb Hart went about saying things in his own way. He never volunteered information, and when he did get to talking, it was a long, drawn-out affair.

"Never mind that, Jeb," she said quickly.

"If you could just tell me where you think she might have gone."

"She didn't say," he answered brusquely, returning his attention to the colt.

"Do you have any idea where she went, Jeb? I'm worried sick."

"It won't relieve your mind none if you know," he warned.

"Please, Jeb!"

He hesitated, then shrugged. "She'll likely be visitin' her Indian friends. And she won't come back until she's ready."

"Indians? But are they . . . will she be safe with them?"

"I reckon she'll be as safe with them as she would be anywhere else."

"I didn't know there were Indians near here," Rachel muttered absently, thoroughly confused.

"There aren't. They're a good three, four days' ride from here, dependin' on how much of a hurry she's in."

"You're not serious!" Rachel gasped, her eyes widening. "You mean she'll be traveling alone for three or four days, camping out alone?"

"She's always done it."

"Why did you let her go?" Rachel demanded, fear making her sound sharper than she meant to.

But Jeb said simply, "You can't stop that gal from doin' somethin' she's set on doin'. Ain't you found that out yet?"

Rachel turned to Chase, her blue eyes pleading.

"Will you go after her? I can't stand to think of her out there alone. She's only been gone a few hours, Chase. You could find her tonight."

"Rachel —"

"Please, Chase."

Looking into those enormous blue eyes, there was no way he could refuse. He sighed. "I'm not the best tracker, but I'll find her somehow. Now where is this Indian reservation she's heading for?"

"That would be the Shoshone reservation, wouldn't it, Jeb?" Rachel said. She didn't wait for him to answer. "It's northwest of here. You shouldn't have to go very far, though. She wouldn't ride all night, would she, Jeb?"

This time she waited for Jeb to answer. He was looking at them as if they were crazy. "I reckon she'll bed down somewhere for the night."

"There, you see," Rachel said to Chase. "If you just follow the mountains north, you should be able to find her easily."

"Just don't expect us back before morning, Rachel. She's got a couple of hours on me."

"No matter how long it takes, I'll feel better just knowing you're out looking for her."

Jeb watched the stranger saddle up and ride out. Nice piece of horseflesh, he admitted grudgingly. Too bad the poor creature would be riding days on end for no reason. Well, it wasn't Jeb's fault they assumed Jessie's Indians were reservation Indians. He hadn't felt obliged to set them straight. His loyalty was to Jessie, no one else. He knew Jessie wouldn't like being followed. Wasn't she in a fit because of that man? Wasn't he why she'd left?

It was just as well Jeb hadn't explained that Jessie was riding to the Powder River region, an area the Army had conceded to the Indians in 1868. It was the hunting grounds of the Northern Cheyenne and their fearsome Sioux allies. When Chase Summers returned, empty-handed, in a week or so, that would be the time to set him straight. He would no doubt thank Jeb for saving him from venturing into hostile Indian territory.

Why, I probably saved his life by keeping my mouth shut, Jeb reasoned. After that, he didn't give the matter another thought.

Chapter 4

It was after midnight when Jessie reached the grubshack used by men working the northern range. No one slept there in the warmer months, so she had the little one-room storehouse to herself. There was even a cot. The next morning at dawn she gathered some supplies and set off. Making excellent time, she reached her destination on the evening of the third day.

Then she found she had made the trip for nothing. She stared across the winding creek at the area where, in winter, fifty tepees crowded beneath the trees. Either she was early, or they were late returning from following the buffalo north. White Thunder's small tribe had not arrived yet.

She watched a squirrel running through the tall grass. The grass had grown well during the spring and summer. It would support the tribe's horses for most of the winter, until the tribe

33

moved on. Jessie stood looking around her wistfully. She had looked forward to talking to White Thunder, and she was terribly disappointed. She had not seem him since the spring, so he didn't know that her father was dead. Now she probably wouldn't see White Thunder until later in the fall. She wouldn't be able to get back this way until after the fall roundup.

Jessie crossed the creek, deciding to make camp for the night. She went directly to the spot where she had spent so many nights, the place where White Thunder's mother, Wide River Woman, always erected their tepee. But it was lonely there without her friend and his family, without the sounds of the children, without the women telling stories as they worked and the men calling triumphantly after a hunt. It seemed more lonely there than any other place on the trail had seemed.

As she spread out her bedroll and gathered wood for a fire, Jessie recalled the first time she had come to this region, eight years before. She had followed her father without his knowing it, followed him because he had a newborn baby with him, and she feared he meant to leave the baby somewhere to die. He had been furious because it was a girl. Jessie wasn't so ignorant that she didn't know the baby was her half sister.

Her father had brought the baby here, and she had been rclieved. She wasn't aware that he was leaving the baby with its grandmother. The

Indian mistress who had lived with Thomas for a year had died giving birth. She was White Thunder's older half sister. Jessie learned all that much later.

Wanting assurance that the baby would be safe, Jessie revealed her presence to the Indians after father had left the camp. White Thunder's mother guessed who Jessie was by her resemblance to her father, and because she could speak English, she and Jessie became friends. Even White Thunder's austere stepfather, Runs with the Wolf, tolerated Jessie. He had known Thomas Blair from his early trapping days in the late 1830s, and they had long been trading friends.

Jessie came to see the baby every month that year, until the weather got too harsh for the journey. She grew close to White Thunder and his younger sister, Little Gray Bird Woman, and she flourished, having friends for the first time. Her father was not a warm man, and the Indians filled a gap in Jessie's life.

The following year, when the weather finally permitted Jessie to travel north again, it was to find that her baby sister had died during the cruel winter. Jessie might have stopped going, but she'd found that the Indian camp was the one place where she could be herself. She could even dress like a girl, which her father wouldn't allow. She found deepening friendships there, particularly with White Thunder.

She had the best of both worlds when she

stayed with the Indians. She could stay by the tepee as young girls were supposed to, learning to sew and create beadwork, to cook, to dress and tan buffalo hides. But it was not frowned upon if she wanted to go hunting with White Thunder, or enter a horse race, or join in the boys' games. She could get away with all of that because she wasn't one of them, and also because she had come to them in male attire and displayed excellent male skills.

They accepted her. They called her Looks Like Woman. With her midnight hair and summer-bronzed skin, she looked like an Indian. Jessica loved her Indian name.

Thinking about the people she loved most brought to mind the man she hated most — Laton Bowdre. Middle-aged and balding, he had brown eyes that were most expressive, telling of the lechery that moved constantly through his mind. There wasn't much to recommend the man, not his ostentatious clothes, certainly not his gaunt body. He was ugly. He reminded Jessie of a weasel, intent on nothing but his own pleasure.

The first time she met him, even while he was demanding payment on the note he had won from her father, his eyes strayed boldly over Jessie's body. She had the feeling that if others hadn't been there, his hands would have followed his eyes.

How right she had been. Her second run-in with the man hadn't been so easy. Bowdre cornered her on the way to the train depot when she was about to depart for Denver and a shopping spree. There was no one around to rescue her.

She could clearly remember that purring voice.

"Fancy meeting you, Miss Blair. I barely recognized you, my dear, in a dress."

"If you'll excuse me," Jessie tried to pass, but Laton Bowdre blocked her way.

"Perhaps you have something for me?" Bowdre asked smoothly.

Jessie was furious. "We agreed you would get your blood money in three months."

The man shrugged. "I just thought you might like to pay sooner. But of course you can't afford to, can you? How could I forget?" He grinned. "It was rather generous of me to give you time, wasn't it? I never was thanked properly for my kindness."

Jessie gritted her teeth. "It was decent of you," she said woodenly.

"I'm glad you realize that. Of course, a little interest on the side wouldn't hurt." Before she could answer, he went on. "My dear, I might even be persuaded to wipe out a portion of your debt if you —"

"Forget it!" Jessie snapped. "You'll get your debt — in money!"

Bowdre chuckled at her indignation and reached out a bony hand to touch her face. "Think about it. A girl needs a man. I might even consider marriage. After all, you can't be expected to run a ranch on your own. Yes, I might consider marriage." His hand dropped to her shoulder and started to move lower.

Jessie reacted instinctively, slugging the man with a closed fist that ended up hurting her all the way to Denver. His surprise did not appease her anger, nor did the trickle of blood at the corner of his mouth.

"Don't you ever put your hands on me again, Mr. Bowdre," she warned him icily.

"You're going to regret that, little girl," Bowdre said just as coldly, all pretense gone.

"I doubt it," Jessie retorted hotly. "I might have some regrets if I were wearing my gun, because then I'd have to explain to the sheriff why I put a bullet through you. Good day, Mr. Bowdre."

Just remembering that encounter gave her the creeps, and she pushed it from her mind.

With a fire going, Jessie cleaned the large grouse she had shot earlier that day. She cut it up, threw it in a pot of water along with some dried peas, spices, and a bit of flour, then whipped up a thick batter from her supplies and added it to the pot in chunks for dumplings. She had learned long ago never to scrimp on a meal just because she was by herself. A large meal could go a long way. It also provided the nourishment for long, tiring days in the saddle.

With the food cooking over the fire, she turned to Blackstar and gave him a good rub-down. Then she threw a blanket over him for the night. She kept her fringed deerskin jacket on for warmth. Summer was over, she realized. She wrapped her only other blanket around her legs and settled down by the fire to eat.

She was only half-finished eating when Black-star started snorting and stomping his feet, and she knew she was no longer alone. Jessie knew better than to jump up in alarm. That was exactly what Indians would expect of a white, and she might get an arrow in her back for her foolishness. She stayed right where she was.

She waited several moments before she spoke in a loud, clear voice, her tone friendly: "I can use the company, and I've food to share, if you'll just come by the fire where I can see you."

No one answered. Should she say it again in the Cheyenne tongue?

She still didn't move, but she tried Cheyenne. "I am Looks Like Woman, friend of the Cheyenne. I have a fire to share and food, if you will make yourself known to me."

Still no answer. She moved between fear and relief when ten minutes passed without a sound. Blackstar had quieted down, too. Still, it wasn't like Blackstar to make a fuss about nothing.

And then suddenly he was there, standing beside her. Jessie's hand flew to her chest in shock. She hadn't heard him approach. One second the space was empty, and then those moccasined feet were there, spread apart, inches from her crossed legs.

Her eyes traveled up his long legs in fringed leggings, past the breechcloth that came only to the middle of his thighs, over the wide expanse of chest that was bare and thickly muscled. Scars there attested to his courage and endurance. White Thunder had similar scars, scars from a Sun Dance of several years past.

As her eyes moved upward, she was surprised to see a man not more than twenty-five years old. His face was arresting, with copper skin stretched over high cheekbones, a hawklike nose, and ebony eyes. The eyes revealed nothing. His black hair was long and loose in the back, with two thin braids in the front. In one braid he wore a single blue feather. A bow and arrows were slung over his shoulder. His hands were empty, showing that he did not consider her a threat.

"You're a handsome one, aren't you?" Jessie said as she finished looking him over.

The brave's eyes met hers, and she blushed, realizing what she had said. But his expression didn't change. Had he understood? She got to her feet slowly, so as not to alarm him. Then she got her first reaction from him, as the blanket fell away and he saw her skintight pants and gun holster.

Before she could think what to do, he reached for her jacket and spread it open. His eyes lingered on the soft mounds that pressed tightly against her shirt front, yet Jessie didn't dare jerk away.

Finally he released her, and Jessie let out the breath she had been holding. "Well, now that's settled, perhaps we can communicate. You speak English? No?" She switched to the only Indian tongue she knew. "Cheyenne? Are you Cheyenne?"

He surprised Jessie then by letting off a long stream of words in a deep, resounding voice. Unfortunately, the single word she recognized was a Dakota word.

"You are Sioux," she concluded, disappointed, because although the Cheyenne and Sioux dialects were similar, they were not the same.

Jessie had never talked with a Sioux warrior, had only seen a few over the years, a few who had visited White Thunder's camp. This brave was of the tribes still actively hostile to whites, tribes so powerful they had forced the Army to abandon territory. The Sioux and Northern Cheyenne had not been subdued by the whites, unlike nearly all the other Plains Indians. They had demanded the whole Powder River region as their hunting ground — and gotten it, too. And here she was, facing a Sioux warrior, and he had found her in his territory.

The direction of her thoughts was alarming, and Jessie put a stop to them right there. She had no reason to fear this brave. Yet. He had condescended to speak to her, which was a good sign.

"I am called Jessica Blair by the whites, and

41

Looks Like Woman by the Cheyenne. I come here often to visit my friend White Thunder and his family, but I am early this year, so I will return in the morning to my home in the south. Do you know White Thunder?"

She helped the lengthy explanation along with what sign language she knew, but he gave no indication that he understood. She fell silent, and he looked away from her toward her horse.

He moved over to examine Blackstar, and she called, "He was given to me by White Thunder."

The brave said something at last, but she didn't understand. He reached out and ran a hand over the horse's flanks, laughing when Blackstar turned his head and tried to bite him.

Jessie lost her patience then and snapped, "Damn it, you can stop looking my horse over right now. You can't have him!"

The anger in her tone was unmistakable, even if the words were alien. She had managed to get his attention again, and he sauntered over and stood in front of her. This time he was so close she was forced to look up to meet his eyes.

His expression was not so austere now. He spoke again, indicating with signs that he was telling her his name. She tried to decipher his words, and finally grinned as she came up with the English equivalent.

"Little Hawk!" she said proudly, but he shook his head. He had not understood.

Jessie smiled as she indicated again that he was welcome to share her food and fire. This time he acknowledged her offer and sat down by the fire. Jessie returned to her place, wrapping the blanket around her legs again. She had only one plate, and she added more food to it and gave it to him. When all that was left of the food was what had been on the plate when he took it from her, he gave it back. He watched her as she quickly finished eating, and when she was done she got up to clean the utensils and put them away. She could feel his eyes following her every move.

When she came back to the fire, she found him stretched out in the grass, leaning on an elbow, facing her place by the fire.

She might have moved to another spot, but she was too wary to make any changes. She lay down and faced him. Their eyes met, and it seemed they stared at each other forever. His look grew bolder. Hadn't Blue looked at her that way? It was obvious that Little Hawk desired her, yet she was surprised when he patted the grass beside him, indicating he wanted her to come to him. She shook her head slowly, her eyes never leaving his. Little Hawk shrugged, gave her one long look, then lay down and closed his eyes.

Jessie continued to stare at him, relieved, yet oddly disturbed. What was the matter with her? It was his eyes, she decided at last, the way he had looked at her, making love to her with those dark, compelling eyes.

But as Jessie drifted off to sleep, it was not Little Hawk's eyes she saw, but other eyes, as dark, the eyes of Chase Summers.

Chapter 5

"You should have seen him, Jeb," Jessie was saying as she unsaddled Blackstar. She had just returned and had been talking nonstop since her arrival, ten minutes before. "He was so proud and arrogant, so utterly Indian, if you know what I mean."

Jes crooked a single brow at her. "And you weren't scared, him bein' a Sioux?"

"Well a little, especially when he made it known he . . . wanted me."

"Did he?" Jeb said. "Well, you sure don't look any the worse for his havin' you."

"Because he didn't," Jessie said simply. "I refused, and he respected my wishes."

"Is that right?"

"You don't believe me?" she demanded. "The fact is he couldn't very well attack me after I had fed him. They do have a very rigid sense of honor, you know. Or is it that you doubt that he wanted me at all? Some men find me attractive, Jeb Hart, even dressed like this.''

''Now, don't get riled, gal.''

She wasn't. ''Well, anyway,'' she went on, ''he was gone before I got up the next morning. I even thought I might have dreamed it all.''

''You sure you didn't?''

She gave him a withering look. ''Yes, I'm sure. The grass was still matted where he'd slept, and he left this behind.'' She brought out the blue feather she'd been keeping in her pocket.

''Why'd he leave that, do you think?''

Jessie shrugged. She didn't know. ''But I think I'll keep it.'' She grinned. ''To remind me of a handsome man who desired me.''

Jeb grunted. ''You're getting' to be a naughty gal, Jessie Blair. I never heard the like, all this talk of desire, and you just eighteen.''

''That's because you think of me as a boy, Jeb, just like you always have. But lots of girls are married before they're my age, so I reckon I'm long overdue to be talking about romance.''

''Well, just don't let Rachel hear you goin' on,'' he mumbled. ''She's worried herself sick over you this last week.''

At mention of her mother, Jessie's whole appearance changed.

''She's been pesterin' the hell out of the rest of us with her worryin'. She even sent that fellow out lookin' for you the night you left.''

''She did what?'' Jessie stormed. ''How dare

she —?"

"Now hold on. He didn't find you, did he? And the fact is, he ain't back yet."

Jessie let it sink in. She grinned. Then she laughed. "Really? That's wonderful! So he got lost after all."

Jeb watched her for a moment before he asked, "You don't think too kindly of him, do you?"

"How would you feel if some stranger started messing in your affairs?"

"Is that what he's done?"

"Not yet," she said tersely. "But I heard Rachel asking him to, and I heard him agree. So if he never comes back, that suits me just fine."

Chase came back five days later. He was bone-weary, saddle-sore, filthy, and not looking forward to telling Rachel he'd failed her. More than two hundred miserable, dusty miles just to get to that damned reservation, and for what? The agent there had never heard of Jessica Blair. Nor had the Indians who spoke English been able to tell him anything at all. He spent a day covering the area, asking questions, but he was sure no one knew anything.

Jeb was in the tack room at the front of the stable when Chase led Goldenrod in. Chase stared at him, all the weariness and anger of the last week and a half boiling to the surface. But if Jeb had learned anything in sixty years, it

47

was how to talk his way around a mean polecat.

"Well, now, you made good time, didn't you, young feller?" Jeb commented congenially.

"Did I?" Chase replied harshly. "Aren't you a little surprised by it?"

"Don't know that I am."

"Really? Being a gambler, I think I can safely bet every cent I have that you didn't expect me back here at all."

Jeb grinned. "Now, wouldn't that be easy pickin's, but plumb ornery of me to take you up on that bet. Fact is, I figured you'd be back just about this time — and in one piece, too, it bein' safe enough the way you went. Ain't had no trouble along that route in a good many years."

"That's beside the point," Chase said coldly. "Going to the Shoshone reservation was a waste of time, and I figure you knew it would be."

"Well, shoot, I could've told you —"

"Why didn't you tell me?"

"You didn't ask," Jeb replied with a shrug. "It ain't my fault you and the lady figured Jessie's Indians were Shoshone. Mister, I was doin' you a favor keepin' my mouth shut, bein' as how Rachel was so set on you ridin' outta here. You wouldn't have cared to go the way the little gal went. No white man goes that way if he's got any sense."

"What way? Just where the hell *did* she go? And don't tell me any more nonsense about

Indians!"

"I don't see what you're so riled about," Jeb grumbled. "I probably saved your life, and this is the thanks I get!"

"Damn you, old man!" Chase exploded. "If you weren't already close to your grave, I'd sure as hell put you there. Now I want some straight answers, not —"

"Leave him along!"

Chase whirled around to face that angry voice and was stunned to see the girl who had sent him off in the wrong direction when he'd approached this ranch the first time. "You again! What are you doing here, kid?" When she didn't answer, he asked Jeb, "Who is she?"

Jeb tried to suppress his amusement, but he couldn't quite manage it. He knew sparks were going to fly, and there was little doubt who would get burned. It would serve the feller right, he thought.

"Why, she's the gal you been lookin' for," Jeb answered innocently.

Chase turned back to the girl, anger overcoming all sense. "Sonofabitch!" he swore furiously. "I ought to tan your hide!"

Jessie stepped back, her hand automatically going to the gun on her hip. "I wouldn't try it, mister," she told him in a cold, calm voice. "I wouldn't even think about it if I were you."

Chase eyed her warily. He hadn't noticed the gun before, seeing only that delicate oval face, a face that for some annoying reason had come to his mind often over the past week and a half. The time he'd wasted looking for her, *this* girl, not Rachel's faceless daughter but this little hoyden in boy's clothes. Christ, he wanted to get his hands on her!

Chase continued to boil, but he managed to get his anger under the surface. "Would you really shoot me, kid?" he asked.

"You better believe she would," Jeb volunteered from behind him.

Chase softened his expression and repeated in his most beguiling voice, "Would you, Jessica?"

Jessie didn't know what to make of this about-face, but she wasn't mollified. Part of her anger was a defense, for she had lied to this man and they both knew it. But most of her anger was because he had no business shouting at Jeb.

"Just stay away from me, and you won't have to find out."

"Then I guess I'll keep my distance," he conceded, leaning back against the wall. "But you will agree you and I are due for some straight talk?"

"No," she answered flatly. "I don't owe you any talk, but what I got to say you better pay attention to. Don't you ever badger Jeb again. He works for me, and he doesn't have to answer your questions. He doesn't have to give you the time of day if he doesn't want to. You don't work here, so you got no business interrupting his work. Is all that clear to you, mister?"

"Perfectly," Chase replied, undaunted. "And since you're the one with the answers, why don't you tell me why you lied to me."

Jessie glared at him. "Because I don't want you here!" she snapped. "And that's all you need to know."

She turned on her heel and started out of the stable, but Chase stopped her with the ominous cocking of his gun and the icy warning, "Just hold it right there, shortfry."

She was not more than a foot away from him, and she turned around to look at him in disbelief. She stared for a moment at the gun he was aiming at her, and then her expression changed to contempt. "You wouldn't," she stated flatly. "How would you explain shooting me to your precious Rachel?"

With that she passed on through the stable doors. Chase angrily put his gun away. Jeb's scratchy chuckling only made him angrier. In fact, he couldn't remember when a female had ever made him so mad, and he wasn't going to put up with it.

He went after Jessie, catching up with her halfway between the stable and the house. Too late she heard him coming up behind her, and before she could react, he had jerked her to a stop, getting to her gun before she could and throwing it across the yard.

"We'll talk," Chase said brusquely.

"The hell we will!" Jessie shouted each word just a little louder than the last. Before she had finished, she was swinging a fist at him.

Chase caught her wrist and jerked it up behind her back, then went for the other one and did the same, leaving her feet kicking at him. "You were only half-right back there," he told her sharply. "It's not that I wouldn't dare shoot you, kid. It's that I wouldn't want to. But I'm not opposed to giving you a richly deserved spanking if you don't settle down."

Jessie stopped all resistance instantly and relaxed against him. Chase held her like that, waiting for her to calm down a bit. As he waited, he became acutely aware of her body. Confusion set in. How old had Rachel said her daughter was? Eighteen! She was full grown, even if she didn't act it and her clothes hid the fact. Soft, full breasts were pressed against his chest. No wonder he was beginning to respond to the closeness.

Chase swore softly and set Jessie away from him, holding her wrists in front of her. He looked her over, seeing the alluring curves he had missed before, the way her pants fit like a second skin, the way her shirt strained against her breasts.

"Are you ready to behave now?"

Jessie's head was lowered, and she seemed subdued. "You're hurting me," she said.

He relaxed his hold. The second he did she jerked loose and started running for the house. When he caught up with her, she had reached the porch steps. This time he was fed up. Jessie screamed when he sat down on the steps and pulled her across his lap. She squirmed with all her might, trying to face him, yet he kept pushing her down. She kept screaming.

Rachel heard the yelling, and when she rushed to the porch and saw, she was shocked. "Stop it, Chase!"

With his hands full of a hissing, spitting wildcat, Chase couldn't turn to look at her. He said angrily, "She deserves it, Rachel!"

"That's not the way to handle Jessica, Chase." She came around to face him. "Now let her up."

Chase stared hard at her, and slowly some rationality returned. "You're right. It's not my place to discipline your kid, no matter how much she needs it."

He let Jessie go, and the moment her feet were planted firmly in front of him, she hauled off and socked him on the nose. He was so surprised that she was able to run past him and into the house before he could react. He growled and got up to go after her.

Rachel caught his arm. "Let her go, Chase."

"Did you see what that little bitch did to me?" he shouted furiously.

"Yes, and it was no more than *you* deserved," Rachel told him sharply. Then she said in a calmer tone, "She's a young woman, Chase. You can't manhandle her like you did."

"Young woman, hell! She's a spoiled brat." He felt his nose, and his hand came away smeared with blood. "Is it broken?"

"Let me see." Rachel felt around the edges and along the ridge and shook her head. "I don't think so, but you're bleeding pretty badly. Come inside, and I'll take care of it."

Chase stepped through the door, but he did so warily, as if he expected Jessie to be waiting to clobber him again. Rachel saw him looking around and said, "The door to her room is open, so she has probably taken off out the back."

"If you mean Jessie," Billy Ewing volunteered, coming up the hall, "she just left on Blackstar."

"She's probably going off to sulk," Chase said.

"Jessie?" Billy scoffed. "Nah, she's got work to do. She said so, when I asked where she was going. What happened to you?"

"Never mind!"

"Boy!" Billy cried as he turned around and went back down the hall the way he had come. "You never get a straight answer out of grown-ups."

Rachel smiled after her son. He was so different from her first child. Having the love of two parents made such a difference. Billy was so good-natured, not at all like Jessica. It was all such a shame.

"You can't get straight answers out of willful little chits, either," Chase grumbled.

"What?"

"Did your daughter happen to tell you where she went? When did she get back?"

"Five days ago," Rachel replied. "And no, she wouldn't tell me where she'd been. I tried to talk to her, but she accused me of only pretending to be worried, of putting on an act. She said it was none of my business and I'd had no right sending you after her. I really think she was most angry about that, that you went after her."

"I'm beginning to think your Jessica is perpetually angry. You want to know why she took off that night? It's because I was here."

"Did she tell you that?"

"She didn't have to," Chase replied. "She happens to be the kid I told you about, the one who sent me off in the wrong direction that day, lying to me. That's why she left, I'm sure. She didn't have the guts to face me after she saw I'd made it here after all."

"But, Chase, you said that girl was with a man, that they were —"

"I know what I said. But that was Jessica, one and the same." And then he added spitefully, whether he believed it or not, "I wouldn't be surprised if that's where she was that whole week, with a man somewhere."

"You're going too far, Chase Summers," Rachel said defensively.

"Okay, but what are you going to do about her? You *are* her guardian, Rachel. Her father left her in your care. Are you just going to let her run wild?"

"What am I supposed to do when she won't talk to me. She doesn't believe I care about her. How do I reach her when she hates me?"

"I'll tell you what I would do."

"I've seen what you would do," she said sternly. "And that's not the answer. There has to be some other way."

"You ought to just find her a husband and get her off your hands. Let someone else worry about her."

Rachel didn't answer, but she looked at him thoughtfully. An idea began to take shape in her mind, an idea Jessica wouldn't have liked at all.

Chapter 6

"Have you seen my sister?" Billy asked Chase as he joined him on the porch.

"Not since yesterday," Chase grunted. "At least this time your mother didn't ask me to go after her when she didn't come home last night."

"But she did come home," Billy said. "It was late, but I heard her come in and go to her room. I missed her this morning. I was hoping she would let me ride with her today."

Chase smiled at Billy's enthusiasm. "I take it you like it better here than the city?"

"Well, sure! Who wouldn't?"

"I kind of like city life myself."

"But you've been out West a long time, at least that's what Mother said. This is all new to me."

"And what about your schooling? As I remember, that was one of the golden rules in the

Ewing household — thou shalt be educated, or suffer the consequences. Or has that changed now that Jonathan Ewing —" Chase stopped, cursing himself for his stupid blunder. Why had he said that?

"That's all right." Billy rescued him. "Father's been dead three years now. It doesn't hurt to talk about it anymore. But as for schooling, I wish you hadn't reminded me. Mother was saying she'll probably send me back to Chicago soon, since the nearest schoolroom is a day's ride from here."

"And you don't want to go?"

"Not alone," Billy admitted. "But Mother says she can't leave Jessie alone, either, and Jessie wouldn't consider coming back with us. I can't blame Jessie for that, though. I wouldn't give up this ranch, either, if it were mine. I just wish I could stay here, too."

"Well, I don't imagine your mother is eager to part with you." Chase grinned. "So you'll probably be around here for a while. Enjoy it while you can."

"Oh, I will," Billy replied. Seeing Chase unconsciously rubbing the bridge of his nose, he asked. "What happened yesterday?"

Chase looked at him sideways, ready with a sharp retort. Then he shrugged. Billy meant no harm. "Your sister punched me."

"Did she really?" Billy grinned, his blue eyes lighting up with wonder.

"I don't see what's so funny about it," Chase

said testily, his eyes narrowing.

"It's not funny," Billy assured him quickly. "It's just, well, I mean, she's not much taller than I am, and here you are twice her size. But then, it's not so unusual when you consider Jessie. She can do *any*thing."

Chase shook his head. There was obviously some hero worship there, hero worship of a girl. It was absurd. Did Rachel know about this?

"You like her, do you?" Chase said dryly.

"I sure do. I never even knew I had a sister, not until Mother got that letter, and then she told me about Jessica — I mean Jessie," he corrected. "She doesn't like to be called Jessica, you know. And she's so different! And beautiful. The boys back at home will never believe me when I tell them about her." His voice dropped. "I just wish she liked me a little."

Chase drew himself up. "What do you mean? Has she been taking that foul temper of hers out on you, too?"

Billy looked away, embarrassed. "I only wish she would," he said. "But the fact is, she ignores me. I'll win her over, though," he added confidently. "She only tries to act rough because she thinks she has to. I can understand that. After all, she's only eighteen, and she has to boss men older than she is. A girl's got to be tough to do that. A girl's got to be tough just to be a girl, out here."

Chase sat back in bemusement. All that logic

pouring out of a boy nine years old. He was amazed. Every bit of what Billy said made sense. It certainly explained the girl's attitude. Chase was suddenly seeing Jessica Blair in a different light.

Chase looked at Billy. "How about us going for that ride? As you pointed out, your sister has a ranch to run and is probably too busy to ride with you."

Jessie was worn out when she rode into the yard late that night. She might have stayed out on the range and gotten an early start the next morning. The roundup of the cattle that would be driven north to fulfill her contracts had started, and work would be long and hard over the next weeks. But Jessie's curiosity had gotten the better of her, so she rode in, wanting to see if her mother's friend had moved on.

She knew the answer as soon as she led Blackstar into the stable, for there was that beautiful golden palomino bedded down next to Jeb's old roan. Strangely, Jessie didn't know what she really felt. But she was too tired to give it any thought just then.

The prospect of removing Blackstar's thirty-pound saddle in her exhausted state made Jessie's movements slow. She lit a lamp and turned him into his stall, sorry Jeb had gone to bed.

There was nothing for it but to get it done and turn in for the night. Though she was starving, she was too tired even to scrape up something to eat. She had left the men just as they were settling down to eat, so she could ride the three-hour journey back to the ranch.

"Can you use some help?"

Jessie started and looked over to see Chase Summers leaning against the railing of Blackstar's stall. He was dressed in a blue cotton shirt tucked into black pants. His open shirt front revealed a dark mat of curls across his chest. Jessie was struck by his powerful attractiveness and felt a pang of regret that she could never like him.

"I couldn't sleep, and I happened to see the light go on," he was saying in a friendly voice, "so I thought I'd come out to see who was still up."

Jessie made no comment, leery of this sudden overture. She wouldn't forget what he'd tried to do to her. Why was he being so friendly after she'd socked him? She noted that there was no swelling around his nose, only a slight discoloration that was hardly noticeable. Disagreeably, she vowed to punch him harder next time.

She turned away from him and began unbuckling the cinches, hoping he would go away if she continued to ignore him. But when she began to lift the saddle, he was there beside her. Taking hold, he easily tossed the saddle over the side railing. Jessie didn't thank him for his help or even look at him as she went about giving Blackstar a brisk rubdown, then seeing to his food and water.

When she had finished, she walked past Chase, still without a word, turned out the lamp, and headed for the house. He fell into step beside her.

"You're not going to make this easy, are you?" Chase asked softly. When she didn't reply, he sighed. "Look, Miss Blair, I realize you and I have gotten off to a bad start, but is there any reason to continue that way? I'd like to apologize if you'll let me."

Jessie didn't stop walking, but after a while she asked, "What exactly are you apologizing for?"

"Well . . . everything."

"Are you really sorry, or did Rachel Ewing put you up to this?"

Chase winced at the coldness in her voice when she said her mother's name. Rachel hadn't been exaggerating. The girl did hate her. He wanted to find out why, but right now wasn't the time. He finally had her talking to him, and it was best to proceed cautiously.

"I don't apologize often, Miss Blair. If it weren't my own idea, I wouldn't be doing it, believe me."

"Then you'll leave?"

Chase stopped short, stunned. "Can't you just accept my apology?"

"Sure I can," she said lightly as she continued walking. "But you haven't answered my question."

Jessie didn't wait for him to answer, either.

As she reached the back door to the kitchen, she stepped inside. Rachel had left a lamp burning low, and Jessie turned it up.

Chase followed her inside, finding her by the kitchen counter, her back to him, opening a can of beans. When she began to eat the beans cold, right out of the can, he grimaced.

"We missed you at dinner," he said as he closed the door behind him. "I believe there are some leftovers on the stove if you're hungry."

She turned, her eyes flashing, and he realized he must have picked a sore subject. It was a sore subject in fact, for Jessie hadn't sat down for one of Kate's excellent hot meals since Rachel and Billy had come. It was a reminder that they had succeeded in pushing her out of her own house. Her own choice, but that didn't change it any.

"Then again, dinner wasn't that good tonight," Chase added quickly, an outright lie, but it seemed to mollify Jessie. She stopped glaring at him and continued to eat her cold beans.

Jessie hadn't planned to eat anything, hadn't planned to let anything keep her from her bed. But for some reason she wasn't quite so tired anymore.

"You haven't answered my question, Mr. Summers," Jessie pointed out casually.

"I don't recall your being too willing to talk to me." Chase grinned, trying to keep it light.

Jessie frowned. "I answered the one question

you had a right to ask. I told you why I lied to you. But my question does concern me, Mr. Summers. I would appreciate it if you would give me an answer."

"What was your question?" Chase hedged.

Jessie slammed the can of beans down on the counter. "Are you deliberately trying to provoke me, Summers?"

"Is everything so serious with you? Don't you ever get any fun out of life?" When she started to walk away, Chase caught her arm, gently this time. "Will you just hold on a minute?"

She didn't look at him, but at his hand, and he released her. "Well?" she demanded.

"I just don't know how to answer you. I know you don't want me here, but Rachel has asked for my help, and I can't very well refuse her."

"Why not?" Jessie asked.

He replied in a tight voice, "She's got no one else to help her. *You* certainly aren't cooperating."

"Was I supposed to?" Jessie snapped. "I didn't ask her to come here!"

"No, you didn't. But your father did."

Her turquoise eyes were stormy, but she kept her voice low as she said, "You want to know why? I heard you and her talking about it that night, and I can give you a better reason than she did. He hated her so much that he wanted more revenge even after he was dead! He wanted her to see what he'd made of me. He wanted her to see this fine house and be sorry it's not hers."

"But she's rich, Jessie, or didn't you know that?" Chase said quietly. "Why, her home in Chicago is four times the size of this house."

"But *he* didn't know that. All he wanted was for us to be thrown together so the sparks would fly. He knew they would. He knew I hated her. He made sure I would."

"Why do you hate her so, Jessie?"

"Damn you, Summers!" she hissed, her lips thinning. "Don't start prying. And I didn't give you leave to call me Jessie!"

"All right, I'm sorry."

"And another thing," she continued. "I also heard what she asked you to do when you were discussing me — which you had no business doing. The fact is, I am well aware of the kind of man Laton Bowdre is. I don't just *think* he'll try something crooked, I *know* he will. I'm already prepared for it. So you'll only be wasting your time concerning yourself." Then she added, just for meanness, "But you waste your time a lot, don't you?"

The gibe hit home. Chase's eyes turned quite black. "I wonder why. Could it be because a certain girl we both know hasn't grown up yet?"

"You're looking for another sock on the nose, mister!" Jessie retorted hotly.

"Look," he replied. "I'm only pointing out

that spiteful lying and going off to sulk do not make a mature young woman."

"And a fool's errand makes for a fool!"

Having reached a stalemate, they just stood glaring at each other. Jessie told herself to walk away, but something compelled her to stay. Matching wits with him was stimulating, exciting. She wondered what he would do next.

As usual, he surprised her. He admitted softly, "You are right, of course. I was off on a fool's errand and was quite the fool for it."

"Well, *you* were wrong," Jessie said. "I didn't go off to sulk."

"Then why stay away for a whole week?"

"That's how long it takes to get where I was going and back.

Chase sighed. "And where did you go?"

Jessie frowned. "Why are you asking me? Jeb already told you where I went."

"No," he said. "He fabricated some nonsense about Indians, but I know for a fact you've never been to the Wind River Reservation."

Jessie smiled. "That's where you went?"

"Of course," he replied tersely. "But the question is, where were you?"

Jessie shook her head. "You really should find out about a territory before you enter it, Mr. Summers. I take it you've never been this far north before, or you'd know that the tame Shoshone are not the only Indians we have in our area. There are the Cheyenne and the —"

Chase interrupted. "I've been west of the

Missouri long enough to know that the Cheyenne were defeated long ago, and what's left of them are confined to a reservation about five hundred miles south of here."

Jessie's hands went to her hips. "So you think you know everything, do you? Okay. Black Kettle's Cheyenne, the ones you're talking about, were confined to a reservation, yes. They had no choice after the cavalry attacked their peaceful village and massacred most of them. That Army butchery was what enraged the northern tribes and allied them more closely with the Sioux. They are not all confined, Mr. Summers. The Northern Cheyenne still roam the plains and protect what little land they have left."

"And you expect me to believe you went to visit them?" he asked, truly incredulous.

"I don't give two hoots what you believe," she said levelly. Then she turned away and went to her room, leaving him standing there.

Chase heard the door to her room close. He ran a hand through his hair, exasperated. She wouldn't be back to finish the argument. Argument? Hell, he had not meant to fight with her again. He had meant to be reasonable. Apologetic. Charming, even. He had sincerely wanted to end the animosity. Damn! What had gone wrong?

Chapter 7

Jessie didn't usually sleep late, but she woke to find her room quite bright. Several hours of the morning were gone. Why? Usually, if she wasn't up by seven o'clock, Kate would come in to wake her. Maybe Kate had assumed she was up and gone.

As Jessie dressed, she wondered what Kate thought about all the uproar in their lives. But then, Kate probably wouldn't have told her even if she'd asked. For as long as Jessie could remember, the Indian woman had been there, like so much else on the ranch. But she had never gotten close to Kate. The older woman never encouraged overtures. Often, especially lately, she was downright sullen. Had Kate ever been her father's mistress? Jessie knew she'd never learn the answer to that. She often felt sorry for Kate, wasting her life there, having no family. But any time she had ever asked

68

Kate why she stayed, Kate had replied that Thomas needed her. And even after he died and Jessie offered to settle Kate anywhere she liked, Kate declined. There was nowhere she wanted to go. The ranch was all Kate had anymore.

Jessie let it go then, grateful that the Indian woman was there to see to the house, for Jessie certainly didn't have the time. And the house was kept immaculate, Jessie's bed always made when she returned at the end of the day, her clothes washed and hung in her wardrobe, hot meals waiting.

As soon as she was dressed, Jessie hurried to the stable, furious with herself for being late. She barely noticed Rachel's voice coming from the porch, but stopped when she heard Chase Summer's raised voice. For once, he was angry with someone other than Jessie.

"Rachel, I wouldn't marry that spoiled brat of yours if you paid me! Where in hell did you get such a fool idea?"

Jessie froze.

"From you," Rachel replied calmly. "You said I ought to find her a husband if I wanted her off my hands."

"But I was angry, not serious. She's just a child. She needs a father, not a husband."

"She *had* a father. A lot of good it did her," Rachel retorted bitterly. "And you know perfectly well she's old enough to marry."

"Age has nothing to do with it. She still acts like a kid. Forget it, Rachel. Find someone else

to dump her on if you must, but I want nothing
to do with that brat.''

"Won't you at least think about it?" Rachel's
voice turned soft and appealing. "You've been
wandering for years, Chase. This is nice country
to settle down in, and the ranch is established,
a fine spread.''

"With a debt," he reminded her.

"I would pay off the debt," she said quickly.
"She wouldn't have to know.''

"Would you listen to yourself, Rachel?"
Chase snapped. "I hope you don't make that
offer to anyone else! Another man would jump
at it, and you wouldn't be doing the girl any
favor. Now, I'm willing to help you, but not to
the point of human sacrifice. And you're not
that cold-blooded, either, so just pretend you
never had this idea.''

"Then, for God's sake, tell me what I'm
supposed to do!" Rachel started crying. "I can't
take much more of this. I'm not used to such
hostility, and from my own daughter — it's
unbearable! She doesn't want me here. She
would be happier if I left, yet I can't leave her
here alone. I just can't do that. She has to have
someone to look out for her.''

"'Take it easy now, lady.'' Chase began to
comfort her. "Perhaps it's time you considered
paying someone to be her guardian so you don't
have to do it.''

"But who could I trust with the responsibility? Who wouldn't take advantage of her? . . .''

She brightened suddenly. "I could trust you, Chase. Would you —"

"No, I wouldn't! I couldn't handle it, Rachel. For some reason I lose my temper every time I talk to that girl. I'd end up wringing her neck if she were left in my charge."

Jessie left then, horrified and humiliated beyond anything she had ever felt before. An agony of pain swelled in her chest, constricting her throat, pain of contempt and scorn, pain of utter rejection. It hurt, it hurt so bad she wanted to cry. But she wouldn't cry because of them, she told herself. She wouldn't.

The tears were blinding as she reached the stable. She was about to collapse when a child's voice said, "What's wrong, Jessie?"

She couldn't bear for anyone to know, let alone Rachel's son.

"Nothing's wrong," she snapped. "I just got some dust in my eyes."

"Can I help?"

"No! I'm fine. The watering washed away the dust."

She walked past him to Blackstar's stall, but Billy followed. "I didn't know you were still here."

"Well I am, aren't I?"

He was not put off. "Are you going out on the range now?" he asked as she saddled Blackstar. When she didn't answer, he persisted. "Can I go with you this time?"

"No!"

"But I won't get in your way, Jessie, I promise I won't. Please?"

The pleading eagerness in that voice broke through, somehow, and she relented.

"All right." Then she added sternly, so he wouldn't think she was easily swayed, "But only this time. You can use that sorrel over there, if you know how to saddle him."

Billy let out a whoop of delight and ran to the horse. But the fact was, each time old Jeb had showed him how to saddle a horse so he could ride around the valley, Jeb had actually put the saddle on himself. Billy found himself stumped. He couldn't even get the heavy saddle off the railing, let alone onto the horse's back. The horse was higher than he was, and so was the railing.

Jessie finished with Blackstar and led him over to where Billy was struggling, shaking her head in amusement. The saddle he was fighting with was an old forty-pounder. Yet there was no other saddle in sight. She had to admit, the kid had determination.

She helped him tug the saddle down from the railing. "Now, together . . . one, two, *three*." They swung the saddle up into place, and Jessie stepped back. "Can you manage now?"

"Sure. And thanks."

Jessie waited impatiently as he tried to do the girth that was tucked under the saddle. His short arms couldn't reach it. He finally went around the horse and carried the strap under him, then buckled it too loosely.

"Honestly, can't you do anything?" she said gruffly as she came forward again to help.

Billy watched her stern expression as she finished the job. He grinned, happy. What she was doing spoke better than words.

"You don't really hate me, do you, Jessie?"

She looked up, startled. Why was he able to see through her like that? "Of course I do."

But Billy persisted, still grinning. "I think you like me just a little."

"Well, that just goes to show how much you know," she said lightly. She'd meant only to tease, but when she looked at him, there were tears glistening in his eyes. "Oh, Billy, I was only teasing. Honestly. Of course I like you." He looked relieved, and she added. "But don't you dare tell your mother I said so, you hear?"

Chapter 8

Old Jeb was in his glory when he was storytelling, and he had a rapt audience in Billy Ewing. Jessie was amused, leaning back against a railing and watching the expressions on her half brother's face as he listened to Jeb recount the time he'd come *that close* to being hanged.

Back at the end of '63, the Vigilantes of Montana had nearly sent Jeb to Boot Hill. The Vigilantes were formed in Virginia City, a town known to its shame to have been the scene of two hundred murders in only six months. Jeb had simply been mistaken for a member of a large gang. He was tried and sentenced to hang. The only reason he was spared was that the gang member he was mistaken for happened to wander into the crowd to watch the hanging. As he approached the crowd, he was recognized. It was an experience Jeb loved to talk about.

Jessie had heard it so often, though. She left

the stable without even being noticed, so engrossed were the young man and the old one.

She moved on slowly toward the house, stopping at the porch and stretching out on one of the leather settees. The air was still and not too cold. Jessie didn't want to go in just yet. It was late, but not too late.

Jessie closed her eyes against her thoughts, hoping the clear air would clear her mind so she could sleep. Just as she was beginning to feel peaceful, she heard, "Where's the boy?"

Jessie opened her eyes slowly. She didn't see Chase at first, and had to look around to find him sitting on the steps, leaning back against a post so he could face her.

"You'll find Billy in the stable with Jeb."

"I wasn't looking for him, just wondering where he was. I thought he might have turned in early, as much riding as he did today."

Jessie grinned to herself, remembering how hard Billy had tried to keep up with her. "He'll probably be sore in the morning, but I think he enjoyed himself."

"I've no doubt of that. He's wanted to go with you for a long time."

Jessie sat straight up and looked at him. "How would you know?"

"He tells me things," Chase replied a little proudly. "Will you be taking him out again?"

"I haven't thought about that." Jessie shrugged. "Not tomorrow, anyway. I won't be here tomorrow."

"Oh?"

Jessie felt her anger rising, and underneath that, she felt some of the pain Chase had caused her that morning.

"Yes, 'Oh,' and it's none of your business why, mister."

"I wish you'd consider calling me Chase," he said nicely.

"I don't know you well enough."

He grinned. "That can be easily rectified. What would you like to know about me?"

"Nothing," she said stubbornly, closing her eyes again.

"That's too bad, because I find myself infinitely curious about you."

She looked at him sharply. Was he teasing her?

"Why?" she demanded.

"You're so different from most girls. I find it fascinating, the way you've been raised. Tell me something. Is it what you wanted, this kind of life?"

"What difference does it make?" she said. "It's done. I am the way I am." She tried hard to keep the bitterness out of her voice. She would never admit to this man or to Rachel how much she hated her life. She wanted more than anything else to look and act like other girls. She'd had a chance to change herself when her father died, a chance to be normal at long last. She would have her chance again when the two interlopers were gone.

"Yes," Chase was saying pleasantly. "You are certainly unique. You can't blame a man for being curious, now, can you?"

He had such an engaging smile. His teeth were so white and even, his lips generous, yet not too full. And his dark hair waved across his forehead like . . .

Jessie shook herself. What was the matter with her, staring at him like that?

"Men out here, whether they're curious or not, don't ask so many questions," she said to him. "But I forget, you're not from out here. I'll be going to Cheyenne tomorrow, since you're interested. I have to hire a few more men for the roundup."

"Mind if I ride along?"

"Why? So you can do Rachel's bidding? I told you you'd only be wasting your time."

"Well, why don't you let me be the judge of that? I won't be moving along until I've done what you mother asked of me, you know." He tried to say it as gently as possible.

"Then by all means, you can come along with me tomorrow," Jessie said quickly.

Chased laughed heartily. "How eager you are to be rid of me. You wound me terribly, Jessica. Most women find me charming and witty. Women usually like having me around, believe it or not."

"But then, I'm not a woman, am I?" Jessie said in a perfectly calm voice, her expression unchanging. "I'm just a spoiled brat. So what I think of you can't make any difference one way or another, now, can it?''

Chase frowned. That echoed too closely what he'd said to Rachel that morning. She couldn't possibly have overheard, could she? No. She wouldn't be speaking to him at all if she had.

"Where's Rachel?'' Jessie broke into his thoughts.

"She's gone to bed,'' he answered, giving her a measuring look. "And don't you think it would be more appropriate if you called her Mother?''

"No, I don't,'' she replied simply. "And I think I'll be turning in myself now.''

Jessie sat up and stretched her arms outward and back, emphasizing that she was worn out, not just eager to end their conversation. His eyes went to her body, particularly to the area where her breasts pressed against her shirt front.

So that was all it took to get him to notice her as a woman! Jessie stretched a little harder before she stood up. She delighted in his expression. He seemed unaware that he was staring rudely.

"I'll be leaving before dawn, if you're set on riding with me,'' Jessie volunteered.

"Yes, well —''

"Good night, Mr. Summers.''

Chase watched her walk into the house. In the privacy of her room she would be removing her clothes, those male clothes that didn't really hide her femininity at all. What would she be putting on to wear to bed? A nightshirt? Nothing at all? He found he could easily picture her completely nude.

He began to wonder if his image of her would match the reality. Were her breasts really so full and rounded as they seemed, her waist so tiny? Her face and hands were sun-kissed, but he imaged the rest of her as delicate as a white rose. Her legs would be her worst feature. They were beautifuly long in proportion to her body, but she spent long hours riding astride every day, and that had to make for hard, bulging muscles. Yet those legs would be powerful, with the strength to trap a man between them and keep him there until she was through with him. Yes, she would be aggressive in making love.

Good Lord, what the hell was he doing, sitting here thinking those thoughts? Regardless of her shapely body, she was just a kid. He had no business stripping her clothes off, even in his mind. She was pretty enough — beautiful, really, if he cared to be honest. Downright stunning when she smiled.

But he didn't even like her. No, he didn't even like her.

Chapter 9

Jessie had no trouble waking up early. It was still dark, and she lit her lamp to get ready. She dressed with care, choosing her softest buckskin pants, a light cream color, and a matching vest set with silver conchas down each side. Silver chains held the vest together. A black silk shirt completed the outfit. Before she left her room, she did something she'd almost never done before. She opened the chest under her bed and took out a bottle of jasmine perfume, and applied just a touch behind each ear. Now, what will he think of that? She smiled to herself.

Kate was in the kitchen, and she served Jessie steak and eggs as soon as she sat down at the table. Kate sniffed at the flowery scent coming from Jessie and raised a brow, but made no comment. Jessie stared after her, grinning. Of course Kate wouldn't say anything, she never did.

Then Jessie frowned, looking at Kate's slumped shoulders. "Why don't you go back to bed after you serve Mr. Summers his breakfast, Kate? You're looking tired," Jessie said. "Rachel can see to herself."

"I do not mind." Kate spoke softly. "And Mr. Summers has already eaten."

That surprised Jessie. She wouldn't have expected him to be up so early. She finished eating quickly and hurried to the stable with the cold lunch Kate had prepared. Chase was talking to Jeb, his horse ready to go. She greeted him with a smile, determined to start the day out right, and he returned it more than generously.

She was pleased by the admiring way Chase looked her over, watching closly as she saddled and mounted. She had never been so conscious of her own movements as she was just then. It was exciting, this game. Could she hold his interest long enough to make him admit she wasn't a child, a brat?

The sky was growing pink as they rode out, Jessie leading the way out of the valley. The trail was still in shadow. As soon as the sun was up, they rode side by side, but they didn't talk. It was not a leisurely ride. Jessie needed to reach town by early afternoon, and she kept them at a steady pace, even breaking into a gallop on the plains.

Five hours later, they stopped at the little creek she always rested by when she went to Cheyenne. It was a nice spot, tree-shaded, level all the way to the water, beautiful with red and gold autumn leaves. It was safe, too, because the land all around them was flat. A stranger's approach could be seen right away.

They saw to their horses first, then sat down under the trees to share a loaf of bread, sliced beef, and cheese. Jessie washed up when she'd finished eating and leaned back against her saddle to rest for a while. Chase, still eating, sat near her.

Jessie put her arms behind her head, forcing the brim of her black felt hat over her eyes. She raised one knee and lazily moved it from side to side so he'd know she wasn't sleeping. The position thrust her breasts forward and drew attention to the flatness of her belly, as she'd intended. His eyes were on her, and she kept the hat over her face, allowing him full freedom to look.

Jessie's voice was startlingly loud when she asked, "How long have you known Rachel, Mr. Summers?"

He sighed. "If you're going to start to get to know me, don't you think it's time you called me Chase?"

"I suppose so."

She didn't see him grin. "I've known your mother for about ten years."

Jessie stiffened. Ten years ago Rachel had left Thomas Blair. Jessie had been eight. She didn't realize that Chase could only have been about fifteen or sixteen ten years ago. So she immediately assumed that Chase had been Rachel's lover just after Rachel left Thomas.

"And do you still love her?" Jessie asked tightly.

There was a pause.

"What exactly do you mean by that?"

Jessie changed her tone, trying to make light of it, as if she didn't care one way or another. 'You're one of her men, aren't you?"

Chase took a deep breath. "Hold on, kid. Is that what you've been thinking?"

Jessie sat up then and faced him squarely. "You came running when she called, didn't you?"

He laughed at her hard, accusing look. "You've got a dirty mind, Jessie, Or is it that you just think the worst of your mother all the time?"

"You haven't answered my question," she said stubbornly.

He shrugged. "I suppose I do love her, as much as I can love any woman."

That stopped Jessie. It took her a while to decide what she ought to say next. "Sounds like you don't like women very much."

"Now you've got me all wrong. I like all women. It's just that settling for one in particular isn't necessary."

"You like to spread yourself around?" she said nastily.

"You could say that." He grinned. "But only because I've never found a woman I could bear staying around for any length of time. Once they think they have you hooked, the romance is over and the pettiness begins, the nagging, the jealousy. That's the time to move on."

"Are you trying to tell me all women are like that?" Jessie asked quietly.

"Of course not. There are all kinds back East, but you have to understand that certain, well, types come west: those already married, their daughters looking to get married, and women who pretend they're not interested until they're asked."

"This latter group of women includes saloon and dancehall girls, I take it?"

"They are the most fun," he said, knowing he was in dangerous territory.

"Whores, in other words?"

"Now I wouldn't call them that," he said indignantly.

"Is that how you met Rachel?" she sneered.

He frowned, annoyed. "Obviously no one's told you, so I might as well. Rachel was alone, starving, and obviously pregnant when my step-father Jonathan Ewing brought her home."

"Your stepfather?"

"That surprises you?"

Jessie was a good deal more than surprised. She had thought Ewing was Billy's father, but obviously Will Phengle was. Did Billy know that? And then it came to her that Rachel was thirty-four now. Ten years ago, at twenty-four, she would have been a lot older than Chase. So they probably hadn't had an affair.

"Where was your mother?" Jessie asked.

"She had died not long before."

"I'm sorry."

"Don't be," he said flatly.

There was obviously bitterness there, but Jessie didn't want to know about it. She had enough bitterness of her own.

"So your stepfather married Rachel, even with her carrying another man's child?"

"Because of that child," Chase replied curtly. Good heavens, Jessie thought, what was going on? "The bastard waited to marry her till after she'd given birth to a son. I've no doubt he would have kicked her out if the baby had been a girl."

Jessie gasped. "Another man just like Thomas Blair! And I thought he was one of a kind."

"Well, there was a reason. Your father could have children. Jonathan Ewing couldn't. He was a rich man and wanted a son to take over his small empire. It was the only reason he married my mother. He didn't love her, he just wanted me. And she didn't care about anything except his wealth. Well, I cared all right. I hated his guts." He was silent, then went ahead.

"I was old enough to understand his motives, old enough to resent his high-handedness. He thought wealth could buy him anything. I wasn't willing to accept him, because I already had a father somewhere. So Ewing and I had a long, drawn-out battle. It never ended. Rachel made it easier, though, in the last year I was there. She was kind. She cared about me, and she was a good buffer between us. She helped me then. Do you see now why I want to return the favor?''

Jessie was silent. His childhood had been awful, fighting a father, losing a mother. But his earlier confession showed him to be a philandering bastard nonetheless.

"You don't really know Rachel," Jessie said.

"I think I know her better —" He stopped, staring into the distance behind her. "Someone seems awfully curious about us."

"What?"

"One of your friendly Indians, no doubt."

Jessie swung around quickly and followed his gaze. An Indian sat on a spotted pony a good distance away. He just sat there, staring toward them. Was it White Thunder? No, he would have come forward to greet her. Jessie got up and rummaged through her saddlebags, got her field glasses, and turned them on the Indian.

She lowered her glasses after a moment and said, "Now why would *he* be here, do you suppose?"

"A reservation Indian?" Chase asked.

She glanced at him and shook her head. "All Indians are reservation Indians to you, aren't they? God, but you're a hardhead. I tried to explain to you . . . Oh, what's the difference!"

Chase's eyes narrowed. "Are you saying we're in danger?"

"I'm in no danger, but I don't know about you," she replied cruelly.

"Look," he said impatiently, "will you explain?"

"That's a Sioux warrior out there. They don't leave their territory unless it's for a good reason, and they don't sit and watch you without a reason, either."

"You think there might be more of them?"

Jessie shook her head. "I don't think so. When I met Little Hawk last week, he was alone."

"You met him last week?" Chase echoed.

She turned away to put her field glasses back, delighted by the confusion she was causing him. "He shared my food and camp one night. He wasn't very friendly about it. He was quite arrogant, in fact. But that's often their way." And then she grinned at Chase. "Actually, he did want to be friendly with me in one sense, but I said no."

Chase managed to conceal his disbelief. "So he wanted you? I suppose that's why he's here now."

Jessie looked at him sharply, but his expression revealed none of what he was thinking. "I can't imagine what he's doing out there, but I'm not conceited enough to think he would come looking for me."

"Well, just in case he did, why don't we show him you're not available?"

Before she caught on, Chase pulled her into

his arms, and his mouth came down on hers. The contact was as jolting as being knocked off a horse. She was stunned, leaning back against his arms, letting herself succumb to the pressure of his lips. But even as she came to her senses, she didn't move. She liked the feel and taste of him, the heady sensation overcoming her. She'd certainly never been kissed like that before, and she realized it was because he knew what he was doing.

Why, it was experience, of course! Chase knew women very well, she reminded herself. Even as Jessie became indignant, however, she couldn't quite bring herself to pull away.

But they had both forgotten Little Hawk. Chase released Jessie as soon as he heard the horse galloping toward them. In a second, the Indian was leaping off his horse. Chase didn't even have time to raise his hands in defense before Little Hawk, flying through the air, caught him at the throat and threw him to the ground.

Jessie stared, wide-eyed. She had never seen such a graceful leap from a galloping horse. But why wasn't Chase getting up to fight? He wasn't moving. Little Hawk pulled out his knife.

"No!" she shouted at him. "Little Hawk!"

She ran forward, getting there just as he reached Chase, and stepped between them. She and Little Hawk stared at each other for several moments. Finally he put his knife away and looked down at Chase. He spoke angrily, then fired rapid signs at her.

She was confused, interpreting as best she could. "You want to know what he is to me? But I don't see —"

She stopped, remembering that he couldn't understand her. "Maybe you're just crazy," she muttered. "I can't explain . . . He means nothing to me."

"Then why do you kiss him?"

Jessie gasped. "Why, you bastard!" she cried. "You knew English *all the time*. You let me rack my brains to try to remember sign language, so — Oh! When I think how frightened I was, and all you had to *do* was tell —"

"You talk too much, woman," Little Hawk grunted. "Tell me why you kissed this man."

"I didn't. He did the kissing, and he did it so you would go away. There was no other reason for it, since he doesn't like me and I can't stand him. And why the hell am I explaining this to you? Why did you attack him?"

"Did you want his attention?"

"No, but —"

Little Hawk didn't stay to listen, but went to his horse. He mounted and came back, sitting looking down at her.

"White Thunder has returned to his winter camp," he said casually.

"So you do know him?"

"I have made his acquaintance since I met you. He tells me you have no man, only your father."

"My father recently died."

"Then you have no one?"

"I need no one," she answered, exasperated.

Little Hawk smiled, surprising her yet again. "We will meet again, Looks Like Woman."

"Damn!" she swore, turning back to Chase as Little Hawk rode away. He was lying still but breathing normally. She examined his head for damage and found a thick lump. She went to the creek, filled her hat with water, and threw the water in his face.

He came up sputtering and groaning, and she breathed a sigh of relief.

"Did that sonofabitch attack me?" Chase asked, feeling his head. He winced as he found the tender bump.

"He could have killed you," Jessie said harshly. "You're not much of a fighter."

He frowned. "What are you so riled about? Did you have to shoot him?"

"No, I didn't have to shoot him. And I wouldn't trade his life for yours, anyway."

Her venom stung him. "You really hate me, don't you?"

"Does it show?"

She moved away to saddle her horse. He was okay. She didn't have to tend to him anymore.

With care for every movement, Chase went to his own horse to saddle up. "Why did he attack me? Do you know?" he asked.

"Figure it out for yourself, tenderfoot."

"Damn it!" he swore. "Is it too much to ask

for a little kindness from you? I'm the one who got hurt, you know."

"And do you know why?" Jessie sneered. "Because of your showing off, that's why."

He looked at her thoughtfully. "Is that why you're so angry? Because I kissed you?"

She didn't answer. She silently mounted and rode off, leaving him to follow if he could. Chase climbed into the saddle, his head throbbing. He wasn't sure anymore why he had kissed her, but it had been a stupid thing to do. He would make sure he was never tempted to do it again, ever.

Chapter 10

Trouble began soon after they rode into Cheyenne. They left their horses at the livery stable, and Jessie went on to the hotel to get a room. She hadn't told Chase her plans, so he was obliged to follow her, wondering what she had in mind. They were barely speaking. Jessie told him where he could find a doctor if he thought it was necessary, and then she continued to ignore him. Her set features and angry stride told him she didn't want his company, and he knew damned well that if he asked about her plans she would tell him it was none of his business.

At the hotel, Jessie signed the register, and then Chase started to do the same. But before he could even finish, the book was suddenly snatched out of his hands.

"It's just like he said, Charlie," the man next to Chase called over his shoulder, chuckling.

"There's a *K* in front of her name."

"Do you mind, friend?" Chase said angrily.

"Oh, sure thing, mister." The man shoved the register back in front of Chase. He grinned. "Just wanted to check something."

As he walked away, Chase glanced at Jessie's name. Yes, there was a *K* in front of it. He then turned around to see that her path to the front door had been blocked by a squat, barrel-chested fellow. The lanky man who had just left Chase came up behind Jessie and slipped her gun out of her holster before she could stop him.

Chase waited for her reaction. It would be nice to see her let loose her terrible temper on someone else for a change.

But Jessie was just standing there, her back stiff, her hands on her hips, glaring.

"So Laton wasn't joshin'." Charlie laughed. "He said the name on the deed was Kenneth Jesse Blair. But I said no, old Blair must have a son somewhere. That's who he's left his ranch to. Couldn't be no girl named Kenneth. Didn't I say that, Clee?"

"Your exact words," the lanky Clee agreed, nodding.

"But Laton was right as usual," Charlie went on. "We got us a *bona fide* Kenneth here. Don't she look just like a Kenneth?"

"Britches and all," Clee agreed again, snickering.

"You've had your fun, mister, and I've had

93

enough of you," Jessie said in a low voice, looking at Clee. "I'll take my gun back now."

"Will you?" Clee grinnned. "What for, unless you're man enough to use it. Are you man enough?"

The men laughed, delighted at the jest. Jessie didn't think twice before she threw a punch at Clee's mouth. Her gun dropped out of his hand, and Charlie's face mottled with rage. He kicked her gun out of reach and grabbed her arms.

Chase had seen enough.

"Let the lady go, friend," Chase said, shoving Clee against a wall.

"You call this wildcat a lady?" Charlie growled.

He released Jessie, however, and she retrieved her gun. "Did Bowdre send you to harass me?" she demanded, facing Charlie squarely.

Charlie didn't like this turn of events. Laton wouldn't like to hear about this. If she went to him and made a fuss in front of others, he would be furious. Laton wanted to be sure no one would point a finger at him.

"Laton don't want no trouble with you, gal. All he wants is his money. It was Clee's idea to have a little fun with you. And we *were* only funnin'. You just ain't got no humor, gal," Charlie grumbled.

"Oh, I've got humor." Jessie smiled unpleasantly. "I'd think it was real funny if I put a ball in your gut." And then she said, "Just stay away from me, mister."

"Real pleasant, ain't she?" Charlie sneered as he and Clee watched her stalk out the door.

Chase caught up with her in the middle of the street. "Hold up, kid." He had to grab her arm to make her stop.

"What do you want?" she snapped.

He looked at her incredulously. She was actually angry because he had interfered!

"I swear, kid, someone ought to take a stick to you. You can't go around throwing your fists at anyone you please. Next time you might not be so lucky."

"Who the hell made you my guardian angel, Summers?" she spat.

They were at a standoff — again. And she was right. He wasn't her keeper.

He grinned. "I thought we agreed you would call me Chase."

"I have a name, too, and it's not 'kid,' " Jessie said stonily.

He laughed. "Touché." She continued walking and he fell into step beside her. "Where are you going now — if you don't mind my asking?"

"To the sheriff's office."

"Because of what just happened?"

"Now why would I bother the sheriff about that?" She seemed truly puzzled.

"Then why?"

"Who would know better who's in town, who's just passing through, who's looking for work? I'm hoping he'll have a few suggestions so I can finish my business today and head back to the ranch in the morning.''

"Then I'll just come along with you, if you don't mind," he said. "The sheriff should be told about our encounter with that Indian.''

Jessie stopped short. "Why?''

"There could be others in the area," Chase replied. "Don't you think he should know?''

"No," she said emphatically. "Look, the sheriff would only laugh at you if you started jabbering about hostiles in the area. He knows better. But if other people heard you, it could cause a ruckus. Then you'd look mighty foolish, because Little Hawk was alone, and I'm sure he's already gone back north.''

She walked on, but Chase didn't follow any longer. He stared after her with eyes like burning coals. She'd done it again, made him feel like a complete ass. Damned if she didn't do it on purpose!

He found a saloon without much searching. After several drinks he was able to cool down. He even joined in a card game. It was a surprise to find himself introduced to Laton Bowdre, sitting in on the game. The skinny, mustached man with thin, wispy hair, sharp cheekbones, and a decidedly avaricious look about him was just what Chase had pictured. The day wasn't going to be a total loss after all.

Chapter 11

The knock on the door caught Jessie as she finished pulling her boots on. It was Chase. She had decided to make an effort to be nicer to him, so she let him in with a "good morning" that was almost cheerful.

He looked terrible. His chin was darkened with stubble, his clothes were rumpled, and his eyes were red from too much smoke and not enough sleep. Maybe he hadn't slept at all.

Chase wasn't too tired to notice immediately the change in Jessie. Besides looking fresh and clean and lovelier than any girl had a right to look first thing in the morning, she was actually smiling.

He came to his own conclusion. "I take it you hired your hands and are pleased to be going home?"

"As a matter of fact, I only found one man worth his salt," Jessie replied. "The other two

I talked to didn't know a cow from a steer."

Chase chuckled. "City boys."

"City boys," she agreed, grinning along with him.

"So you won't be leaving today after all?"

"I guess not, unless I get lucky this morning. I sent Ramsey, the fellow I hired, on out to the ranch. No point in wasting him here, even for a day."

"Are you sure you told him how to find the ranch?"

He was teasing her, showing her there were no longer any hard feelings about the day she had given him the wrong directions.

She grinned. "I reckon he'll manage, since he's from near here."

It was pleasant to see her in an agreeable mood for once, and he said impulsively, "Look, there's really no point in your hiring another man when I'll be at the ranch, anyway. I might as well do something to earn my keep while I'm here."

Jessie didn't take him seriously. "You don't know cattle," she said, startled.

"Who says I don't? I've driven cattle from Texas to Kansas."

"How often?" she asked.

"Once," he admitted. "I hired on for the trail drive just for the company, since I was heading in the same direction and I wasn't in a hurry. Once was enough."

She was amazed. "So you really know cattle?

I never would have guessed it."

"I'll admit I've never done any branding, but I learned to handle a rope fairly well. And I can carry a tune passably. And I know the difference between a steer and a cow."

She laughed. "Then I guess you're hired — Chase."

He smiled. "Give me an hour to freshen up, and we can start back together."

She smiled again. "I'll meet you downstairs for some breakfast."

But Jessie shook her head as she watched him leave the room. She never would have believed it. He didn't have to earn his keep at the ranch. Rachel had invited him as her guest. So why had he made the offer to help out?

Chase was wondering exactly the same thing. What made it especially confusing was that he had Thomas Blair's note in his pocket. It had taken him all night to win it from Bowdre, but he had done it.

Why he hadn't come right out and told Jessie about winning the note, he wasn't sure. Perhaps he had the feeling she'd be angry with him — again.

He sighed. He wasn't at all sure her worries were over, not as gracelessly as Bowdre had lost the note. Chase recognized that he might actually have made things worse.

They returned to the Rocky Valley late that afternoon. Jeb eagerly told them about the big pronghorn that had been dumped on the back-door steps sometime after Jessie rode to Cheyenne. No one had seen who brought the animal, freshly killed. No one knew who it might have been. If someone was going to give away fresh meat, he usually waited around for a thank-you.

But Jessie knew instantly who the mysterious provider was. It could be none other than Little Hawk.

As they bedded the horses down, she said to Jeb, "You remember the young Sioux I told you about? Little Hawk? Well, we met him on the plains yesterday afternoon."

"Is that a fact?" Jeb whistled. "He's the one?"

"It looks that way."

"Mighty nice of him." Jeb chuckled.

Jessie glanced at Chase. He was rubbing down the golden palomino, pretending he wasn't listening.

"I suppose you don't agree?" Jessie asked pointedly.

He didn't look up. "I'm sure you both have good reason for thinking it was Little Hawk. I'm just dying to know what his purpose was, that's all."

"You don't know much about Indians, do you, young feller?" Jeb chuckled.

"I'm beginning to think not," Chase answered without rancor.

"Indians don't like to be indebted to anyone, especially to a white. Little Hawk took Jessie's food and shared her fire without givin' anything in return.'' Jeb cackled. ''That must have rankled him. So now he's paid his debt and then some. Generous of him, too. That big pronghorn would've fed his whole tribe.''

''Now you see why he was so far south,'' Jessie added. ''He had to let me see him, or I'd never have known he had paid his debt.''

''Yes, but that doesn't explain the rest of what happened yesterday,'' Chase said shortly.

Jessie laughed as she approached him and put her hand on his arm. ''Come on. I'm sure Billy will love to hear how you were attacked by a savage Sioux and lived to tell about it. And I promise not to interrupt you if you embellish the tale.''

She was teasing him, but he didn't mind. In fact, what they were talking about went right out of his head the moment she touched him. Her touch seemed to burn his arm, even after she had moved away.

Chapter 12

Exhausted though he was, sleep still eluded Chase that night. His mind wouldn't let him rest. What the hell did a man do when he found himself desiring a girl who was off limits?

Jessie was just a kid. Well, maybe not a kid. But she was Rachel's daughter. So even if she were willing, he couldn't have her without marrying her, not Rachel's daughter.

Chase wasn't anywhere near ready to settle down. He was only twenty-six, and there were too many things he wanted to do first. Finding his real father was one thing. He had put it off for quite a few years after he'd had no luck in California, where his mother claimed to have met Carlos Silvela. Perhaps now was the time to continue the search. Should he go to Spain, where his father's home was supposed to be? Anyway, it was better thinking about that than about an eighteen-year-old woman-child he had no business thinking about.

But it didn't work for long. Nothing did. He kept seeing those bright, turquoise eyes, that pert nose and stubborn chin, that softly rounded bottom.

"Damn!"

He jumped out of bed as if he'd found her there. He needed some air, some cool air, maybe even a swim in the stream that ran behind the house.

Throwing on some clothes in the dark, Chase stepped out of his room, only to have the cause of his turmoil step right into his arms. For a second, he wondered if he was dreaming. But the warmth, the smell of her was real. Then he saw that her falling into his arms had been an accident. She pushed away from him.

"I'm sorry," she whispered. "I didn't see you."

"It's so dark here," Chase managed to reply, having no idea what he was saying.

"I couldn't sleep," Jessie explained. "I thought I'd go for a ride. The moon's bright enough."

"I've been having the same problem. Why don't we go together?"

"If you like," she said, walking on toward the kitchen without waiting for him.

Chase didn't move. He wanted to wring his own neck. For the life of him, he couldn't understand why he had offered to go with her. That was the last thing he wanted. He needed to get away from her. Then Chase pulled himself together, chastising himself for being afraid of a slip of a girl. He couldn't very well let her go off alone, anyway.

Jessie led the way up into the lower hills of the mountains, rather than out over the plains, prodding her horse upward to a spot that offered a beautiful view of the valley. It wasn't too long before they reached the place. Trees parted on a ridge before a view so breathtakingly beautiful, especially in the moonlight, that both were enthralled.

"It's lovely, isn't it?" he said softly as they dismounted.

"The stream looks like liquid silver in this light," she answered, pointing. "And over there you can see several more creeks. There's one farther up where I like to swim, a nice sunny area that's completely secluded."

"You're not thinking of swimming now, are you?" Chase asked in alarm.

Jessie laughed softly. "Of course not. It's too cold at night." She looked at him carefully and frowned sternly. "Look at you. Why didn't you bring a jacket?"

"I didn't think about it," he said lamely. "But I'm fine, really."

"You are not." She went to get the extra blanket she always kept in her saddlebag. "Here. You can wrap yourself in this for the ride back."

She leaned close to him to drape it around his

shoulders. That closeness was just more than he could bear. She was only inches away. His arms acted of their own accord, circling her, gathering her to him. His lips sought hers. He was powerless to obey his better instincts, so he left it up to Jessie, silently begging her to fight him off. Maybe she could bring him to his senses.

But Jessie had no thought of fighting him. She was caught off guard and considered nothing except the sensations fluttering in her belly and the warmth spreading through her. The pressure of his lips increased, and with it her yearning grew.

His tongue forced its way between her lips next, and she opened her mouth to accommodate him, liking the new assault. She moaned softly and pressed closer to the hard, muscular length of him. She could feel the evidence of his desire and was extremely excited by it. Chase gave up his silent battle and succumbed. She would be his. There was no further thought to the consequences.

He pulled her down to the ground, the blanket spreading out under him. He managed to keep her in the same position, so that she lay on top of him, her legs between his. The full weight of her pressing on him was a lightning shock. He rolled over, placing her beneath him. There was a frantic urgency to his movements.

Jessie felt him opening her belt and tugging at her shirt. His hand moved up under her shirt and reached her breasts, and little sounds of pleasure escaped her, driving him wild. He was too inflamed to be gentle, but so was she. She ripped a button from his shirt, trying to reach his bare flesh. His skin was hot, burning her, and the muscles on his back were hard and tense. She dug her fingers into those muscles, clasping him savagely.

A little voice inside her head asked her what the hell she was doing, but she ignored it. She moved both hands to his chest, running her fingers through his hair, reaching his shoulders, his thickly corded neck, grasping his hair.

His lips were devouring hers now, bruising her, but she urged him on. He tugged at her pants, and she helped him push them down to her feet. But when he moved to fight with her boots so as to remove her pants completely, she stopped him. She was on fire. She couldn't bear to have him move away from her even for a moment.

She caught his hair and pulled him down on top of her. "I want you now," she whispered huskily. "Now."

His lips seared her throat, moving to her ear. "But I want to feel all of —"

"Now, Chase!"

His desire to have her skin molded to his, to look on all of her in the moonlight, was not as strong as her urgent plea. He undressed in an instant, and she brought her knees up on both sides of his. Her moist warmth made it easy for him to enter her, but Chase restrained himself, holding back for one delicious moment, wanting to savor that first thrust. And then he found his way blocked by the last thing he had expected to find.

"Oh, my God," he gasped, never more miserable in his life. "I'm sorry, Jessie."

She paid no attention, thrusting her hips upward insistently. Jessie gasped. No one had ever told her there would be any pain. But it faded, and then it was gone, the urgent need returning and washing through her like a flood.

He was moving in her, and she delighted in the full length of him. He was gentler than she would have liked, slower, but she found the exquisite torture had its rewards, intensifying her need, prolonging the craving. And when she hurtled over the crest, the explosion that followed went on and on.

A few moments later, when Chase collapsed and was still, Jessie hugged him to her tenderly. "Wonderful," she murmured dreamily.

He raised his head. "More than you realize," he said softly.

His lips caressed hers with a feathery touch and moved down to her neck, her ear. He laid his head on her shoulder with a deep, contented sigh. Chase had never felt more relaxed, more blissful. Sleep beckoned, but he fought it, wanting to savor the feeling of her clasping him.

She was like no woman he had ever been with. Such intense passion from a woman was unknown to him. She had been as wild to have him as he was to have her. Even her virginity hadn't restrained her. Her virginity! Ah, he had forgotten. Damn! He was done for now!

Jessie felt him tense suddenly. "What's wrong?" she asked.

"Nothing," he replied too quickly.

Jessie frowned. "You're sorry we did this, aren't you?"

"Aren't you?" he countered.

"Why should I be?"

"You were a virgin!" he said painfully.

Jessie smiled. "Of course I was. Did you think otherwise?"

He was feeling trapped. "Well, you weren't behaving like a virgin the first day I saw you."

"Oh, that," Jessie scoffed remembering. "That was nothing. I just wasn't aware of what Blue was doing."

"I suppose you'll say that about what happened here tonight."

Jessie grinned, thinking he was jealous. "I was quite aware of everything *you* were doing."

He was silent, which began to confuse her.

"I don't understand what you're upset about," she said.

"You were a virgin! I had no right . . . I would have stopped."

"I know," she said softly, remembering when he had indeed stopped. "But I'm glad you didn't."

"You made sure I wouldn't, didn't you?"

She giggled.

"I don't see anything funny about this, Jessie."

"I don't see what the problem is. I wanted you, too, you know. If I'm not upset over what happened, why should you be?"

"You're not going to expect . . . anything . . . because of this?"

He rolled over even as he asked the question and began dressing.

"What do you mean, expect anything?" she asked warily.

"Come on, Jessie, you know what I mean. I'm sure you're not like most virgins, who give themselves up just to trap a man, but if Rachel should find out about this she would insist —"

"We marry," Jessie finished for him, her eyes blazing with sudden and complete understanding. "And of course I'm not good enough for you to marry."

"I didn't say that."

She slapped him then with all the fury growing within her. "Bastard!" she hissed, getting to her feet. "It didn't matter while you were getting what you wanted, but afterward you started fearing the consequences, didn't you?"

"Jessie —"

"Damn you, I hate you! You've made me feel dirty and calculating and deceitful. But I'm not like that! I hate you for it."

He could have cut his tongue out. "Jessie, I'm sorry," he began contritely, but she was walking away so as to dress apart from him. Once dressed, she grabbed her blanket and mounted.

"You've ruined what happened, and nothing can change that," she called to him. "I wouldn't marry you if you begged me. So you needn't worry I'll tell Rachel about it. I don't need her reminding me of something I'm going to forget."

Jessie rode off. At least he knew better than to follow her.

Chapter 13

Chase woke at dawn. He took his time getting back to the ranch, trying to think what to say to Jessie. He had ruined her first taste of love, and he wanted terribly to make her feel better.

Rachel was on the porch, looking especially lovely in a dress of spring green with rows of white ruffles that swept back into the bustle. Her golden hair was caught in a tight bun at her neck, with wispy curls at her temples.

She looked elegant. Rachel always looked elegant, demure and poised, as if nothing could ruffle her. It was one thing Jonathan Ewing had admired about her. And it was the only thing that irritated Chase about Rachel, that unnatural self-control.

"Goodness, Chase, you look like you've been out all night," Rachel said as he drew up by the porch.

He looked down at himself and grinned,

rubbing his stubbly chin. "I was. I couldn't sleep last night and went for a ride. Only I got lost in the dark, so I bedded down until daylight."

She shook her head. "Honestly, Chase, that's not like you."

"Well, I haven't exactly been myself since I came here, Rachel," he retorted. "That daughter of yours has a way of changing people."

She ignored that. "Weren't you supposed to begin work this morning?"

He was ashamed. He'd forgotten. "I guess I was. I suppose Jessie has already left?"

"I don't know," Rachel sighed. "She never tells me anything."

"Well, mornin', young feller." Jeb came around the porch and spotted Chase. "Noticed your horse didn't sleep in his stall last night. You just gettin' back from somewhere?"

"Yep," Chase replied, offering nothing further.

Jeb grunted, seeing he wasn't going to get any more information. He turned to Rachel, dismissing Chase by giving him his back.

"Thought you'd better see this, so you don't go gettin' all fired up like before," he told her grouchily.

She snatched the note from Jeb and read it quickly, groaning. "Not again."

Chase dismounted and read the piece of paper.

Jeb,

I need to get away for a while. Look after things for me. Tell Mitch to start the drive without me if I'm not back before he's ready. He can handle things. You know where to find me if I'm needed.

Jessie

"So where's she gone this time, Jeb?" Chase demanded.

"Where she went last time," Jeb said none too kindly.

"Are you going to start that again?" Chase exploded.

"You know where to find her, Jeb. You have to go after her," Rachel said.

"Can't do that." He shook his head stubbornly. "Not unless she's needed, like she says."

Rachel turned to Chase, those big eyes so full of anxiety. "All right, Rachel," he groaned. "I haven't done this much riding since I covered California searching for my father."

She placed a hand on his arm. "I can't tell you how much I appreciate this, Chase."

"I know," he said. "But that daughter of yours won't appreciate it when I catch up with her."

He wasn't at all pleased about this second wild-goose chase. And the fact that Jessie had run away made him feel decidedly uncomfortable after what had happened the night before. She was gone because of him.

113

Chapter 14

It was so wonderful to be with White Thunder and his family again, wonderful to put away her guns and wear the Indian dress Little Gray Bird Woman had helped her make, to braid her hair and wrap fancy beaded and quilled thongs around her braids. It was wonderful. But it wasn't the same as before, because there was an intruder this time.

Little Hawk had followed her to the Cheyenne village. He had not returned north at all but had stayed in the area. If he'd been skulking around, watching her, couldn't he have seen her with Chase that night? She was more embarrassed than she'd ever been in her life. Why did he persist in following her? White Thunder couldn't explain, saying only that Little Hawk had requested to speak with her.

She had managed to forget about Little Hawk the night before. She and White Thunder spent long hours talking, and she had unburdened herself to him, especially about her father's death. His sympathy had managed to make her cry, which was good. Then she went on to tell him about Rachel and her recent troubles, but he had no solutions to offer. For some reason, she said nothing about Chase. Perhaps she was too ashamed.

This afternoon, Jessie waited in the tepee with her friend for Little Hawk's arrival. They had the large tepee to themselves. White Thunder's little brother was off with his friends, using half-sized bows and arrows to hunt for prairie dogs and rabbits. Runs with the Wolf was outside gambling with some of the older men. Wide River Woman and Little Gray Bird Woman were tanning a buffalo hide behind the tepee, and their soft voices came to Jessie every so often. She had to grin at their conversation.

"I saw you smiling at Gray Kettle, daughter, and I have told you many times you must never exchange glances or smiles with a man, and certainly not one who is courting you."

"But it was only a little smile, Mother," Little Gray Bird Woman protested.

"Every little smile will lessen your worth. He will think he has already won you, so he will not offer so many horses. Do you want to be a poor wife?"

"No, Mother." Little Gray Bird Woman's voice was submissive. "And I will remember not to smile so much."

"Not to smile at all, daughter," Wide River Woman reprimanded. "And you must not let Gray Kettle or White Dog stay so long when they come to visit."

"Yes, Mother."

"Has either of your young men asked you to marry?" Wide River Woman's voice grew even more serious.

"No, not yet."

"Well, you must remember to refuse the first time you are asked. Refuse gently, but let them know you are not an easy conquest."

"But, Mother —"

"Listen to me. I tell you these things for your own good," Wide River Woman said patiently. "Do not let either of your young men see you when you are alone, even the man you prefer. You must not let a man touch you, daughter, especially your breasts. If a man touches your breasts, he considers that you belong to him. Would you have your two men fighting each other because one boasts that he has won you before he has consent? No, you would not, for the one you prefer may lose. Have you made a choice yet? My husband favors White Dog, as I do, but if Gray Kettle should offer more, then . . ."

Their voices trailed off. Jessie's face was bright red. She had let Chase Summers touch her breasts and do a great deal more. But he wasn't an Indian. He'd not think she belonged to him. No, quite the opposite. Chase had known her in the most intimate way, then wanted nothing more to do with her!

White Thunder had been watching Jessie closely, and he'd known her for a long time.

"You blush. Have you been touched by a man, Looks Like Woman?" he teased.

Jessie gasped. Could he see into her mind? It was eerie and it had happened many times before.

"Do you wish to speak of it?" he asked hesitantly.

"No, not yet."

"It was not Little Hawk?"

She laughed bitterly and he was shocked.

"At least he wouldn't want a woman one minute, then decide she was unworthy of him the next."

"Who has treated you this way?" White Thunder stood up. He was very angry.

"Sit down, my friend," Jessie said gently. "I was probably as much to blame for what happened as he was. I was naive."

"But you are hurt."

"I will get over it."

Jessie returned to pounding the wild cherries, pits and all, in a stone mortar. Later they would be dried and mixed with strips of buffalo meat and fat to make pemmican, a food that would keep for months.

He moved away from her, leaving her to her thoughts. Jessie was glad she had told him. He would understand now if she suddenly became moody.

White Thunder was such a wise, thoughtful man for one so young. He was, in fact, only two years older than she was. How she loved him, her dear friend! She glanced at him and smiled as he looked up at her.

The Cheyenne were the tallest of the Plains tribes, and White Thunder was six feet in height. He was disturbingly handsome, too, with those startling blue eyes inherited from his father. His skin was copper, but mostly from the sun. He was a young warrior who had already proved himself as fit as any man, stronger than most. She was proud of their friendship.

Little Hawk came in a few minutes later, entering the tepee silently. He wore a shirt reserved for special occasions, one made of the hide of the bighorn sheep. The long sleeves were fringed, as were his leggings, and the bead work was beautiful. There were also tassels and bits of metal and shells hanging here and there. On his braids were wrappings of white fur, and a single blue feather was attached, just like the feather he had left her.

White Thunder was impressed, and concerned. The way the Sioux was dressed portended something important, and he was afraid he knew what that something was. He was not pleased.

Little Hawk, following protocol, waited to be invited to sit. White Thunder let him wait for a moment, looking at Jessie to see if she understood the meaning of this visit. Finally he sighed and bade Little Hawk welcome, speaking in the Sioux tongue. Jessie watched them talking, growing impatient as the conversation continued without her understanding a word of it. She had thought Little Hawk was there to talk to her. She was becoming annoyed.

At last Little Hawk turned to her, and White Thunder said, "He asks permission to speak to you."

Jessie replied, "But I have already agreed to speak to him. Isn't that why he's here?"

"He is asking formally now."

Jessie repressed a grin at the absurdity of it. "Then I agree, formally."

White Thunder continued solemnly, "He has also asked that I interpret for him."

"But why? He speaks English."

"He disdains to use it when it is not necessary," White Thunder explained.

Jessie was irritated. "Then why did he learn it to begin with?"

"You wish me to ask him?"

"*I* can ask him," she said curtly.

"Do not speak with him directly," White Thunder warned quietly. "Do not look at him so boldly, either, or reveal what you are thinking."

She laughed. "Do you know you sound just like your mother?"

"Be serious, woman." White Thunder

frowned at her. *"He* is serious. Besides, for what he intends, it is customary for him to speak through a third person." He raised a questioning brow at her. "Do you understand now?"

Jessie's forehead crinkled in a frown. What was he trying to tell her? She had never known White Thunder to be so cryptic.

"Perhaps if we just got on with it," Jessie suggested, glancing apprehensively at Little Hawk.

The two men spoke at length, and Jessie's apprehension grew when it became obvious that they were arguing. If she only had some inkling of what the meeting was all about.

The men fell silent, and Jessie found she'd been holding her breath. When neither man spoke again, she prompted, "Well?"

"It is as I guessed," White Thunder told her shortly. "He wants you to be his woman."

Jessie was speechless. She told herself she ought not to be surprised, but she was.

She turned to Little Hawk then, and their eyes locked for a moment before she looked away. Yes, he did want her. Suddenly she was flattered. This was soothing balm after the despicable way Chase had treated her.

"Just his woman, or his wife?" she asked hurriedly.

"His wife."

"I see . . ." Jessie gazed up toward the top of the tepee, musing.

White Thunder was taken aback. "You are not considering accepting?"

"What did he offer for me?"

"Seven horses," he answered.

"Seven?" Jessie was impressed. "Why so many? Is he rich?"

"Simply determined, I think. One horse would be for me, for agreeing to speak for him, since he has no close friend here to do so. Two horses would be given to Runs with the Wolf, since it is his tepee you occupy. The other four are for you, and will remain yours, along with all your own possessions."

"And the tepee," she prompted, knowing that a tepee was considered the wife's property.

"No, not the tepee," White Thunder confessed gently. "This was the main reason I told him it would not work. He already has a first wife."

"He does?"

"Yes."

"I see," Jessie said stiffly.

Why she was suddenly so angry she didn't know. Perhaps because it had been nice to feel wanted, to forget about her troubles at the ranch. A fairy tale, however.

"Tell Little Hawk I am flattered," Jessie said, "but I cannot possibly accept. Tell him white women do not share their husbands. I will not be a second wife."

To Jessie's relief Little Hawk accepted her refusal gracefully. He had a few more words

121

with White Thunder, then left the tepee.

"He said he expected your refusal this first time," White Thunder told her gravely. "He seems to think you will get used to the idea and change your mind."

"Oh!" Jessie was getting worried. "I suppose he will stick around, to press his suit?"

"I can guarantee you have not seen the last of him," replied White Thunder.

Jessie shook her head. A few days before, she had been without a man and as free as you please. Now she had more than she cared to handle.

Chapter 15

It was late afternoon of the fourth day that Chase had been on the trail. He had never thought he would have to come this far. He had stopped at Ft. Laramie, spending a night there, and had been directed to White Thunder's village. He knew this would be the right place. It had to be. There was no other settlement nearby.

The village looked peaceful enough in the late afternoon sun. Children were playing. He could see women working, men gathered in groups. There were many horses tethered by the tepees, meat hung up to dry, skins spread out for tanning. It seemed a prosperous village, and tranquil. He crouched near a creek, watching. Could this be where she was?

His question was answered immediately, when he moved a little way down the creek to where an overgrowth of shrubbery and trees blocked the village from view. He had meant to hide there, but he stopped when he saw a woman bathing in the creek. She was naked to her waist, and she wore an Indian breechcloth. Chase moved closer to the bank, leading his horse carefully. He was far enough away that she couldn't see him.

He forgot about the village, forgot everything as he watched her bathing. It was Jessie. He was sure of it. Her hair was loose and clinging to her wetly. Lord, she was beautiful, a goddess kissed by the sun. Her breasts were much fuller than he remembered, unencumbered by a shirt. They stood high and proud above her tiny waist and gently swelling hips. Chase was mesmerized. Why was she so special, so lovely?

His musings came to a sharp halt when he saw that Jessie was speaking to someone. Then he saw the Indian. He was sitting, with his back against a gnarled tree. The Indian wasn't facing Jessie, but he turned to look at her when she spoke to him.

Chase was furious. A man was watching Jessie bathe! It was a shame that his fury overcame him, because he lost all awareness of his surroundings. Black Bear Hunter, White Thunder's older brother, was moving slowly toward the white stranger. From his position, he could not see Jessie or White Thunder, the man who was talking to her. It appeared only that the white stranger was spying on his village. Black Bear Hunter approached Chase ever so cautiously.

Jessie managed to put Little Hawk from her mind as she let the cold creek water trickle over her body. She and White Thunder had often taken baths together when they were younger, but Wide River Woman had put a stop to that when Jessie's body began developing curves. White Thunder still accompanied her, however, to protect her.

It was really because of Black Bear Hunter that White Thunder was there. He was the only one in the village who had never tolerated Jessie's visits. Twice the brothers had argued over her. And several times Black Bear Hunter had come upon Jessie alone and frightened her terribly.

She had not seen Black Bear Hunter last year, or during this visit. She knew he had recently taken a wife and had his own tepee. She wondered if he was perhaps less severe now.

Jessie broached the question to White Thunder, calling over her shoulder, "Does your brother still hate me?"

White Thunder was so surprised by the question that he forgot himself and turned to look at her. "But he has never hated you."

"Of course he has."

White Thunder turned away quickly. It had been a long time since he had seen her without clothes. His face heated. It had happened before, and he was furious with himself whenever it happened. He could not bear what he sometimes felt for her. They were friends. He would not jeopardize that.

"Did you hear me, White Thunder?"

"Yes," he called back without looking at her. "But you are wrong in mistaking what he feels for hate."

"But you know how he's always been," Jessie reminded him.

"He did not like it that you came here, but only because you were white like my father, the one who took Wide River Woman away from her first husband, Black Bear Hunter's father. He lost his father because of that, and he bears a grudge against whites, all of them."

"But I was a child. I was blameless."

"He knew that. He even came to regret his treatment of you, but it was too late by then."

"Why? I would have understood."

"Yes, but would you have understood all the reasons for his change? You see, he found himself wanting you."

She was surprised, and a little disbelieving. "He had a funny way of showing it," she scoffed.

"Because you are white. Because he could not permit himself to want a white woman. He took pains never to let you know. He was harsh because it was not easy to conceal what he felt for you."

"But how do you know this, White Thunder?" Jessie asked. "Did he tell you?"

"No. I just know."

"Well, you could be wrong, couldn't you?"

"I doubt it. But would you prefer to go on thinking he hates you, when that is not true?"

"Yes, I would." She was quite serious. "It is rather disconcerting to suddenly find I am wanted by so many men. I am not used to it, and I don't understand it. It is not as if I am a vision of beauty, you know. I'm usually sweaty and dusty from work, and dressed in pants. Why, Little Hawk didn't even see me in a dress until today. Yet he and Chase —"

"So that is the name of the other one?" White Thunder interrupted.

"We will not discuss *him*," Jessie said stonily. "Just tell me, is Black Bear Hunter happy with his wife? Can I expect less hostility from him now?"

"He is happy, but how he will feel about you I cannot say."

"Where is he?"

"He went hunting, and he should return any time. In fact —" White Thunder stood up, his expression alert. "I believe that is his victory cry. You hear it?"

"Yes. You go ahead, White Thunder. I'm almost finished."

"You are sure?"

"Yes. Little Hawk will be inspecting Black Bear Hunter's prize, so he won't bother me, and I'm not worried about anyone else. Go on."

Jessie finished washing her hair. She didn't hurry. As much as she had on her mind, she wasn't curious about Black Bear Hunter's prize. She would hear of it later, she was sure.

Imagine Black Bear Hunter wanting her, too! She shook her head, bemused. It was all so strange, the different aspects of wanting. Blue had wanted her. Little Hawk wanted her. Chase had wanted her, but only for the one time. And Black Bear Hunter fought his desire, continually hostile because he wanted her. In all of that, where was love? Rachel had only pretended to love Thomas, and what Thomas had felt couldn't be called love, for it had turned to hate. In books, real love was bountiful, but Jessie had never seen two married people display the kind of love she had read about. Was there really any such thing as love?

A little while later, dressed, her hair still wet but braided in two neat plaits, Jessie turned toward the narrow path leading up to the camp. Little Hawk stood there, blocking her way, standing with his feet slightly apart, his arms crossed over the wide expanse of his chest. He had removed his ceremonial shirt and his leggings, and was wearing only his breechcloth and moccasins.

Jessie managed to hide her surprise. She stared levelly at him.

"If you are finished, I will walk you back," Little Hawk offered.

"So now you will speak English?"

"When it is only the two of us, it is necessary," he replied with a shrug. Then he said abruptly, "You should not be here without the gun you carry on your hip."

"It wasn't needed. I wasn't alone until just before you came. You did *just* come, didn't you?"

"If I say yes, will it make you happy?"

"What kind of answer is that?" Jessie snapped.

"You would rather hear that I came while you were still drying yourself?"

Jessie's eyes blazed. "Why didn't you make yourself known? You had no right to . . . to stand there and watch me!"

"You let White Thunder watch you." He made the observation calmly.

"He didn't watch me," she insisted. "He wouldn't do that. He's my friend. I trust him."

Little Hawk grinned. "You will learn to trust me."

"How can I when you sneak up on me?"

"Hold, Looks Like Woman." He cut her off and in two steps he was beside her, forcing her to look into his eyes. "Why are you angry? Do you begrudge me the sight of you when I have made my intentions clear? Is it not reasonable for a man to seek out the woman he has asked to marry? I did not know I would find you as I did, but I am not sorry. The sight of you gave me much pleasure."

He went on to say something more, but he had switched to his own language, and while Jessie was confused at the change, he kissed

129

her.

It was a shock. She felt it right down to her toes. It frightened her, and she was powerless to resist.

When he finally let her go, he stood looking at her intently, passionately. He smiled, thinking he had won that round. "You have the sky and the forest both in your eyes, and when you are angry, they light up like the stars. But you must learn to curb your temper, Looks Like Woman. My first wife is a gentle woman — she would not understand these emotions of yours that rage like storms."

"You needn't worry!" she said hotly. "I won't be meeting your wife — ever. And I can walk back to camp myself, thank you."

She tried to pass him, but he caught her arms. "Does it bother you this much that I have a first wife?" he asked softly.

"Of course it does."

"But I can love you both."

"I know your customs," she said defensively. "But I am from a different culture, and I couldn't be happy sharing a husband."

"Then I will give up my wife."

"Don't you dare!" Jessie gasped. "I couldn't bear that. I couldn't live with myself if you did that. You must care for her."

"Yes, but I want you, Looks Like Woman."

Jessie wanted to scream. "Look, I'm not even a virgin," she said quietly, her cheeks turning rosy. "So forget about me and —"

"That does not matter."

"It doesn't?" she asked, disbelieving.

"No."

Having nothing further to say to him, she pushed away and ran up the path.

He let her go but called after her, "A Sioux does not give up easily, Looks Like Woman."

"You'd better learn to!" she shouted back at him just before she broke through the bushes and saw the camp.

She heard him laugh and ran faster, running all the way to Runs with the Wolf's tepee.

Chapter 16

Chase woke slowly, the pain in his head making him groggy and disoriented. His shoulders hurt and his hands were numb. What the hell?

His eyes flew open. There were tepees around him, and a group of Indians sitting about a fire, not far away from him. He tried to move his arms, and rawhide cut into his wrists. The pain cleared his senses. Chase moaned, wishing he hadn't awakened.

One of the Indians heard Chase and motioned to the others. Two rose and approached him, looking down at him. He was sitting on the ground, his hands tied to a pole behind his back. As he looked at them, he tried not to look afraid. Both Indians were young, probably younger than he was, but that didn't make him feel any better.

"You have broken our treaty, white eyes," the taller man said. "You will suffer the penalty for that. But first you will tell us who sent you here to spy on us."

Chase didn't recognize the man who spoke to him as the one he had seen by the creek with Jessie. But he noted the blue eyes, the difference in his facial structure, and he took heart.

"You're half white, aren't you?"

"You will answer questions, not ask them," was the harsh reply.

"This is ridiculous," Chase said impatiently. "I don't know who attacked me, but he's made a mistake. I'm not from around here, and I know nothing about your treaty. And I'm *not* a spy."

Chase waited while the two men conferred in their own language. Then the taller man faced him angrily.

"Black Bear Hunter says you lie. It was he who captured you. He found you concealed on the creek bank, watching our village. He thinks the Army sent you here, and he will know the truth of it even if he must force it from you."

Chase felt his insides tighten. "This is all pointless. I came here to find Jessica Blair. And I know she's here. Ask her about me."

The two Indians spoke again, and this time the shorter one stalked off angrily. Chase dared to take hope when the other one turned to him, his features relaxed, beginning a slow smile.

"You should have said that much sooner," the brave scolded.

"I can see that," Chase replied. "But your

friend wasn't too happy about it, was he?"

"No. He would have preferred to kill you."

Chase paled. "Is *that* the penalty for breaking a treaty? But the Army wouldn't stand for that."

"The Army left this area at our demand. We destroyed their forts, we drove them back. They would not break the treaty for one man, even if they had sent the man themselves. This region belongs to the Cheyenne and the Sioux, and the Army agreed that no whites should trespass."

"Yet you allow Jessica Blair to break the treaty?"

The Indian frowned. "She is a friend to us. And just who are you?" he demanded, his expression solemn.

"Jessie knows me. If you'll just tell her Chase Summers —"

"Chase!" the Indian echoed. His eyes narrowed. "I think Looks Like Woman would prefer to let my brother have you."

With that, he walked away. Chase tried to call him back, but he wouldn't stop.

What the hell had made him so angry all of a sudden? All he had said was his name. Chase grew very uneasy. Jessie must have said something about him, and whatever she had said, it couldn't have been good.

The sun set. No one came. The Indians at the fire drifted off, and still no one came. Chase tried working on his bonds, but they were firm. He began to feel desperate. Where was Jessie?

When Jessie did come, she came with the

blue-eyed Indian, and Chase didn't recognize her at first. She looked like an Indian, wearing the Indian dress and knee-high moccasins, her hair fastened in two braids. Her expression was impossible to read. Was she there to help him or to gloat over his predicament?

"You could have come a little sooner," Chase said, trying to make his tone light.

Jessie's expression didn't change. "I was sleeping. White Thunder saw no reason to wake me just to tell me you were here. You weren't going anywhere."

"Thanks."

Jessie's eyes narrowed. "Keep your sarcasm to yourself, Summers. No one got you into this mess except you."

"Damn it, all I did was come here to get you!" Chase snapped.

White Thunder took a step closer to Chase, and Jessie grabbed his arm. She pulled him away, and Chase watched them arguing. Then Jessie came back alone.

Chase was amazed. "You speak their language."

"Yes."

"What was that about?"

"He didn't like your shouting at me. Now look, I can understand your being upset, but I suggest you keep a civil tone. There's no point in angering him, when he already wants to just leave you here."

"Why?" Chase demanded. "What the hell

did you tell him about me?"

"Just the truth. That you used me. You had your fun and then were terrified that I might want to marry you because of it. Do you deny it?"

"You never did let me explain, Jessie."

"There was nothing to explain. It was all quite clear," she said stiffly.

God, how he wanted to shake that composure out of her. "What about you, Jessie? I could say the same damn thing about you. You had your fun. You used me. What if I had insisted on marriage because of it?"

"Don't be absurd," she snapped.

"No, you think about it. Who would have been the one to back off then?"

"But you wouldn't have insisted on marriage," she said quietly now. "And you never even gave me a chance to find out what I was feeling."

The hurt in her voice caught at his heart. "I told you I was sorry, and I meant it. You may not have thought it was such a big deal, losing your virginity, but I was so shook up about it I didn't know what the hell I was saying, Jessie."

"This is all beside the point. I told you I wanted to forget it."

"It's not beside the point when your Indian friend wants to slit my throat because of what you told him."

"If you must know, I told him very little. He saw that I was upset and drew his own conclusions. He just happens to be very protective of me."

"What is he to you, if I may ask?"

"A very close friend. And you've put off long enough telling me what you're doing here."

"How close?"

"Never mind!" Jessie snapped. "What's wrong at the ranch to bring you here?"

"Nothing is wrong at the ranch."

"Nothing?" A fiery gleam entered her eyes. "Don't tell me Rachel sent you after me again."

"She was worried."

"Damn!" Jessie exploded. "What are you, a puppy, to jump to her every bidding? She could have gotten you killed.

"Hold on." Chase grew uneasy, for White Thunder was watching them closely and frowning.

"You listen to me." Jessie lowered her voice. "You had no right to follow me. I don't need a watchdog, and if I did, it certainly wouldn't be you. This region is a second home to me, but it's a death trap for you. You're damn lucky Black Bear Hunter didn't kill you outright when he found you. And you'd better hope your luck continues, because you're leaving here alone. I won't be there to help you. You've wasted your time — again."

At least she had said he would be leaving. But Chase didn't dwell on that. He was staring at White Thunder by the fire. The Indian had turned away when Jessie lowered her voice.

Chase saw only his profile. It reminded him of the scene at the creek. Unbidden, his anger returned.

"When do I get released, Jessie?" Chase asked.

"White Thunder will cut you loose," she told him.

"Before you call him over here, answer me something, will you?"

Jessie should have been wary. But she missed the icy tone in his voice. "Answer you what, Summers?"

"Am I responsible for turning you into a whore, or did you always have the potential? I'd just like to know if I should feel guilty about that."

Jessie gasped. "Are . . . you crazy?"

"That *is* what you meant by your friend there being a very close friend, isn't it?" Chase questioned, deliberately cruel. "Or do you just like to put on a show for him sometimes?"

"What are you talking about?" Jessie whispered.

"I saw him with you down by the creek," Chase snarled. "I wasn't watching this camp when that other Indian found me, I was watching you. And I wasn't the only one watching you," he sneered. "Had he already —?"

Jessie didn't let him finish. She slapped him viciously. "You bastard! How dare you insinuate something like that? He's like a brother!"

She was so angry she shook. White Thunder

138

came up behind her and turned her around to face him. Her eyes wouldn't meet his.

"You heard what he said?" she asked miserably.

"Yes. You are ashamed?"

She didn't have to answer. White Thunder led Jessie away and asked, "You wish me to kill him for you?"

Chase heard, but he didn't hear Jessie's answer. He watched them until they disappeared around a group of tepees on the other side of the camp. Then he closed his eyes. It was odd, but he was quite calm. Maybe he was crazy. Why else would he antagonize a person who held his life in her hands? He didn't seem to know himself anymore.

Chapter 17

Jessie knelt beside Chase. It was still dark. She had brought food, and a knife to cut his bonds, and some other things. He was sleeping, and she didn't wake him. She looked him over carefully, thoughtfully. Why did he have the power to make her cry? Thomas Blair had once been the only man who could do that.

White Thunder had suggested that Chase hadn't meant what he'd said. He had actually defended Chase, even after offering to kill him for her. She was shocked. But afterwards, alone, she'd considered what he'd said and realized it was probably true.

White Thunder had suggested other things, outrageous things, and she had disregarded them completely. He'd said it might be that Chase felt she belonged to him after what had happened between them, that his accusations were prompted by jealousy. Jessie knew better. Her

140

belonging to Chase was the last thing Chase wanted. He had made that clear enough.

"How long have you been here?"

Jessie's eyes met his, but she looked away quickly. "I just came."

She moved around him and slit the rawhide at his wrists. Chase moved his arms carefully, but he gasped when the blood began rushing back into his hands. He shook them, but it didn't help.

Jessie came back to his side, sticking her knife in her knee-high moccasin. "I brought you food and your belongings."

He saw the saddle on the ground, with his guns and other things. He looked sideways at Jessie. "Thanks. I really had my doubts about your helping me."

"Helping you?"

"To get out of here. After what —"

"I should let you think that." She cut him off bitterly. "It would serve you right to feel indebted to a whore."

"Ah, Jessie," he groaned. "You must know I didn't mean that."

"Yes, I know," she said sullenly. "White Thunder pointed out that you've been through a lot today. A man faces death bravely or badly. You handled it badly. Of course."

He liked that explanation better than the right one and agreed readily. "Yes. Well, I haven't been handling anything too well lately, have I?"

"No, you haven't."

He stood up and stretched, reveling in that simple act. "Thanks for releasing me. I didn't see anyone else coming forward to do it."

She shrugged it off, uncomfortable with his gratitude. "Someone would have, eventually. They're not savages, you know. You ceased to be a prisoner the moment they knew you were here because of me."

"It didn't strike me that way."

"If you were inconvenienced, it serves you right for coming here in the first place," she told him pointedly. "No one invited you."

"That's true," he conceded. "And I'll be damn happy to leave. Can we go now?"

"You can leave any time. I suggest you wait until morning, though. A hunting party will be leaving then, and they'll escort you out of Indian territory. You'll be safe with them. Otherwise, well . . ."

He looked at her thoughtfully for a moment before he said, "I'd be safe with you, wouldn't I?"

"Yes, but I'm not leaving."

"Yes, you are, Jessie. I didn't come all this way for nothing."

"Don't you start with me, Summers," she warned him coldly. "This isn't open to debate. Even if I were ready to leave tomorrow, I wouldn't go with you. I don't happen to like your company."

Chase moved toward her, but Jessie quickly

stepped back from him.

"Perhaps I should put it another way," Jessie said. "One shout from me, and every tepee around here will empty within moments. And I'll leave you to explain your way out of it."

Chase sighed, "You win."

Jessie's temper rose, now that she didn't feel threatened anymore. "You're crazy, you know that? What the hell were you intending to do, anyway?"

He shrugged and said coolly, "Collect a little compensation for my trouble. And maybe make you eat your words about not liking my company."

Jessie gasped. "You think all you have to do is kiss me and I'll forget everything else? God, you're conceited!"

"Afraid it might be true?"

"I won't even answer that. And I don't know why I'm still standing here talking to you. If you're going to leave now, I'll go get my horse."

"So you *are* going with me?"

"No," Jessie replied hesitantly. "I'm letting you borrow my horse." She prayed he wouldn't explode.

His voice rose. "Is something wrong with Goldenrod?"

"No, but —" He didn't let her explain, but turned and started walking away from her. "Where are you going?"

"To get my horse."

Jessie saw the animal, and realized whose tepee he was tethered at. She ran after Chase and grabbed him.

"You go messing around Black Bear Hunter's tepee, and you'll find yourself in a whole lot of trouble."

"How else am I going to get Goldenrod?"

"You're not. He's keeping your horse. You think I'd lend you mine if I didn't have to?"

His eyes turned black as coal. "You damn well better be joking."

"Well, I'm not," she said stiffly.

"Is this another custom here? Like leaving a man tied up all day for no reason?"

"No. It's just your rotten luck that Black Bear Hunter is the one who found you. He hates whites — including me. If he hadn't jumped to the wrong conclusion about you it would be different, but he did, and he was furious to learn he was wrong, especially since I was involved. He was made to look like a fool. He's saving face by keeping your horse. You don't have a choice."

"Forget it, Jessie. I've had that horse too long to give him up."

"Look, damn it, just be glad he doesn't want your saddle and guns, too. He could have left you nothing, you know. He did capture you, spy or not, mistake or not."

"I'm not leaving here without my horse, and that's all there is to it."

"Don't be ridiculous," she hissed. "You'd

144

have to fight for him and —"

"Then I'll fight for him."

Their eyes locked. "You showed yourself to be ten kinds of a fool for coming here," she said with forced evenness. "What chance would you have against a Cheyenne warrior? He'd kill you in one minute."

"He'd have to win first."

"Damn it, we're not talking about a test of strength here! I told you he doesn't like me. He wouldn't go easy on you because of me, as one of the other braves would. He will *try* to kill you!"

"You don't think very much of me, do you?"

She stared at him, aghast. "No, Summers, I don't."

"Just arrange it, Jessie."

"Why won't you listen?"

His brow quirked. "Since when do you care what happens to me?"

"Oh!" Jessie fumed. "Fight him then!"

She stalked off. Chase took a long, deep breath. He wasn't leaving here without Goldenrod — or Jessie, either.

Chapter 18

Jessie and White Thunder went to Black Bear Hunter to tell him of the challenge for the golden horse. He agreed eagerly, too eagerly. Jessica pleaded with him not to kill Chase, to let it be only a battle of strengths, but Black Bear Hunter stared at her stonily. Nothing had changed. He would not be merciful.

The whole tribe turned out to watch the entertainment. Wagers were placed, for the Indians loved to gamble. There weren't too many takers until Chase stripped down to his pants, and then betting began in earnest. Jessie took heart. She should have remembered those thick muscles. Luckily, Chase and Black Bear Hunter were about the same height, and equally muscular.

"You can still change your mind, you know," Jessie said to Chase.

But before he could answer, his face hardened, and he said, "What's he doing here?"

She followed his gaze and saw Little Hawk nearing the crowd.

"I got a good look at him before he knocked me down that day, Jessie," Chase said angrily.

"Watch what you say! He speaks English," she hissed at him.

"Is that a warning?" Chase asked disdainfully. "Can I expect him to jump me again?"

Jessie quickly pulled Chase back a few feet and whispered, "Damn it, keep your big mouth shut." Did he have no sense at all? "He's not from this tribe, but what you do still matters. You came here because of me, so what you do here reflects on me."

"But he —"

"I'm not referring only to him. Black Bear Hunter happens to be White Thunder's brother. I'm asking you not to kill him, Chase."

"Oh, I'm supposed to just let him kill *me?*" Chase cried. He no longer cared who heard.

"Of course not," Jessie hissed impatiently. "But if you kill him, I won't be able to come here again. I'm just saying . . . don't if you don't have to. Just subdue him. See?"

"Sure, I see," Chase said sarcastically. Then he turned away from her and walked to the center of the circle. Black Bear Hunter was waiting, and as soon as Chase stood before him, White Thunder stepped between them. He said a few words — Jessie couldn't hear — and then he tied a long sash around both men's waists.

It bound them together for the contest, making it impossible for one to get away from the other. The struggle was more dangerous that way, because it kept the men within easy cutting distance of each other's knife.

Chase appeared quite calm. Jessie had warned him about the sash, also telling him there were no rules to the contest. He had shaken his head. No rules?

Black Bear Hunter made the first move, an unexpected leap that caught Chase off guard and sent both men crashing to the ground. They were both on their feet again in an instant, the Indian slashing with short jabs, Chase just barely staying out of reach of each thrust. Then Black Bear Hunter charged, his knife held high for a downward thrust. They locked wrists, each one holding the other's knife hand. The straining of muscles was awesome. The blades were close, but neither man could gain those extra few inches to draw first blood.

Jessie was horrified when she saw the blade turn in Black Bear Hunter's hand, stabbing Chase's forearm. Chase lost his hold, and the blade continued downward, slicing his side. The Indian prepared for another thrust, but Chase blocked it with his bloody forearm, then skillfully tripped him.

Black Bear Hunter was down. The sash brought Chase down with him, but he managed to land on top of Black Bear Hunter. they rolled again and again, each one fighting for the upper position. Chase tried to stand, but Black Bear Hunter used the sash to pull him back down and, with a skillful maneuver of his feet, sent Chase over backward. He landed with a thud.

They were stretched out on the ground, head to head. Black Bear Hunter leaned upward on one arm and brought his knife down viciously with the other hand. It would have landed in the center of Chase's throat, but Chase saw it and moved, with one second to spare.

The look on his face was murderous, and Jessie felt fear wash over her. Chase's losing control would give Black Bear Hunter the edge he needed, for anger made a man careless.

Chase stood up, waiting for his opponent to rise. Jessie wanted to scream at him to take the advantage while Black Bear Hunter was still down, but she couldn't make a sound. The moment the Indian was on his feet, Chase slammed his fist with the knife in it into his belly. Black Bear Hunter doubled over, his feet leaving the ground from the force of the blow.

The crowd was silent. Jessie felt her stomach turn over. Chase had won, but she had begged him not to win *that* way. And he wasn't finished yet! His anger drove him to strike Black Bear Hunter again, slamming his other fist into his face, laying the man out cold on the ground.

Then Chase was calmly cutting the sash with his knife. But there was no blood on the sash . . . or on the blade. Her eyes flew to Black Bear Hunter. There was no blood on him anyplace! Chase had turned the blade away before punching him!

She wanted to laugh. And she nearly did when, at that moment, Chase let out a roaring victory cry and the crowd echoed him. Those who had bet on Chase rushed to congratulate him.

"He did well," Little Hawk admitted.

It was all Jessie could do not to grin. "Yes, he did," she said solemnly.

She didn't know why she was so pleased. Was it only because Chase had vanquished Black Bear Hunter without hurting him?

"Jessie!" Chase was calling her cheerfully. "Get your gear, lady, we're going home!"

Jessie stiffened. "I'm not leaving with you," she said.

"But I'm not leaving without you," he answered firmly, reaching her side and standing there, unmoving.

"You'd better go," Jessie said uneasily. He looked so determined.

"If you don't come along with me agreeably, I'm going to pick you up and carry you out of here," Chase announced.

"They'll kill you!"

"Then my death will be on your conscience, won't it?"

They both knew she had no choice. She stared at him, wide-eyed, and fumed. "Damn you, I'll get even with you for this, Chase Summers. You see if I don't!"

Chase grinned as he watched her stomp off to the other side of the camp. He turned to fetch his gear and Goldenrod, but he had to pass by Jessie's two champions. He was in too good a mood to feel intimidated. He stopped for a second, smiling agreeably. "Looks like she'll be coming home with me, fellows. You see, her mother sent me to get her. She may have put up a fuss about it, but she always makes a fuss about something or other, doesn't she?"

He nodded to them politely, then kept on going. White Thunder had to restrain Little Hawk from going after him. Chase chuckled to himself, knowing damned well what was happening behind him, without having to look. He didn't care. Damn, he felt good!

Chapter 19

They were only three hours on the trail when Little Hawk caught up with them. Jessie heard him calling to her and stopped. Then Chase heard the name being called and grabbed Jessie's reins. Little Hawk stopped, watching them.

"So *you're* Looks Like Woman?" Chase said.

"The Indians call me Looks Like Woman," she said flatly.

"Your friend said the Sioux was there because of you. Is that true?"

"Yes. He never left the ranch area, and followed me to the village. He's asked me to be his wife."

Chase stared at her for a few moments, then said, "So he did attack me that day because I kissed you?"

"Yes, I suppose he did. But I didn't know that at the time."

Chase laughed derisively. "But that's ridiculous, him wanting to marry you."

"Why ridiculous?" she said in a deadly voice.

"He's an Indian, for God's sake!"

"My closest friend is an Indian," she said smoothly. "I've been visiting him and his people for eight years. I know their culture as well as I do my own. You think I can't be happily married to an Indian? Well, let me tell you something, Summers. The only place I've found *any* happiness these last ten years was with White Thunder and his family. So don't tell me his being an Indian should have anything to do with my decision."

Chase was left speechless. Little Hawk was watching them, and he could feel it. "What did you tell him?"

"That, Chase Summers, is none of your business," Jessie said, yanking her reins away from him. Turning around, she rode straight for Little Hawk.

They didn't say anything at first, just stared at each other, Little Hawk searching her eyes, Jessie wishing they were alone.

At last Little Hawk said, "I did not mean to let you go without speaking to you, but I was angry."

"I'm sorry."

"It was not you who caused my anger, but that one. He upsets you."

"Do not trouble yourself about him. He's just a stubborn cuss who does my mother's bidding."

"I do not like it that you ride alone with him. I will ride with you."

"No." She shook her head emphatically. "And have you two battling? No."

"If he touches you —"

"Stop it," she said quickly. "I can handle that one. I'm armed again, see?" She patted her gun before she added gently, "You have got to stop concerning yourself with me. I will not marry you, Little Hawk, and I will not change my mind about it. So go home to your wife."

He avoided replying to that, asking instead, "You will come again to White Thunder's camp?"

She frowned at him. "You mustn't look for me."

"Looks Like Woman —"

"Oh, please, don't make this so difficult," she pleaded. "We are not fated to be together. I know it. Ask your medicine man, he will tell you. Do not look for me. My spirit cannot meet yours with ease. You understand, Little Hawk? You are too . . . too much for me."

She turned away then, riding back to Chase. She looked back once to see Little Hawk sitting there, watching her, his expression unreadable. How it hurt her to say those things to him. But it wasn't to be, and she'd had to stop him from hurting himself more.

She passed Chase without a word, galloping steadily. She didn't see the two men staring at each other for a long time before they simultaneously turned away, Little Hawk to the north, Chase to follow her. She could feel Chase's eyes on her from time to time as they crossed the plains. It was beautiful country. The Big Horn Mountains were directly west, joining many other ranges stretching across the land to form the Rocky Mountains. The Black Hills were to the east. Even the rolling grassland that seemed infinite was beautiful. Trees along creek beds were bursting with brilliant autumn leaves. A slow-moving herd of buffalo seemed from a distance like great-backed turtles.

Jessie knew this land and loved it. She loved the ranch, too. She had nothing else, really. She certainly didn't want to live anywhere else. Yet she felt she had reached an impasse in her life. She felt changed, but without a new direction. She felt she needed *something,* only she didn't know what that something was.

They didn't stop that day, except to water the horses. It was late when they finally came to the creek where Jessie meant to camp. The sun had set, and the moon had yet to rise, but she knew just where to find firewood. She got a fire started before Chase had even unsaddled his horse.

With Jessie leading the way home, Chase had no recourse but to let her make the decisions. He wouldn't have thought of asking her to stop sooner. He was drawing on his last reserves, however. The fight with Black Bear Hunter had been a hard contest. Still, he kept silent.

His cuts were bleeding again. An Indian woman had put salve on them and bandaged him while he was waiting for Jessie that morning, but the cut on his side was bleeding through his shirt and needed tending. He was too tired even to do that. If he could just get his horse rubbed down . . .

"Sit down before you fall down!" Jessie commanded in a no-nonsense voice from behind him. "Honestly, if you were this tired you should have said something."

He hadn't known she was watching. "Didn't want to trouble you," he offered lamely.

She sighed as she grabbed some grass and finished rubbing down Goldenrod for him, saying, "There's food by the fire. White Thunder's sister prepared it for us. Help yourself."

"I think I'll just get some sleep."

"You'll eat first," Jessie said firmly. "You'll need the energy to withstand tomorrow's ride."

Her tone promised that the next day would be another grueling one. "What's the hurry?" Chase grumbled.

"I told you. I don't like your company. The sooner we get back the better."

Chase scowled. "Then by all means I'll eat. We can't have you fretting over the few extra hours you might have to spend with me."

"Thank you."

How she drove him with that unbending hostility. Whoever would believe they had shared a night of the most incredible loving he

156

had ever experienced?

He sat down and picked through the food laid out on a thin hide wrapping. He had eaten several pieces of meat by the time Jessie sat down. She sat next to him, with the food between them. Her expression was as unfriendly as possible.

"I'm in pain, Jessie," he ventured.

"From what?" Her tone was a little less frosty.

"From this gash in my side."

"How bad is it?"

"I didn't get a good look at it," he confessed.

He managed to get the left sleeve of his jacket off. When it fell back, the blood soaking his shirt became visible. He felt Jessie's shock and was pleased. Then he looked down at himself and saw the blood ruining a damn good pair of pants.

Jessie was up instantly, helping him remove his jacket all the way. She went for his shirt next, pulling it out of his pants and over his head. She said nothing until after she had unwrapped the bandage and inspected the wound carefully, making him move closer to the fire-light so she could see.

"It's not so bad," she murmured. "All that jarring from the ride kept it from clotting is all."

Chase raised his arm to get a better look while she went to the creek for water. It looked bad to him, a good quarter-inch deep and at least ten inches long. Jessie hadn't been at all squeamish, he reminded himself.

When she came back, she carefully cleaned the cut. Chase was gazing at her face, the way her brow wrinkled in concentration, the way she chewed at her lower lip. She was too close, and he was beginning to think about things he shouldn't think about.

Jessie had to use the same bandage for want of another, but offered, "If you have a change of shirt, I'll wash this one for you."

"In my saddle bag. How about washing my pants, too?"

"You'll need your pants for warmth. It's going to get chilly tonight."

"All I need is a blanket and a warm woman." Chase grinned.

"All you'll get is a blanket," she retorted.

Chase was grinning when she tossed his clean shirt and a blanket at him before she went back to the creek. She was less hostile, and he was delighted.

He had the blanket wrapped around his waist and was struggling to get the shirt buttoned when Jessie came back. She finished buttoning it for him, then helped him get his jacket back on. He lay down, and she knelt beside him to straighten the blanket. When she leaned over him, his arm came around her and drew her close. She didn't think to pull back before it was too late. He whispered, "Thanks," and then his lips brushed hers lightly. His arm fell away, and his eyes closed. Jessie moved away to settle down a few feet from him. She lay facing him, and for a long while she watched him as he slept.

Chapter 20

Jessie stirred the pot of beans one more time before she brought it to the table. Chase was already helping himself to the hot biscuits and fried rabbit. She'd made a suet pudding for later, just like Jeb's, with the raisins, nuts, brown sugar, and spices she'd found.

They were making use of the supply shack on the north range. Jessie had pushed hard, trying to get home before the day was out, but it just hadn't worked out that way. The sky had clouded up, and it had gotten dark early, with the ranch still three hours away.

She had kept her distance since that surprising kiss, and he hadn't made any other overtures. Still, being so near him was disconcerting. She needed a distraction.

"Where did you learn to handle a knife so well?" Jessie asked tentatively.

Chase didn't look up. "San Francisco. I met

an old sea captain who taught me a few tricks so I could handle myself on the waterfront. That waterfront wasn't the most sociable of places at night, or even during the day for that matter."

"Why were you there?" Jessie prompted.

"I worked there for a few years."

"Doing what?"

Chase looked up at last. "My, but you're full of questions tonight." He smiled at her.

"Do you mind?"

"No, I guess not. I was a dealer in a gambling house. It's where I got my first taste of gambling."

"You like to gamble?"

"You could say that."

"San Francisco is a long way from Chicago. Had you always lived in Chicago before San Francisco?"

"I was born in New York, but my mother moved to Chicago when I was a baby. She was hiding, really. Her first name was Mary, but she changed the last to Summers. She never did tell me what her real last name was."

There was the bitterness in his tone that had been there before when he spoke of his mother.

"Hiding from what?" Jessie asked hesitantly.

"I'm a bastard," he replied nonchalantly. "She couldn't bear the shame of it. She never let me forget it, either, or that my father hadn't wanted her or me. I sometimes wonder, though. When she was drunk, she would let certain things slip that she denied when sober, like the fact that she hadn't actually seen my father once she knew she was pregnant."

"You think maybe he never knew about you?"

"It's possible," he replied. "I mean to find out, someday. But anyway, she brought us to Chicago and started a seamstress shop that did very well. She met Ewing through the shop. I was ten when he started bringing his mistresses there for fancy outfits. He was looking for a respectable wife, one with a child, and the widow Summers seemed ideal. She didn't love him, though. And it wasn't as if we needed his wealth, for we were doing fine. But she claimed to love him. That was her excuse, when all she really wanted were the luxuries his wealth could buy."

"Was that so wrong? It couldn't have been easy, raising you alone. Perhaps your bitterness stems from having to share her after all the years when it was only the two of you."

"Share her?" Chase said. "I hardly ever saw her. She was always at social functions, on shopping sprees. She turned me over to Ewing completely."

"You resented that?"

"I'll say! Here's a perfect stranger treating you like you were born to him, but with an iron hand. Beating you for the slightest wrong, the tiniest assertion of your own will."

"I'm sorry."

"Don't be. I was only under his rule for six

years."

Jessie knew he was trying to make light of something that held terrible memories. He was frowning at some unbidden memory, and she left him to himself for a while.

"You left home when you were only six-teen?" she ventured a little later. "Weren't you frightened? How did you manage, so young?"

"You could say I joined another family, the Army."

"They accepted you that young?"

Chase grinned. "This was in '64, Jessie. They were taking anybody then."

"Of course," she gasped. "The War between the States. You joined the North?"

He nodded. "I signed up for the duration, a green kid learning the hard way how to be a man. I took off for California after that."

"Why California?"

"That's where my mother met my father."

"So you went there to find him?"

He nodded. "But I didn't find him. The Silvela ranch was sold when the gold rush started. So many years had passed, there was no one to tell me where the Silvelas had gone, but I figured they went back to Spain."

"Your father was a rancher?"

"It was his uncle's ranch, according to my mother."

"A Spaniard," she commented thoughtfully. "You must take after him."

"I guess so." Chase smiled lazily. "My

mother was a redhead with bright green eyes."

"But I gathered she was from New York. What was she doing in California?"

"The way she told it, her mother had just died. It was only her and her father, and he lived more at sea than at home. He was captain of a tallow ship that made regular runs from the California coast to the East. It was the first time she had ever gone with him, and the Silvelas were one of the rancher families her father dealt with. Apparently Carlos Silvela, young and handsome, swept her off her feet. He did not promise marriage, though.

"She realized she was pregnant before her father sailed back East, and she told her father. He insisted on marriage, and I've heard several versions of what happened then. One was that my mother begged Carlos Silvela to marry her, but he wouldn't. Another was that the uncle, the head of the clan, refused to give his consent, humiliating my mother by saying an *americana* was not good enough for his nephew. Then there was my mother's drunken version, where she swore Carlos loved her and would have married her *if he had known.*"

"Don't you know which one is true?"

"No. But I'll find out someday."

"You'll have to go to Spain to do that. Why haven't you gone?"

Chase shrugged. "It seemed hopeless. I didn't know where to start. Spain's a big country. Also, I don't speak the language."

"Spanish isn't difficult to learn," she scoffed.

"I suppose you speak it?"

"Well . . . yes," she admitted.

Spanish happened to be the only language John Anderson knew besides English, and Jessie had been eager for him to teach her everything he was capable of teaching. But she wasn't going to explain that to Chase.

"Why didn't you learn it, if it would help you find your father?" she pressed.

"I was too disappointed and angry in not finding my father where I thought he'd be. It had taken me a hell of a long time just to get to California. then to find I had made the trip for nothing . . ."

"So you just gave up?"

"I was twenty and restless, Jessie. I didn't have the money to get to Spain, anyway."

"That's when you got a job dealing cards in San Francisco?" she concluded.

"Yes. I drifted back East after that. Thought I'd see a bit more of this country," he explained. "I tried life on the Mississippi for a couple of years, but one too many boiler explosions and collisions made the river steamers unappealing. A big game down in Texas drew me there, and then I drifted to Kansas. They have some fancy saloons in the cow towns there, if you don't mind the wild goings-on at the end of every trail drive."

"You're a gambler!" Jessie realized finally. "My God! Of all the shiftless, lazy things!"

Chase chuckled at her contempt. "It's a living. I can take it or leave it. It's made traveling easy. I just happen to have uncommon luck at cards. Why shouldn't I take advantage of it?"

She calmed down a little. "Can you really make a living at gambling?"

"Enough to live quite comfortably in the good hotels," he admitted.

"But what kind of a life is that?"

That hit a sore spot. "Let's just say, a life with no ties. Now it's my turn to ask a few questions, don't you think?"

Jessie shrugged, reaching for the last biscuit. "What do you want to know?"

"You said you've only been happy with your Indian friends. Why is that?"

"They let me be myself."

"I saw you looking and acting like one of them. You call that being yourself?"

"I looked like a girl, didn't I?" Jessie threw back at him.

"You looked like an Indian."

"But a girl," she persisted.

"Yes, of course, but what has that —"

"It's the only place I can be a girl — what I am. My father never let me, you see. He burned all the clothes I came here with and never let me buy a dress. Dresses weren't appropriate for the things I had to learn to do. Nothing could remind him I was a girl."

Chase hissed. "I thought you dressed like

166

that by choice."

"Hardly."

"But your father's dead now."

"Yes," Jessie replied without thinking. "But my mother is here."

"But she doesn't approve of the way you dress and act. You must know that." And then he whistled softly. "Yes, of course you know it. I see."

"It's none of your business," Jessie snapped.

"Anytime I hit a touchy subject, it's none of my business." He sighed. "I'm not judging you, Jessie. I don't care how you dress. You looked mighty pretty, though, in that Indian dress," he said nicely, trying to cool her temper.

But Jessie wasn't having any of it. She got up, her eyes flaring. "I cooked, now you can clean up. I'll be back."

He sat up straight. "Where are you going?"

"Out back to wash."

But before she could leave, he was up and facing her. "What did you tell Little Hawk about marrying him? You did give him an answer, didn't you?"

"If you must know, I refused him. I won't share the man I settle for. Little Hawk already has a wife."

Chase let that sink in. "And if he didn't?"

"I probably would have agreed."

She went outside, and Chase stared at the closed door for a long time.

Sometime later, Jessie came in shaking her

wet hair. It was loose and as black and glossy as sable. Without a glance in his direction, she walked to her saddlebags on the foot of her cot, got a brush, and sat down cross-legged on the shaggy fur by the fire.

Chase watched her as she began running the brush through her hair, but then he turned away, feeling edgy. He moved to his own cot, only a few feet from hers. He stared at the narrow thing, looked at hers, and realized it would be easy to push the two together. The thought made him edgier.

"Thanks for cleaning up the mess," she said suddenly.

"Thanks for making dinner," he returned.

They fell silent. She turned back to face the fire, giving him her profile. Chase couldn't take his eyes off her. Absently, he began to unbutton his shirt. She was raising her hair to the heat, shaking it, swaying it, then brushing it. He became mesmerized by that floating black hair. It was so shiny, reflecting the fire. And when she leaned back, tilting her head back to shake her hair, the smooth contour of her throat enraptured him.

Chase didn't know what he intended when he got up and started toward Jessie. He knelt behind her and gathered her hair in his hands, pressing his lips to the side of her neck. She tried to pull away from him, and he came to his senses and let her go.

Jessie scrambled to her knees to face him.

"What —?"

"I want to make love to you."

His eyes were smoldering as they caressed her face, her neck, her hair. All she could think of was that other night when he'd looked at her the same way. Funny, but that was all she could think of. Jessie moved toward him and let him gather her into his arms. One hand entwined in her hair, the other held her lower back, pressing her close to him. His mouth captured hers in a kiss that inflamed her, and it went on and on until she lost all sensation but that. His lips moved to her neck, and she groaned with the tingling they caused. He lowered her to the rug, and she tried to pull him down on top of her, but he held back, shrugging out of his shirt first. She devoured him with her eyes, watching the hard muscles that played under his skin, such darkly tanned skin. She ran her fingers through the hair on his chest, over those muscles that fascinated her so, down those strong arms.

Chase was watching her watch him. It excited him until he was so hard inside his pants that it was painful, and he quickly removed them.

Jessie reached out and touched the thick, hard shaft that stood so proud. He groaned, and she wrapped her arms around his hips, pressing her cheek against his hard belly. He jerked her upward, fastening his mouth on hers again savagely. She dug her fingers into his hair, and he undid her buttons, quickly removing her shirt. There was no bashfulness as she shed the rest of her clothes. There was only the heat of his eyes, and then his hot hands as he touched each place she bared.

When she was as naked as he was, she leaned back, ready to receive him. He knelt between her legs, but he didn't give her what she craved, not yet. He leaned forward, running his hands down her sides, over her hips. When he laid his cheek against her belly, snuggling there, hugging her to him, she knew what he had felt when she'd done the same thing. It was unbearable.

"You're so beautiful, Jessie."

She believed him. She felt worshiped. She felt completely woman.

Chase kissed the inside of her thigh. Her legs were exquisite, not at all as he'd expected. The muscles were there, but her legs were soft and supple when she relaxed.

He slid his hands up to her breasts. They were so soft, so full, the nipples hard and pointed. He tasted them, licking her until she cried, "No more!"

Her fingers dug into his hair, and she pulled him up. Her mouth fastened to his with such urgency that he was lost in her. She arched to meet him, molding her skin to his wherever she could and he entered her. She wrapped her legs around him, and he sank deeply into her. "Oh, yes! Jessie . . . Jessie."

She exploded in a burst of ecstatic throbbing. He had not moved once after entering her, and did not need to. Her fulfillment coming so quickly was enough to drive him over the brink, and he spilled his seed into her, his throbbing making her own pleasure go on and on.

Jessie floated off to sleep. Chase got up to fetch a blanket to cover them, then snuggled down next to her and slept a deep sated sleep.

Chapter 21

Jessie woke first. She understood what had happened, got up quickly, and silently gathered her things.

She pushed Blackstar to his limit, riding not to the ranch but to the range, wanting to throw herself into hard work so she wouldn't have to think. How had it happened? She could have stopped it. It wasn't as if he'd forced her. She had wanted him. But *why?* Damn!

It was quite late when Chase woke, and it didn't take long for him to see that there was no trace of Jessie in the cabin. Damn all independent women, he swore, feeling as though he'd been taken advantage of.

His irritation increased as he rode back to the ranch, thankful that he knew the way, at least. He was fed up with having this one particular woman turn him inside out. He didn't act the

172

same when he was with her, couldn't even think straight when she was near him. He would tell Rachel what she needed to be aware of, give Jessie her father's promissory note, and light out.

When Chase entered the house, Rachel was in the parlor. She was sitting in a rocker, crocheting, looking fetching and demure in a gown of moss green with black lace. He remembered the Ewing household, how soothing it had been to sit and watch her crocheting or knitting, or arranging flowers. Gazing on Rachel's beauty eased his troubles, always had. Without Jessie on his mind, it might still have worked.

"Is she here?" he asked.

"No. A young man, Blue, rode in for supplies about noon," she explained. "He told Jeb she was out on the range working."

Chase sat down heavily and sighed. "I might have known she'd get right back in the thick of things. Are they still rounding up the herd?"

"Yes. Jeb says it'll only be a few more days before they're through. He's going to town tomorrow in fact to get the supplies they'll need for the drive." She looked back to her lap as if she weren't going to say any more, but she added softly, "Chase? She wasn't really with Indians, was she?"

He wondered how she knew he'd found Jessie, then decided to skip it.

"Actually, Rachel, she's been visiting these Indians for about eight years."

"Then it's true!"

"You haven't heard the worst. I found her with the Cheyenne. They're friendly with her, but other whites are not welcome in their territory. I nearly got killed, in fact. My horse was stolen, and I had to fight to get him back. I was kept tied up for half a day, and if Jessie hadn't told them she knew me, I'd have been tortured, maybe killed. That's the kind of company she keeps. Nice, isn't it?"

Rachel stared at him, knowing he had more to say.

"The closest friend your daughter has is a half-breed Cheyenne called White Thunder. They're so close she bathes naked in a creek with him standing a few yards away."

"I don't believe it." Rachel was shaking her head.

"I saw them. And I still haven't gotten to the worst. She has a suitor, a Sioux warrior. He wants to marry her, and the only reason she refused him is that he has a wife. She said as much! She claims the only place she's found happiness is with the Indians. Who knows? The next warrior who asks for her might not already have a wife. You just might find yourself with an Indian for a son-in-law, Rachel."

She was so stunned she couldn't speak. Finally she said, "What am I going to do?"

"You're her mother," Chase replied angrily, "not to mention her father's choice of guardian. You've got the power to control her. Do it.

Stop letting her do as she pleases."

"But how?" Rachel implored.

"How the hell should I know?" he snapped, then relented. "Oh, Rachel, stop it, please. You'll think of something. But you've got to stop putting me in the middle of it. I've done what you asked, and I'm lighting out of here in the morning."

"But, Chase —"

"You're not talking me into staying her any longer. I checked on Bowdre, and he's just what you thought he was. But he no longer has any right to bother Jessie," he said proudly.

"Why not?" she cried.

"I played cards with him." He paused. "I won the note."

She gasped. "You won the note? What did Jessie say?"

"She doesn't know yet, but I'll give her the note before I leave. If there's any more trouble with Bowdre, it will be trouble for the sheriff to handle. I won the note fairly. Bowdre's got no further claim. And I'm through here."

"Of course. It is selfish of me to try to keep you if you want to go. Chase," she said softly, "thank you."

Chase grinned despite himself. "Now don't try your tactics on me, lady. They won't work."

"I'm sorry," Rachel said sincerely. "It's just that I feel so helpless when it comes to my own daughter. You don't know how much she hates me, Chase. If I told her to stay away from fire, she would walk into one just to defy me."

"Why does she hate you, Rachel?" he asked quietly.

She looked away, saying evasively, "I told you. Her father taught her to."

"But why?"

"I used to live here, you know. Oh, not in this house. There was only a small, three-room —"

"I know. Jessie told me her father built this house just because you could never live in it."

"Did he? Well, I don't doubt it." She was silent for a long time before she went on. "I came home here one night, and he beat me, then threw me out."

"Why?"

"He accused me of being unfaithful. Called me a whore," she added distastefully. "But he never gave me a chance to defend myself. He beat me so badly I nearly died. I would have if old Jeb hadn't found me and taken me to the doctor at Ft. Laramie."

"Does Jessie know that?"

"I don't know, but I don't think so. I gather that she feels I deserted her. Thomas might have told her that. I wouldn't put anything past a man who would make his daughter believe her mother was a whore! He was so spiteful over the years, never allowing me to see her. Yes, I don't doubt that he told her I deserted her."

"When Ewing found you, you had just come

from here?" Chase asked thoughtfully.

"Yes."

Chase whistled softly. "The boy is his, isn't he? Billy is Thomas Blair's son!" Rachel wouldn't answer or look at him, but Chase pressed her. "You never told him, did you?"

"Thomas has already taken one child from me," Rachel said defensively. "I wasn't going to let him have Billy, too. Besides, he never would have believed Billy was his."

"But why haven't you told Jessie?"

"She wouldn't believe me, either, Chase. She doesn't believe anything I tell her. I think she would rather hate me. It's easier for her that way. She's afraid to care about me, afraid she'll be hurt again. When I think of how she must have been hurt by all of this, my heart bleeds for her. But I can't reach her if she won't let me."

Chase was thoughtful. What Thomas had done to Jessie was unnatural. It was an outrage. But damn it, it just wasn't his concern — it wasn't!

"I'm not going to get involved in this, Rachel. This is between you and Jessie."

"I know." She smiled in understanding. "And don't worry about it. I'll work it out somehow. I've involved you in my daughter's affairs enough as it is."

God, if she only knew how involved he'd become, he thought.

Chapter 22

Rachel waited for Jessie in the kitchen that night. Kate had gone to sleep. Chase had gone to his room after dinner, and Rachel had put Billy to bed.

Jessie came in late. She had washed up at the stable, but her clothes were filthy. She used her hat to whack some of the dust off before she entered the kitchen. When she saw Rachel sitting at the table, she scowled.

"I've kept your dinner warm," Rachel said casually.

Jessie stared at her. "I'm not hungry."

"Have you eaten already?"

"No."

"Then sit down and eat." Rachel's voice was firmer. "I want to talk to you, anyway."

Rachel got up to make Jessie a plate, and Jessie didn't say anything more. She was hungry, after all, and too tired to argue.

She pulled out a chair and plopped down at the table, her legs spread on each side of the chair as though in a saddle. She leaned back, one arm hooked over the back of the chair.

"Do you do that just to annoy me?" Rachel asked quietly as she put the plate in front of Jessie.

"What?"

"Sit like that."

"What's wrong with the way I sit?" Jessie demanded belligerently.

"If you can ask that, then you would benefit from a few lessons in feminine deportment."

"From who? You?"

There was such derision in Jessie's voice that Rachel gasped. "Do you think this is acceptable behavior for a young woman?"

"What the hell is the difference?" Jessie countered. "I live in my own world. I'm not exactly a social butterfly, now am I?"

"You're not alone here, however," Rachel pointed out. "You have a guest. What do you think a man of Mr. Summer's sophistication thinks of such uncouth behavior?"

"I don't give a good God —"

"Jessica!"

"Well, I don't," Jessie insisted. Then she acquiesced. "I haven't forgotten the first eight years of my life, Rachel. I can conduct myself fittingly if the situation warrants it."

"Then for heaven's sake, why don't you?" Rachel asked in exasperation.

"To impress a *gambler?* Why should I?"

"For my sake."

Jessie didn't respond.

"This is not what I wanted to talk to you about, though," Rachel continued.

Jessie sat up to start eating. "I'm all talked out."

"You will spare me a few more minutes."

Jessie raised her brow at the firm tone. She was surprised, and a bit curious.

"I'm here. Talk. I just hope this isn't going to be boring."

"I promise you will not be bored with what I have to say. You may disagree perhaps, but —"

"Get to it, Rachel."

The older woman drew herself up. "Very well, I will come directly to the point. You are not to go off on your own to visit your Indian friends again."

Rachel braced herself for an explosion, but there wasn't one. Jessie stared blankly at her, as though waiting to hear more.

At last Jessie asked, "Is that all you have to say?"

Rachel was amazed. She wasn't putting up a fight. "Well, actually, I had my reasons for insisting on this if you wanted to hear them. But since you are going to be reasonable, I suppose it won't be necessary to get into all that."

"Wouldn't matter, anyway," Jessie said offhandedly. "You can give all the orders you like, Rachel. I do what I want."

Rachel sat back, her face hot. She should have known better. "This time you will do as I say, Jessica."

Jessie grinned, unconcerned. "Will I?"

"Yes, you will, if you want to keep on running this ranch."

"Don't mess with me, Rachel," she warned softly. "You know nothing about ranching. And the men wouldn't listen to you, anyway."

"I didn't think they would, but I'm in a position to bring in outside help if I deem it necessary."

"My men take orders from me!"

Rachel's voice rose, too. "Your men can be fired and new ones hired."

"You have no right!"

"But I do, Jessica," Rachel said more gently. "I am your guardian."

Jessie was furious. "When will you get it through your silly head that my father only made you my guardian so you could see what a proper young lady he'd made of me? He brought you here to spite us both. He knew I didn't really need you. He raised me to stand on my own — like any man!"

"Whatever the reason," Rachel said stiffly, "I am here, and I do have the authority to do exactly as I said."

"Why, damn you?" Jessie shouted, losing control. "What is really behind this?"

"Twice this last month you have left the ranch and gone off where you couldn't be reached for days. That is totally irresponsible behavior, Jessica."

"That won't wash and you know it," Jessie hissed. "Mitch Faber was left in charge, and Jeb could handle anything else that might have come up. So you'd damn well better have a better reason than that!"

"Where you went is reason enough," Rachel said obdurately. "It is unthinkable that you should venture into an area forbidden to whites. I thought your Indians were friendly. If I had known they were not, I would have put my foot down sooner."

"Utter nonsense. You think I could go there if I weren't welcome?"

"You might be welcome, but other whites are not. I will not have you associating with Indians who are hostile to whites. It has obviously been a bad influence on you, and the influence will not continue."

"What is that supposed to mean?"

"For God's sake, Jessica, your behavior here is bad enough, but there, you apparently throw every civilized convention to the wind. I have never heard of anything so appalling as your bathing naked in a creek with an Indian in plain view."

Jessie stood up so quickly that her chair went skidding backward across the floor. Bright spots of color stained her cheeks, and her eyes were wide and sparkling with fury.

"The bastard had to tell you that, didn't he?" Jessie cried furiously. "And I suppose he told you about Little Hawk, too? Of course! That's what this is all about, isn't it? Isn't it?"

"Jessica, calm down."

"Calm down? When you're threatening to take the ranch out of my control because of the distortions that bastard told you? What else did he tell you?"

"This much is certainly enough, don't you think?" Rachel tried to keep her own voice down.

"No, I certainly don't think it's enough, not when he twisted innocent happenings into . . . what did you call it? The most appalling thing you'd ever heard of? What the hell is wrong with my taking a bath in a creek? I do it here every chance I get when I'm alone. There, the village is too close, and White Thunder accompanies me so I won't be disturbed. He didn't watch me, for God's sake! He's like a brother!"

"This Sioux brave was not like a brother," Rachel said stonily.

"So I was asked to marry? So what? I refused. If you want to get up on your high horse about something, ask your friend about what he conveniently *didn't* tell you!"

"If there is more, I'm sure it will only confirm my opinion that you should not go there again, Jessica," Rachel said quietly. "An Indian camp is still no place for a young white girl. I will not relent on this."

Jessie glared, so furious she was shaking. Unfortunately for Chase, he picked that moment to step into the kitchen.

"There's enough shouting going on to wake the dead. What's the trouble?"

Jessie turned eyes on him as stormy as anything he'd ever seen. She picked up her plate and threw it at his head. He ducked, and it bounced off the wall to the floor.

"You rotten sonofabitch! You just had to get her all fired up, didn't you? It wasn't enough that you dragged me back here, you had to malign everything that happened! But you forgot to include *yourself* in those tales, didn't you?"

"That's enough, Jessie," Chase warned darkly.

"Enough?" she shrieked. "You were the one so hot to carry tales to her! Why didn't you tell her the rest of it? If she ought to know about my appalling behavior with the Indians, then she ought to know that her trusted friend seduced me — not once, but twice! I mean, if we're going to wash the dirty laundry, we might as well include everything. Or wasn't the loss of my innocence as important as my sinful conduct with the Indians? Bastard! When you start something, do it right!"

With that Jessie stormed past Chase, shoving him so forcefully that he slammed back into the cupboard by the door, shattering two of the glass panes. A moment later, the door to her room closed just as forcefully, the sound as loud as a gunshot.

"What's going on?" Billy called from down the hall.

"Go back to bed, Billy," Rachel ordered sharply.

He did, without question. Chase would have loved to do the same. The silence that followed was eternal. He was afraid to look at Rachel, afraid to see the accusation in her eyes.

Rachel waited awhile, giving him a chance to speak. When he didn't, she said, "Was she telling the truth?"

He started to speak, but no words would come.

Rachel let out a small cry before she implored, "Chase, you didn't! Not my Jessica!"

He winced but still couldn't answer. He finally faced her. The look in her eyes made him feel about an inch tall. She didn't wait any longer for an answer, but ran past him, crying.

Chase stood there for several long minutes. Was there anything he could salvage?

Chapter 23

"What would you do, Goldy? Would you marry a woman just 'cause you felt a lil' guilty?" Chase asked.

The horse snorted. "Sorry, old fella. Forgot you don't like to be called Goldy. But it was a good question, huh?"

Chase was propped against the wall in Goldenrod's stall, sitting trustingly at the horse's feet, a half-empty bottle of whiskey beside him. He'd found the unopened bottle in the tack room after searching high and low in the kitchen. It was undoubtedly Jeb's stash. He would have to remember to replace it.

Opening the bottle again, Chase drained another half inch and eyed his horse seriously. "I mean, shoot, that lil' minx never made me feel bad, did she? It's that damn Rachel who's got me feeling like a louse. And you know what she's gonna say soon as she gets 'round to it?"

Chase belched, then laughed. "Not that. No, Rachel's gonna say, 'You ruined her, now you marry her.' You think she might hold a gun at my back? No, not Rachel. But she's got another weapon, that damn face of hers, that damn look that says I stabbed her in the back." He took a deep breath. "Why the hell don't I just ride out of here?"

Chase tried to stand but didn't succeed until he'd tried several times. He eyed his saddle on the railing as if it were an ornery critter giving him trouble. And it did. He couldn't get it off the railing. Finally he leaned against it and spoke to his horse again.

"Looks like I might need to sober up first. But I'll be back, Goldenrod. I'll saddle you up, and then we'll hit the trail. I can't marry that hellion. It'd be like tying myself to a cyclone."

Chase made his way out of the stable and around to the stream behind the house. He fell in and for a moment thought he might be drowning. The water was only a foot deep, however. After a considerable bit of splashing, he pulled himself to the edge of the stream and lay there, letting the icy water chill him.

Unbidden, an image of Jessie came to mind. Not the Jessie of tonight but of last night. She had been a tempest then, too, but a passionately loving tempest.

Would it really be so bad being tied to her? he wondered. She was the prettiest thing he'd ever seen. And wasn't he tired of drifting?

Rachel had said it was time he settled down, and, well, maybe it was. With some effort, couldn't he tame the hoyden?

Jessie was too furious to cry but too upset not to. That left her with a choked feeling that was keeping her awake, tossing and turning. Being awake, she heard the soft knock clearly. She wasn't pleased.

She didn't bother to pull on a pair of pants but answered the door in the oversized long-sleeved shirt she usually slept in. She didn't care what Rachel thought of that. In fact, she considered taking the shirt off and letting Rachel think she slept nude.

She was glad she hadn't carried through with that rebellious thought, however, when the door opened to reveal Chase in the hall. Jessie slammed the door shut, but it hit his shoulder and bounced open again. She was forced to step back as he shoved his way in rudely, closing the door behind him.

"Get out," she said.

"In a minute."

"Now!"

"Keep your voice down, damn it. You'll have Rachel in here, dragging us to the preacher tonight. She's ready to. I need to sober up before that happens."

"That won't happen, not for *any* reason!" she assured him. "You stink! You're drunk! Is that what gave you the courage to bust into my room

in the middle of the night?"

"I'm not that drunk, not anymore, anyway. Not enough that I don't know what I'm doing."

She lit the lamp by her bed, then swung around to face him. The sight of him wearing only pants, his hair sopping wet, stopped her fury for a moment. "What'd you do, fall in the creek?"

"As a matter of fact . . ." His grin filled in the rest of the explanation, but Jessie wasn't amused. "I changed clothes, though," he offered sagely. "Didn't want to be dripping water all over your floor."

"Well, you forgot to dry your hair. You think it's appropriate, you coming here half-dressed?"

His grin widened. "I wouldn't talk about being half-dressed, not the way you answered your door."

Jessie glanced down at the cotton shirt that came only to the top of her knees. "I didn't invite you here, so just get the hell out. You've caused enough trouble for one day."

"*I* have?" His humor fled. "And what have you done?"

"Paid you back and nothing else," Jessie said coldly. "No more than you both deserved."

"Oh, well, I'm glad to hear I wasn't the only victim of your vicious attack," Chase replied sarcastically. "Especially since I'm the one who'll end up paying for it."

Jessie flared. "You think you're the only one hurt? Because of what you told her, she may try to deny me control of the ranch if I go north again. Well, if I had to lose a friend, it was only fair that you both should lose one, too — each other."

"And you think that's the only consequence?"

"What's the matter, Summers?" Jessie purred. "Wasn't she understanding? Did she hurt your feelings?"

"You really don't care that you hurt her, do you?" he asked tightly.

"I don't recall making love by myself," Jessie retorted. "I don't recall making the first move either time. So who's responsible?"

"I warned you what would happen if she found out, Jessie."

Jessie began to laugh, surprising him. "So that's why you're here. Well, I hate to relieve your mind, Summers, I really do, but that isn't one of your worries. All you've done is lost her respect. Why you want the respect of a whore is beyond me, but —"

"She's not a whore, Jessie," Chase said harshly.

"Don't you tell me what she is or isn't! I know better than you ever could!"

"I didn't come here to fight with you again. I came to ask you to marry me." It took her aback, but she recovered.

"Well, you asked. Now you can go tell her you were a good boy and did as she told you."

"She didn't send me here, Jessie. She hasn't

said anything yet. She left the kitchen in tears, and I haven't seen her since."

"Then what are you doing, being noble?" she sneered. "Or are you just trying to score a few points by doing right by me before you're told to?"

"What's wrong with our getting married?" he asked reasonably, knowing every reason she would think of.

"What do you take me for?" she demanded. "You think I can't remember that the thought of marriage scares you?"

"That was before," he insisted.

"Like hell. Nothing's changed. You want to marry me as much as I do you, and that's not at all. So get out of here and stop bothering me with this drunken nonsense."

"It's not nonsense, and I told you I'm not drunk. Rachel is going to insist we marry, anyway, so why not deny her the chance to make a big issue of it?"

"Why? And spoil her righteous fun? How often does a whore get to be righteous?"

"You're not being serious, Jessie," he said wearily.

"Because there's nothing serious about this!" she snapped. "I may have to give in on some things, but marrying you? I'd take off from here and make myself scarce for as long as necessary before I'd let her force me to marry someone I can't stand."

"You didn't feel that way last night."

"I was a fool last night."

That made him angry. "Maybe we both were fools. But the fact remains that there's a special spark between us, Jessie."

"Don't kid yourself. You just happen to be the first man who touched me. You won't be the last, believe me."

He reached her in two strides and grabbed her, his eyes dark with anger and desire. "What happens with you and me doesn't happen with just any two people," he said huskily. "You can deny it, but you know you want me, Jessie. Marry me. Say yes."

He wouldn't let go of her, so she punched him, hard enough to gain her release but only surprising him. She followed that with a stinging slap.

"Does that prove I don't want you?" she cried, her chest heaving. A lump in her throat made it difficult to get the words out. "You might give a good tumble, but I sure as hell wouldn't marry you for that. It takes a little respect to make a marriage, and I've got none for you!"

"Then maybe I ought to give you some," Chase growled, a threatening glint in his eyes.

Jessie backed away, but not quickly enough. He caught her wrists and dragged her to the bed, but his intention was not what she thought it was.

"Damn, but I've wanted to do this since I first met you," he told her. His voice held pure satisfaction.

He pulled her onto his lap. Jessie gasped at the first stinging blow to her backside. Another followed, and another. She wanted to scream but refused to give him the satisfaction. She fought instead, struggling and squirming to get off his lap, but he threw one leg over both of hers, clamping her legs between his, and pressed the palm of his free hand into her back to hold her immobile. Her struggling had caused her shirt to rise, and his hand was striking bare skin.

Jessie had to bite her lips to keep from crying. He wouldn't stop.

"I'd like to say this hurts me more than it does you, but it doesn't," he said as he continued to hit her glowing backside. "Someone should have done this a long time ago, Jessie. Maybe then you wouldn't be so quick to throw punches anytime you feel like it."

Her eyes were overflowing with tears, but he couldn't see that. He saw only the fiery red of her bottom. Forgetting why he had been so brutal, he leaned over and kissed the injured area.

Jessie didn't feel it. She was burning too much to feel anything but pain. Chase didn't know that, either, and he was annoyed with himself for feeling the need to comfort her at all. He lifted her off his lap and onto the bed. Then he stood up and stomped to the door. He opened it and was even out in the hall before he remembered the note in his back pocket and pulled it out. He went back inside just as Jessie was sitting up, her back to him, her glorious hair spilling around her. The sight stirred him, and every muscle in his body stiffened.

"I have something for you," he said. He dropped the note on the bed, but she didn't turn around. "It would have been a wedding gift, but since it cost me no more than the turn of a card, why don't we call it payment for pleasures received. That way, we're even."

He had hoped for some kind of response to his cruel barb, but he got nothing, not even a glare. She wouldn't look at him. He left the room and closed the door behind him. He was *not* going to let it bother him. His parting shot hadn't been any meaner than many things she had said to him. It would *not* bother him. He was free of her now.

Chapter 24

Jessie didn't sit a horse too comfortably for a week, and every time she rode, she thought of Chase. He had left that following morning. She had stayed in her room until after he was gone, and he hadn't come to say good-bye. He had argued with Rachel before he left, and Jessie couldn't help but hear most of it.

"I asked her to marry me. She refused. Damn it, Rachel, what more could I do?"

"You could have left her alone!" Rachel had actually screamed at him. "I trusted you!"

"What do you want from me, Rachel? It happened. You think I didn't regret it when I found she was a virgin? But it was too late to stop."

"You didn't want to stop!"

Their voices lowered after that, and Jessie didn't hear any more until the final slam of the door when Chase left the house. She was curious about his attempt at being noble. They both knew that she was the one who hadn't let them stop. Yet he let Rachel think he was wholly to blame. Stupid. What was he trying to prove?

Jessie thought a lot about that in the weeks that followed. She couldn't help but think about it. Rachel reminded her of it constantly with her woebegone, pitying expressions. It was absurd. The woman acted as if the most heinous of crimes had been committed. How could she be such a hypocrite, whore that she was? The loss of virginity had not mattered to Jessie, but Rachel acted as if she'd been raped.

Rachel didn't speak Chase's name again, either. It was as if Jessie were suddenly break-able, as if the slightest wrong word would shatter her. Utterly ridiculous.

Rachel's behavior was irritating in another way, too. Her sympathy was not only unwel-come, it also made it impossible for Jessie to forget about Chase Summers, which she dearly wanted to do.

Both mother and daughter despised him now, but for different reasons. For his ill treatment of her, for his getting in the last lick but good before riding out of her life, Jessie would never forgive him. But she would never see him again, never have a chance to even the score. It infuriated her beyond measure.

It was a blessing when Jessie got sick in the middle of October, for the illness served to take her mind off everything but herself. The first few days she was ill, she figured it would run its course quickly. She was annoyed to be sick at all. But when it didn't pass quickly, she began to worry. She managed to keep her illness from everyone, although that was difficult. She didn't want anyone fussing over her, especially Rachel. She'd hardly been sick a day in her life, and she wasn't used to it. After a week, she decided it was time to see a doctor, but she wasn't feeling up to a long ride on Blackstar. She came up with an excuse for using the buggy simply by breaking the heel on her riding boots.

Jessie hadn't counted on Billy wanting to come along, but she didn't refuse him. It was easy to shake him once they got to town, for he was only too willing to go and register them at the hotel for the night. As soon as he was out of sight, she headed for Doc Meddly's office.

Whether he was a real doctor, a horse doctor, or just a man who knew a little about doctoring, she didn't know. But Cheyenne was lucky to have any medical help at all. Many western towns didn't. And he seemed to understand his business, asking the right questions, concentrating like he knew what he was doing. The trouble was, he wouldn't stop frowning when she finished explaining. She was getting awfully nervous.

"Well, what is it?" she demanded. "Is it contagious? Am I dying?"

The man was clearly flustered. "Fact is, Miss Jessie, I got no idea what's ailing you. If I didn't know better, I'd say you were pregnant. But you being an unattached youngun, I have to scratch that. But nothing else fits. You get gut-sick only in the mornings, and you're fine the rest of the time."

Jessie didn't hear a thing he said . . . beyond the word *pregnant*. "But it's too soon . . . I mean, it's only been three . . . no, four weeks since — damn!

After the stammered confession, Doc Meddly cleared his throat uncomfortably and set about rearranging the papers on his desk, avoiding Jessie's eyes. "Yes, well, it don't take long at all to figure if you've conceived . . . ah, that is, if you've been with a man . . . ah, shoot, Miss Jessie. I ain't used to discussing this. The women round here don't come to me for such a delicate matter. They see to each other."

"Then you really think I'm pregnant?"

"If you were married, Miss Jessie, I wouldn't hesitate to say yes."

"Well, I'm not married!" Jessie said sharply. "And I'd rather think I was dying."

Outside the doctor's office, Jessie stopped and leaned back against the door, desperate to get her thoughts together without letting rage interfere. But there was too much to think about. A baby!

Jessie got to the hotel without even being aware of having crossed town. Billy was waiting for her, and he followed her to her room, perplexed. He'd never seen her so preoccupied.

"Is something wrong, Jessie?"

"What could be wrong?" She laughed in a high-pitched voice, on the too-soft bed in the bleak room. She groaned and put her hands to her temples, as if warding off pain.

Billy frowned. "I . . . I thought maybe you heard about Chase Summers, that you were upset because he's still here."

Jessie sat up very slowly. "Here? What do you mean?"

"He's still in town. He didn't leave like we thought. He's staying here in the hotel, in fact."

"You saw him?"

"No."

"Then how do you know?" she snapped.

"Two men told me." He shrugged. "They said they saw you and me come into town. They said they knew Chase worked for you, and if you were looking for him, you could find him over at the saloon. I suppose they were just being obliging, Jessie."

She jumped off the bed. "It's been three weeks since he left the ranch. He's got no business still being here."

"Are you going to see him?"

"No!"

Billy took a few steps away from her. "Are you sure you're all right, Jessie?"

"No . . . yes . . . oh, I've just got a splitting headache that's going to have me climbing the walls soon if it doesn't go away. I need some quiet. Why don't you go down and get yourself some supper, then go to bed?" Then she added, giving a thought to him at last, "Will you be all right alone?"

He drew himself up, insulted. "Sure. But you need to eat, too."

"No, I don't, not tonight. I think I'll just go to bed now, to sleep this headache off. I'll wake you in the morning when it's time to leave."

"What about your boots?"

"I'll get them before we leave. And, Billy, if you happen to see Chase, try not to let him see you, okay? I'd rather he didn't know we were here."

"You sure don't like him, do you, Jessie?"

"What's to like about an arrogant, pigheaded —" She caught herself before she lost control. "No, I don't like him."

"That's too bad."

"Why?" Jessie asked incredulously.

"It's just . . . you and him could have . . . oh, never mind. I'll see you in the morning, Jessie."

"Wait a minute —" But Billy had already closed the door.

Chapter 25

Chase had become quite fond of the bottle and its magic cures. He had even gone on a binge for an entire week when he first got to town. But after he sobered up, he got down to the business of making money — money that would get him to Spain. It was time. Spain was so far away. He needed the distance. In Spain, he wouldn't be tempted to come back to this area.

It was difficult staying there in the meantime, though, and that was why the bottle was never far from his reach. The point was, he kept telling himself, the railroad came through Cheyenne, and there were many saloons for a gambler's needs. It just didn't make sense to go on to Denver or back to Kansas to catch the train east, not when he could do that from where he was.

The difficulty was in being only a day's ride away from that jewel-eyed termagant who kept coming to his mind no matter how much he drowned his thoughts in drink. Twice it had even been so bad he'd considered riding back out to the Rocky Valley Ranch. But Rachel wouldn't welcome him, and Jessie never had. He got drunk enough to stop those foolish notions whenever they came over him.

He was drunk just then, after hearing that Jessie had come to town. What the hell was it about her that made it so difficult to put her out of his life? She had damn well turned his life upside down already. He had never before had this trouble forgetting any woman he'd gotten involved with. And liquor didn't seem to help this time, not even a little. With Jessie so close, he needed something more.

His eyes roamed the saloon from where he stood at the end of the bar. He saw Charlie and Clee, Bowdre's two obnoxious sidekicks, sitting at a table by themselves. Chase could have shot them for telling him Jessie was in town. To get his mind off her, which the drink wasn't doing, he considered picking a fight with them. But then he spotted Silver Annie crossing the room. She would suit his needs even better than a fight.

Annie was the prettiest of the girls who worked this saloon. Unfortunately, that wasn't saying much. She got her name from the silver ribbons she always wore in her hair and around her neck, and also from the color of her eyes, more silver than gray, especially because of their glassy appearance. Her eyes hinted at something stronger than drink. Chase didn't care. He couldn't judge someone else's weakness when he was developing one of his own.

She had approached him before, but he hadn't been tempted. Maybe that was a mistake. What was the old saying about one woman helping you forget another?

A little while later and a lot drunker, he found himself in Silver Annie's room. The lights were out, and he was inundated by the smell of cheap perfume. Some of him was just sober enough to know he didn't really want to be there. But he was there, and he vowed he *would* forget Jessie in the arms of another woman.

But when he finally crawled naked into bed, Chase couldn't find that other woman. She wasn't there. He felt all around the bed, but she still wasn't there.

"Well, where are you, Annie?" he demanded belligerently, determined to go through with it.

He heard her giggle from one side of the room, and then there was a deeper snicker from the other side. Before Chase could make any sense of it, a man spoke.

"You reckon he never got enough from the mama and daughter?"

"Damn you, now he knows we're here!" growled another man.

"Think I care, when I got this?"

"Shit!"

Chase struggled up from the bed. "What —"

A fiery pain stabbed into his back, driving him facedown on the bed. He tried to rise but couldn't quite manage it. And then it didn't matter anymore. A black void engulfed him.

"You dumb asshole!" Charlie swore. "What'd you do that for?"

"I owed him," Clee said defensively. " 'Sides, I weren't scared of him like you sure as shit were."

"Were we told to kill him?" Charlied asked on a rising note. *"Were we?"*

"Ah, what's the difference?"

"Laton didn't want no trouble, that's what, not when the gal will be hearin' soon about what he did up north. He means to drive her out without the law comin' into it. He likes to do things his way, and you sure as hell just messed that up for him."

"It was stupid, anyway, if you ask me. There was no guarantee the Blair girl would fire this one just 'cause he was found here, passed out. Laton was just gettin' worried with him bein' in town all these weeks. Fired or dead, he won't be tellin' the girl even if he did find out anythin' he shouldn't have."

"You better hope Laton sees it that way. And what about Annie?"

"Shoot, she won't say nothin', not if she wants the stuff she was promised. Will you, Annie?"

The girl could only barely see the outline of the two men. She felt sorry for the good-looking gambler, but he was dead and she was alive, and she did need that stuff they'd promised her.

"It's dark in here," she replied quickly. "I didn't see nothin'."

"That's a good girl, Annie." Clee chuckled.

Charlie wasn't amused. "Well, the sheriff will have to be called. We'd best go through his pockets so they think this was a robbery."

"Well, shoot, if you're gonna do it that way, it'd be better just to take his pants with us, wouldn't it?" Clee suggested reasonably. "See, he's dead, and she's screamin' her head off, so would a robber stick around long enough to go through the man's pants?"

"All right, all right," Charlie grumbled, not liking the way this had turned out. He was just glad that Clee was showing some sense in covering all the angles of the new plan they were now stuck with.

Chapter 26

"Do you know who he is, Ned?" Doc Meddly asked.

The deputy shook his head and looked at Silver Annie. She could hardly sit still.

"He calls himself Chase Summers, but what does that tell you?" she said peevishly, wishing they'd hurry up. "It's prob'ly an alias. They usually are."

"Ned, why don't you get her out of here? She's a bundle of nerves," Doc suggested.

"Well, what do you expect me to be, a man gets stabbed in my bed?" Annie shrieked. "And I'm stayin'. Just hurry up and do what you got to do, then get him out of here so I can clean up this mess. I can't afford to stop workin' tonight just 'cause of this."

"Callous, isn't she?" Doc mumbled to the deputy.

"Aren't they all?" Ned agreed. Annie ignored

them both as she yanked a brush through her flaxen hair.

"Where's he staying, Ned?"

"At the hotel, I imagine."

"Don't you know? Where's the sheriff, anyway?"

"Now don't get all put out, Doc. There wasn't any reason to wake him. I can handle this."

"Find out if this young fellow knows anyone around here. He's gonna need looking after for a few days."

"What about Mrs. Meddly? Don't she usually —?"

"God-fearing folk only, Ned. She'd just have to hear where he got hurt to know he don't fit in that category. Now I could insist she tend him, but I'd be living with a shrew the whole time, and I'd rather not."

"He knows the Blair girl," Annie volunteered. It had been a shock to Annie to find the gambler wasn't dead after all. Clee might pay her extra if she continued with their original plan. It was worth a try.

"Jessie Blair?" Doc said absently as he continued cleaning Chase's wound. "She was in town today. See if she's at the hotel, Ned, and —"

"Get her over here quick," Annie interrupted shrilly. "So we can get this over with."

Meddly looked up sharply. "Miss, this is no place for a young lady like her."

"Why not? I heard she's tough as nails. Any gal who can pack a gun can come into a saloon without fainting."

"Not when it isn't necessary," the Doc told her indignantly, then turned to Ned. "Just tell Miss Jessie this man has been hurt and have her wait for me at the hotel in Summers's room. And send up a couple of men to help me get him over there."

Ned left the saloon for the hotel, but he wouldn't find Jessie there. She had entered the saloon just moments before, and was listening inattentively to the talk of the robbery. She had her mind on other things. She had come to find Chase. She hadn't been able to sleep at all after Billy left her, and she had done a good deal of calm, logical thinking. She'd come to a decision that still surprised her.

She didn't see Chase anywhere in the crowded room. And after she looked a second time, she finally began to really listen to the spurts of conversation going on all around her.

"If you gotta go, by God, that's the way to do it — lovin' a woman!"

"Yeah, but to get it in the back, without even a chance to fight."

"I heard they stole his pants and all."

"He's been winning a lot lately, but I didn't see him gambling today. It'd be a good one on the snake who stabbed him if his pockets were empty."

"Yeah."

"I seen him once with the Blair girl. I think he was workin' on her spread for a while."

"Well, I wish they'd hurry and bring him down. I'd like a turn with Silver Annie tonight to find out what really happened."

Jessie ran to the stairs. Four men were coming down, and farther up, on the landing, more men stood near an open door, peering inside. She moved slowly up the stairs. She didn't realize the saloon below was quieting down, now that she had been noticed.

When she got to the open door, Doc Meddly's voice came to her clearly.

"It might help, Miss Annie, if you happened to have a spare pair of pants around. Do you?"

"What would I be doin' with men's britches? The men who visit me take them off, but they always take their pants with them when they leave. Cover him with a blanket, for cryin' out loud. He ain't gonna know the difference."

Jessie's gaze moved from Doc Meddly's back to the heavily painted face of the blonde, who was clad in no more than a skimpy corset and knee-length drawers. She then looked at the man on the bed.

"Is he dead?" Her voice was harsh, almost a scream.

"Why, Miss Jessie!" the Doc exclaimed. "Now, what's wrong with that deputy? I told him not to bring you here."

"Is he dead?" Jessie repeated in a much louder voice.

Meddly saw the ashen color of face, the horror in her eyes. "No, no," he quickly assured her, trying to make his voice as gentle as possible. "The young man will be just fine, with proper care."

Jessie's body almost collapsed. She grabbed the doorframe for support. Meddly smiled encouragingly. But then Jessie's whole demeanor changed. Her back straightened, and an expression as hard as flint closed over her features as she looked at the injured man sprawled on the bed, and then at Silver Annie.

Doc Meddly hastily threw a blanket over Chase as Jessie walked into the room and approached the bed. "Now, Miss Jessie, you shouldn't be in a place like this. I was just about to have him moved to the hotel."

"What happened?" Jessie asked in a hard voice.

"Robbery."

"Was there a fight?"

"You ought to be askin' me, honey," Annie said in a too-sweet voice. "I was the one in the room with him when it happened."

Jessie whirled around, and the older woman shrank from the look in her eyes. "Is that so? Well, then, why don't you just tell me, *honey?*"

"There . . . there weren't no fight," Annie replied uneasily. Then she continued more confidently, "The gambler was too drunk to fight. But I guess the thief didn't know that and he stabbed him. I thought he was dead, I surely

210

did, and I commenced to screamin', see? Well, that sure made that back-stabber turn tail. He swiped up the gambler's duds and lit out of here like a wolf-chased rabbit."

"Is that what you told the deputy?"

"Well, sure."

"And somebody can verify your story?"

Annie frowned. "Now what do you mean?"

"What I mean, woman," Jessie said in a soft, thoroughly icy voice, "is, who else can prove what you're saying is true? Was this thief seen coming out of your room?"

"How should I know?" Annie retorted defensively. "Men come and go from the rooms up here all day and night. No one takes notice of them."

"Did you see the intruder?" Jessie asked.

"I didn't see nothin'. The lights were out."

"Then how did you know Chase had been stabbed?"

"Know? I . . . just did."

"How? Did he bleed on you? Was she covered with blood when you got here, Doc?" Jessie asked him without taking her eyes off Annie.

"Not that I recall, Miss Jessie. But why are you asking all these questions?"

"That's what I'd like to know," Annie grumbled. "Ned didn't bother askin' me all this stuff."

"Maybe he didn't," Jessie replied. "But he didn't know that man lying in your bed like I do."

"Is he close to you, Miss Jessie?" Meddly ventured.

"Close enough."

"Holy —"

Jessie gave him a sharp look, and the good doctor said no more. He knew exactly what she meant. It was a shame she had to find her man here, but if anyone had a right to be asking about how he got hurt, she did. What a situation! And he couldn't even tell anyone about it.

With Meddly silent, Jessie tore into Annie again. "I want to know why there is blood all over that bed, but none on you?"

Annie crossed her arms stubbornly over her ample breasts. "I don't have to be answerin' your questions."

In a flash, Jessie's compact Smith and Wesson revolver was in her hand. "But you will."

"Doc!" Annie shrieked.

"Jessie Blair!" Meddly exclaimed.

"Shut up!" Jessie said furiously. She moved back to the door and kicked it shut, keeping the gun level on Annie. "Now you tell me, damn you, and if I have to shoot you first, well, that doesn't make any difference to me."

"Tell you what?" Annie screamed.

"You stabbed him yourself, didn't you? That's why there's no blood on you."

Annie backed up against the wall, stunned. "No, no, I swear! I wasn't even near him. I was over there, on the other side of the bed!"

"You expect me to believe that?"

Annie drew frantically from her past experience. "He was so drunk, I was hopin' he'd fall asleep and I could wake him, well, you know, like it was all over with, and get paid for nothin'. I don't do it often, honest, only when a feller's as full to the gills as he was."

"You're lying. You lured him up here and set him up!"

"I didn't! God, I swear! I was after him for weeks, but he wouldn't have nothin' to do with me until today. He wasted half the evenin' drinkin' first, said he had things to forget. I figured he could hold the whiskey, so I waited it out. But he couldn't. A man ain't no good when he's that drunk. But he insisted on comin' up here."

"Liar!"

"Doc, Doc, stop her!" Annie was crying hysterically by then. "She's gonna shoot me!"

"What the hell is going on in here?" The door burst open, and a big, ham-fisted, ugly brute of a man loomed in the doorway.

Jessie swung around. "Who are you?" she demanded, not at all intimidated by his size. She, after all, had her gun.

"I happen to own this place you're causing so much ruckus in, and I'll thank you to take your litle self out of here, pronto."

For all the belligerence of his words, his manner was quiet and conciliatory. He was eyeing her weapon. Jessie lowered it when she

213

felt Doc Meddly's hands on her shoulders.

"Come on, girl," he said gently. "Let's get your friend out of here and into a clean bed at the hotel. I'm sure it happened just the way Silver Annie said it did. Let's go."

Jessie looked back at Annie, who was still wide-eyed, and in shock. "All right," she conceded, and put the gun away. "But no one messes with what's mine and gets away with it. You hear me, Annie? If I find out you lied about this, I'm going to put a ball through your heart."

She let Meddly lead their way out of the saloon, with three men following, carefully carrying Chase wrapped up in an old wool blanket. They handled him like a newborn babe, for they'd been standing outside the door and had heard what the little spitfire said. They weren't going to give her any reason to think they had mishandled what was hers. No, sir!

Chapter 27

Jessie rented a wagon to get Chase to the ranch. They left the next morning, with Billy driving and Goldenrod fetched from the stable and tied to the back. Doc Meddly said Chase was fit to travel.

Jessie sat in back with Chase stretched out on his belly, his head resting on her lap. He still hadn't come to, but Meddly said it would be a while, not just because of the wound, but because of all the liquor.

Damn, but she'd made a first-class fool of herself in that saloon. And for what? A man who consorted with whores. A no-account gambler. An arrogant, puffed-up meddler. She should never have gone looking for him, she realized that. Did she want her child raised by a man like that? No. Never. She had let the wrong things influence her. She could just imagine the talk today, poor Jessie Blair, so in love with her man that she could forgive him anything, even getting stabbed in a whore's bed. She was glad to be out of Cheyenne. She would never be able to live it down.

She shouldn't care. She would have to stop caring what people thought, because women didn't live down having babies out of wedlock very easily. And she was not having that man for a husband.

Jessie had been nauseous from the moment she woke that morning, but as long as she stayed well away from food, it remained just a subtle queasiness. Now as she sat there watching the buckboard and the ground rattle and shake, the bile rose steadily. She heard Chase moan, but by then her complexion was turning green, and her own moan drowned his out. She couldn't move fast enough to get to the side of the wagon, and she let Chase's face fall with a crack to the wagon floorboard.

Chase's eyes flew open, but he squeezed them shut in unbearable agony. If he were on his back, he would only be worrying about the phantoms stomping on his head, but for some fool reason, he was lying on his stomach and something was shaking him to hell and back. He managed to open his eyes again. He squinted disbelievingly, thinking he was enclosed in some kind of wooden box. But the box was open on one side, revealing the brightest blue he had ever seen. It was blinding, and Chase closed his eyes again. But there was to be no respite. The box he was trapped in rattled and shook, and he emptied his stomach over the side, holding on for dear life. It was over quickly, and he actually felt a little better.

With his head cleared some, Chase tried to figure out where the hell he was without having to open his eyes to the blinding light. The shaking, a rock-hard bed, walls two feet high, none of it made sense. And there was the sound of retching even when he was finished.

He had to open his eyes if he was going to make any sense of it. Hesitantly, he looked to one side, following the low wall until it turned, and went on, and turned again. He *was* in a box, an open box! And when he looked the other way he saw silky black hair, a white shirt, and the shapeliest little bottom in skintight pants.

"Jessie?" he moaned.

Jessie wouldn't answer, let alone look his way. She felt like she was dying. The damn retching wouldn't stop, yet she had nothing left to give. She was empty but still gagging, and it hurt, and she wanted to cry.

At last Jessie moved slowly away from the side of the wagon. Chase had closed his eyes again.

"If you're not going to spill any more of your guts over the side, you'd best get back over here and lie down."

Chase's eyes flew open. He couldn't answer.

"Can't you hear?" Jessie demanded.

"I fear . . . I . . . I would not be the best of company," Chase managed to get out despite the thickness of his tongue.

"Company, hell," Jessie grumbled. "I don't want your company any more than you want mine, but it looks like I'm stuck with you, thanks to your drunken blunders."

"I don't . . . understand."

"Oh, God, will you just lie down!" Jessie moaned. "You need to rest, and I'm not up to talking just yet."

Chase thought it was more likely he needed a doctor, or another bottle of whiskey. But sleep might help get rid of this wretched hangover.

The space was small, and Jessie was already lying on half the blankets. "Where am I supposed to lie down?"

Jessie moved back slowly until she lay along the edge of the spread blankets, but there still wouldn't be enough room for him to stretch out unless he continued to use her lap for his head. Yet she couldn't offer it without sitting up and she couldn't sit up right now without being sick again.

Curled on her side, she grudgingly straightened her top leg so only the lower one remained bent. She patted the bent leg. "Your pillow."

Chase grinned despite his pains. "Really?"

Jessie saw that gleam in his eye, but for once she didn't get angry. She felt like laughing.

218

There they both were, sick as dogs, and he probably had a fever as well, besides a nasty wound. Yet he could think of passion. The man was a marvel.

"I'm only offering you the use of my knee, so get all those lecherous thoughts out of your head right now, Chase Summers." She tried to make her voice stern, but there was a laughing note in it. "If I didn't feel the need to rest, be assured I'd be sitting up front with Billy."

"Billy?"

"Yes, Billy. He's got the reins."

Chase looked up front, but the glare was too bright, and he found it easier to stay still, anyhow.

"On your stomach, Chase." Her voice was firm. "Doctor's orders."

He scowled. "What doctor?" he demanded irritably, thinking she meant herself. "I never sleep on my stomach. And I wouldn't have been so sick just now if I hadn't been on my stomach."

"I'm in no mood for you to be difficult, damn it!" Jessie said hotly. "Now lie on your stomach or your side, but stay the hell off your back!"

"Why?"

"If you don't know, then you're not sober enough yet for me to waste my time explaining."

Chase turned on his side angrily, but slowly. Jessie went silent. Later, when she felt better,

219

she would give him a large piece of her mind. The thought gave her something to look forward to.

Chapter 28

Jessie finally woke, disoriented, hearing Billy call her name again and again. She lay there until she understood that he was telling her they were almost home. She sat up, giving thanks that she could move again without having her stomach rise with her. But, of course, it was late in the day, and the sickness never bothered her then.

She hadn't intended to sleep the day away. Had Billy been all right? She guessed he had. Chase was still sleeping. She felt his brow for fever, but it was only slightly warm. The moment she touched his face, his arm snaked up and wrapped around her extended leg, holding her there. Jessie almost said something sharp, then saw it had only been a reflex action. He was still asleep, snuggling back against her groin.

Jessie's eyes became stormy. His movements

were causing unwanted stirrings in the lower part of her body, but he shouldn't have had any effect on her at all, she thought. It wasn't natural, to loathe a man and want him anyhow. Was it?

Thinking about that wasted enough of her time that they were pulling up in front of the house before she knew it. Rachel came out, took one look at Chase in the back of the wagon with Jessie, and went right back inside the house. Jessie shrugged. Rachel didn't know yet that Chase was wounded. She would change her tune when she did. She'd better. Jessie certainly wasn't going to care for him all by herself.

"Run and find Jeb, Billy, and see if any of the other men are around to help get Chase into the house," Jessie ordered, then added, "And thank you, Billy. You did a fine job getting us home."

Billy lit up with pleasure, then went to find Jeb. He appeared again in a moment, running ahead of the older man.

"And what have we here, little gal?" Jeb asked curiously. "I thought never to set eyes on this one again."

"You're not the only one," Jessie replied with a good measure of disgust as she crawled to the end of the wagon. "But he got hurt while I was in town, and Doc Meddly happened to know I was acquainted with him, so he dumped the caring of him in my lap."

"Do tell." Jeb chuckled.

"It's nowhere near funny," Jessie retorted.

"But what was he doin' still in town?"

"Gambling and drinking and whoring."

"Do tell."

"Oh, hush up and help me get him inside."

"There's no one in the bunkhouse, Jessie," Billy announced. "Jeb said so."

Jeb grunted. "We can do this, the three of us." He turned to Jessie. "Can't he walk none at all?"

"He'll have to," Jessie returned. "There's nothing wrong with his feet. Billy," she directed, "Jeb and I will steer him if he's not surefooted enough. Could you go inside and get his bed ready?"

"How bad hurt is he?" Jeb asked seriously when Billy was gone. She explained, finishing, "The Doc seemed to think he should stay off his feet for the next few days, which means someone has to look after him. Otherwise, I would never have brought him back here."

Jessie shook Chase gently, then sighed when he rolled onto his back. "He'll be breaking those stitches for sure. I hope you're handy with a needle, Jeb."

"Don't tell me he got it in the back?" Jeb's voice rose indignantly.

"Yep, but I'll explain the rest later. Let's see if we can get him out of the wagon."

They managed, but it took a while. Chase didn't even open his eyes until his feet were on the ground, and he was so wobbly that they each grabbed one of his arms to pull around their necks.

They put him in Thomas Blair's old room, dragging him all the way. Billy had the bedcovers pulled down and was waiting anxiously. Luckily it was a low post bed with no footboard.

"Let's position him so he can get his knees up on the foot of the bed, Jeb. Then we'll lower him to his stomach," Jessie instructed.

"Christ, no!" Chase growled.

"Oh, shut up," Jessie said impatiently. "I never heard a man bitch so much about sleeping on his stomach."

"Lady, if you had two quarts of raw whiskey in your stomach, you'd bitch, too."

Jessie released his arm and stepped back. "I recall you got rid of that this afternoon," she said in a lighter, amused tone as she rubbed her aching shoulder. He was too heavy to carry.

He grimaced. "And I recall you retching right alongside me, so have a little sympathy."

Jeb and Billy both looked at Jessie strangely, and that heated her temper. "You're talking mighty clearly for a man who had to be dragged in here."

Chase raised his head slightly. There was the tiniest grin about his lips. "Was I supposed to make an efffort? Nobody told me."

Jeb snorted and left the room, mumbling all the way. Billy giggled until Jessie's stormy eyes lit on him.

"I'll, ah, get his things out of the wagon,"

he offered quickly, and left the room.

Jessie turned those flashing eyes back on Chase. "I'm beginning to think you're not as bad off as the Doc told me," Jessie said coldly. "And if that's the case, Jeb can tote you back to town when he returns the wagon tomorrow."

"For another ride like today?" he cried. "Not on your life! And what is all this talk about a doctor? I have a terrible hangover, but what's a doctor got to do with that?"

"You really don't remember what happened to you, do you?"

Chase closed his eyes wearily. "I got drunk, maybe a little more than usual, but so what? I've been doing a lot of that lately," he added, more to himself than by way of revelation.

"Maybe the name Annie will stir your memory."

The anger in her tone disturbed him. Annie? The only Annie he knew was . . .

Chase put his hands to his temples, which caused a stabbing pain in his back. He didn't know which was worse, the physical pain or the memory of him staggering up the stairs last night with Silver Annie. All the while, he'd been thinking of this one, wishing it were Jessie he was with, Jessie he was about to make love to. Had he really gone to Silver Annie's room?

His eyes opened wide. He could see that Jessie wasn't just a little angry, but one hell of a lot angry. She was standing there with her arms crossed over her chest, her body so stiff he thought she was about to break. She was trying to mask her feelings with contempt, but her eyes were shooting daggers at him.

She knew. Somehow, she knew. And she was furious about it. Chase didn't know whether to be pleased or worried.

"I, ah, can explain, you know," he ventured sheepishly.

"Can you?" Jessie said coldly. "Where you were found is explanation in itself, isn't it?"

"Found? You didn't come to the saloon, did you? Is that how you know?"

"Yes, I was there. Half the town was there! It will probably make the paper. I can just see the headlines. 'Drunk assaulted and robbed in whore's room. Thief got away with the victim's pants, since he wasn't wearing them at the time.' "

Chase's eyes narrowed. "Is that suppposed to be funny?"

"*That* is what happened, Summers. Or don't you remember getting a knife in your back?"

He tried to turn over, but he couldn't. "So that's what hurts so much."

"I would imagine it does."

"How bad is it?"

"Doc Meddly said you should stay off your feet for a few days, since you lost so much blood. Other than that, you should heal fine."

"If I was to have bed rest, what did you drag me out here for?"

"I wasn't going to stick around town to take

226

care of you! And Meddly had me believing no one else would tend you, considering where you got your wound. I probably could have found someone to look after you, but it was easier just to bring you here. Rachel can do it. So if you have any explaining to do, you can do it to her."

Chase frowned. "I doubt Rachel would help me now, Jessie. She doesn't think too kindly of me anymore."

"You think I do?"

"No, I suppose you don't," he sighed. "What were you doing at the saloon, anyway?"

"I went there to see you," she said stiffly, unsure of herself for the first time.

That was the last thing he expected to hear. "Why?"

"That hardly matters now."

And with that she left the room, leaving Chase even more befuddled.

Chapter 29

Jessie lingered at the table with Rachel after Billy had excused himself. She hadn't eaten a meal in such uncomfortable silence since those terrible meals she and her father had suffered through when they were angry with each other. No wonder Billy had left as soon as he could.

At least Jessie was used to it and didn't let it affect her appetite. That was important, because evenings were the only time Jessie could make up for the other meals she was missing. She wasn't going to let a little tension keep her from taking full advantage of the times she felt perfectly normal, as if there were no changes taking place in her body.

The silence continued, both avoiding the other's eyes. Finally Jessie's plate was empty, and there was nothing left to do but get it over with. She sighed deeply.

"He won't have to stay here long, Rachel. A

week at the most, until he can sit a horse without opening up his wound. A week isn't that long."

Rachel's eyes were stonily unsympathetic. "But why did you bring him here?"

"Look, I don't like this any more than you, but there was no one else to look after him. I couldn't just turn my back on him, could I?"

"How did he get hurt?"

"The thief who was robbing him panicked and stabbed him in the back."

Rachel lowered her eyes. "Well, I suppose things like that are to be expected," she said harshly, "considering his occupation." It was the most condemning remark Jessie had ever heard from her.

"You knew he was a gambler, Rachel. It didn't seem to matter to you before."

"He is not the boy I used to know," Rachel said coldly.

"It's none of my business what kind of man he is, Rachel," Jessie said. "And it's none of yours, either. He's not answerable to either of us."

"Well, that's a fine attitude after what he did to you," Rachel said tearfully.

"Are you ever going to put that to rest?" Jessie demanded. "What Chase and I did, we did together. You're the only one crying over it!"

"If you feel that way, why didn't you marry him when he asked you?"

229

"His asking came a bit too late," Jessie replied bitterly. "He didn't want to marry me, and I knew it. Whose pride would have been served if I had accepted? Only yours, Rachel."

Rachel's voice turned soft suddenly. "You mean . . . you would marry him if he loved you?"

Jessie shook her head. "Where on earth do you get these ideas? That man doesn't love me. I mean no more to him than any of his countless other women."

"Are you so sure, Jessica? He may very well love you now but hasn't realized it yet. He did stay in town instead of moving on," she pointed out.

"To get drunk."

"But why, unless he loves you so much he —"

"Are you defending him? I wish to hell you'd make up your mind!"

Rachel looked away. "I'm not defending him, not in the least."

"Well, I'm glad to hear it, because I wouldn't marry a no-good, carousing —"

"So you *do* care!"

Jessie could have pulled her hair out by the roots, she was so exasperated. She leaned forward and banged her fist on the table, her cheeks high with color.

"I don't care! I care so little that he can starve to death before I'll put one foot in his room again. He's in this house, but I'm not

230

going near him, not going to set eyes on him again. Now, you brought him here in the first place, he's your responsibility. *You* tend him!"

Rachel stood up stiffly, rigid. "I refuse to care for the man who ruined my daughter."

Jessie's mouth fell open as she watched Rachel walk away from the table. She jumped up, tore around the table, and followed Rachel up the hall. *"I am not ruined!* Do you hear?"

"I cannot help but hear, you're shouting so," Rachel replied without stopping. "But it does not change the facts. I won't help him."

"But he's your friend!"

"Was my friend," Rachel said stubbornly, stopping at her door. "If someone must see to him, get Kate to do it. I'm sure she won't mind."

"Of course she'd mind!" Jessie rasped. "You can't foist him off on her."

"And you can't foist him off on me, Jessica," Rachel countered coolly, going into her room and closing the door.

Twenty minutes later, Jessie carried a platter of food into Chase's room. It would have done her a world of good if he had been awake so she could vent her spleen at him, but he was sound asleep. She simply left the food on the bedside table, made sure he was warmly covered, and left the room.

Chapter 30

Chase was enjoying his convalescence, even if the only cheerful face he saw was Billy's. In the mornings, the boy would bring him breakfast and stay to chat for a while. Too, Chase was seeing Jessie every day, and he definitely liked that, sour-faced though she usually was.

He called the situation poetic justice. After all, he was laid up because he'd gotten drunk and couldn't defend himself, and he'd gotten that way because of Jessie. So wasn't it just desserts that she should have to care for him?

Jessie didn't think so. She did everything in her power to show him how much she resented having to wait on him. His pride should have been stung. He should have reacted angrily. But he didn't. He was amused by her tongue-clicking, her sighs, her brusque manner. She was acting the martyr, yet she might have sent Billy in with his evening meal, or asked him to hold the mirror while Chase shaved in the afternoons. She might have sent Jeb in to change his bandages or sponge him down. but she didn't do any of those things. She even changed his bedding, which was usually Kate's job. In fact, the only thing Jessie didn't do was bring him breakfast.

He didn't see her at all in the mornings. No one did, according to Billy, for Jessie was leaving the house much earlier than usual, heading out to the range. After only two days, he found himself listening for her return, listening for the sound of her voice when she wasn't in his room. If she was late, he fretted. If she was early, he was delighted.

He could hear Rachel occasionally, too, but she never came near him. She made her displeasure felt without directing those accusing blue eyes at him. She even cornered Jessie one day outside his room where he could hear them clearly, and demanded to know when he would be leaving. Rachel must have been quite surprised to hear her reply that he would leave when he damn well please. *He* was certainly surprised to hear Jessie take his side. Of course, she had done it just to go against Rachel. Anything to go against her mother, he knew that. Still . . .

After a week of convalescence, Chase knew he had no business staying in bed any longer. His wound had closed nicely, and he had his strength back. He could undoubtedly sit a horse with only a little pain. It was time to leave the Rocky Valley, and this time not even stop in Cheyenne. Jessie had packed all his gear in his hotel room and brought it here, including the considerable amount of money he'd won during those few weeks gambling in town. The man who'd robbed him had gotten away with only the pocket change he'd been carrying that day. He had more than enough money to head back East and then book passage to Spain. And that was what he should do.

But that wasn't what he wanted to do. He wanted to continue seeing Jessie every day. He had gotten used to her in this last week, seeing her in an entirely different way. He'd come to understand her a little better.

They say the young can see things clearly, he recalled, and young Billy had hit it right on the head that day when he'd said Jessie only tried to act rough and mean because she thought she had to. Anger seemed to be her only defense. She used it to hide hurt, confusion, fear.

Chase knew her better. He could see the frightened girl inside trying desperately to be independent, trying not to need anyone. She'd needed someone once and had been hurt terribly by it. When he saw her in that light, he wanted to draw her into his arms, to hold and protect her. But tough little Jessie would never stand for that. No, her defenses would have to be breached first, and those were defenses built up over ten years. A king-sized effort. Was any man up to it?

Chase knew he had too many strikes against him. It was too much to hope for — Christ, did he hope for it? He wasn't sure. The only thing he was sure about was that he didn't want to leave yet.

He would put it off as long as he could. After all, Jessie was not pushing him out the door. But once he left this room, Rachel would. Damn, but he hadn't remembered Rachel being such an unforgiving woman. Trouble was, she loved Jessie too much. It was too bad Jessie didn't realize that. He wagered that, deep down, Jessie felt the same way. And their rift was at the heart of so much, it would take a miracle to mend it. Chase wished he had that miracle.

Today Chase was having a bath, a longed-for hot bath, with Billy and Jeb's conspiratorial help. The thing was to get the water to him without Rachel knowing that he was well enough to get into a tub unassisted. They managed it, with Jeb heating water in the clothes tub out back and passing it through Chase's window to Billy. Billy thought it was great sport, keeping a secret from his mother. Chase wanted it kept from Jessie as well, for he didn't want her confronted with the truth of his mobility.

It almost worked. But today was one of the days Jessie happened to come in from the range early. They were both quite surprised when she walked in on him as he sat in the skinny barrel. She recovered more quickly than he did and continued on into the room.

She was still wearing her chaps. Her clothes were dusty; her hat was caught by the string around her neck. It was the first time she had come into his room without first cleaning up. But Chase didn't think of that, too embarrassed to think of anything but how to explain himself. He was thankful that Jeb and Billy had left him alone.

"Does Rachel know about this?" Jessie asked casually, indicating the tub.

"No."

"You're going to get your wound all soft. How long have you been in there?"

Chase couldn't seem to think straight with her eyes fixed on him. "Not long."

She came right up to the barrel and stuck her finger in the water. "Too long, anyway. How many other baths have you sneaked in without my knowing about them? Have I been sponging you off in the evenings only for your amusement?"

"Come on, Jessie, this is the first time."

"But I wouldn't have known about it, would I? I mean, there wouldn't have been any evidence if I'd come home later, would there?"

He was guilty of intention, and she knew it. He couldn't tell if she was angry or not. He was also acutely aware that he was naked and she was standing right next to him.

He cleared his throat. "It's no big thing, Jessie. Water hasn't touched the wound or not much. Where's the harm in my having a decent bath?''

"None, I suppose," Jessie conceded. "And seeing as how you've removed your bandage and are already in the tub, you might as well get your back washed, too."

"Jessie —"

"Lean forward, Chase," she ordered firmly. "You do want a decent bath. And I can wash your back without getting the wound too wet."

It was easier to comply than to argue, but he wished to high heaven he knew what was going through her mind. She wasn't acting normal. She hadn't said one harsh word, hadn't made the slightest fuss about his being out of bed. She was too calm. Something was wrong, but he couldn't put his finger on it.

Worrying about that, Chase didn't even take notice of what Jessie was doing behind him until she was finished and she commanded. "All right, stand up now, and I'll rinse you off."

"I can do it," he said quickly.

"And you'll get water all over the floor, too," she pointed out. "That tub doesn't have the widest of rims. In fact, I'm amazed you could squeeze into it."

"I hadn't planned on any help." His embarrassment made him curt.

"Well, you have it anyhow."

"Will you get out of here, Jessie!"

She laughed softly. "You're not embarrassed

to display a bit of that handsome body, are you? It's not as if I haven't seen you in the all-together before this."

"That was different," he retorted.

"Why? Because I was unclothed, too? Well, I'm not about to strip down just to appease your male dignity. Now stand up like a good boy, and let's get this over with." Then she added teasingly, "I promise not to take advantage of you, if that's what has you worried."

Chase looked over his shoulder to glare at her. She really was amused. It wasn't often he saw humor dancing in her eyes, turning them a lighter, brighter turquoise.

He stood up and felt the cool water dribble down over his body. Jessie was pouring it over him, and it felt so good.

"There now, that wasn't so bad, was it?" she said, mischievously giving his backside a pat.

Chase gasped, but he was immediately draped in a towel and thought it best not to comment. He turned to look at her, but she was walking toward the bedside table where a stack of clean bandages was kept.

"If you'll come over here, I'll get you wrapped up again — if you think it's still necessary."

Chase grimaced. She was saying he was well, that there was no reason for her to tend him any longer. Next she would be asking when he planned to leave.

With the towel wrapped around his waist, he

came over to the bed and sat down so she could bandage him, anything to prolong her presence for what would probably be the last time he would have her to himself. He watched her intently as she leaned forward to place the folded cloth over his wound, then began to wind clean strips around him to hold the bandage in place. She was uncommonly gentle about it for once. That, and the unusual way she was behaving, stirred his curiosity almost uncontrollably.

"Why all the tender treatment?" he ventured at last.

She quirked a brow at him. "Tender?"

"You know what I mean."

She shrugged and looked back at the bandage. "I don't know. I guess, since this will probably be the last time I'll see you, I figure there's no reason we have to part on a sour note."

Chase shook his head. "You're kicking me out today, just because I took a damn bath?"

She looked at him sharply. "Don't be ridiculous. It doesn't matter to me how long you want to pamper yourself. I just figured, now that you're able, you'll want to be on your way."

"So we are to part as friends, huh? Just how friendly?" He grinned, running a finger up the side of her thigh.

She slapped his hand away. "Not that friendly."

She stepped a careful distance away from him, and Chase laughed. "Come now, Jessie, I don't bite. You must know that by now."

"Do I?" she retorted, her eyes turning hard as stone.

He frowned. They were both remembering what he'd done to her the night before he left. "I thought you had forgiven me for that."

"Well, I haven't."

"You never mentioned it."

"Was I supposed to shoot you while you were laid up?"

"You're not going to shoot me, Jessie," he said confidently.

"I think you had better drop the subject," she replied stiffly.

"I am sorry, you know. I just wasn't myself that night."

"I said drop it!"

"All right," he sighed, her mercurial moods too much to fight. "What brought you home early?"

"I came to tell you I won't be tending you any more. I see now that I won't have to feel I'm deserting you, since you're so much better."

"You really are angry, aren't you?" he said, sure that was meant as a barb.

Jessie drew herself up. "I'm not being spiteful. I've got more than thirty cattle dead on the south range and a water hole that's apparently been poisoned. I've got no time to be spiteful."

"Are you serious?"

"Of course I'm serious. The only reason I

rode in at all was to tell you I won't be around for several days. The poisoned hole has to be fenced off, and the cattle have to be herded up and brought closer to home. They'll have to be guarded day and night for a while. With the others not back from the drive yet, I'll need every hand on the range, including myself."

"You weren't upset about it when you came in here," he said, surprised.

"You took my mind off it for a time," she admitted. "But the fact is, what's done is done, and there's no point in crying over it. All I can do now is see that I don't lose any more of the herd."

"I'm sorry."

"It's none of your concern," she said. "So I guess this is good-bye."

"Why?" he asked quickly.

"I won't be getting back to the house even for a change of clothes, not for a while. And you've got no reason to stay anymore."

"But you could use my help."

"I'm not asking for it. And Rachel won't want you around."

"Whose ranch is this, anyway?" Chase said angrily.

"Oh, so now it's up to me? But when I wanted you gone, it was Rachel's place to make decisions."

"There's real trouble involved this time, not just the threat of trouble. Do you think it was Bowdre? He wasn't pleased that I won that note back from him."

"I'm sure he wasn't. But there's no way in hell I can prove it. Poisoning cattle is pure vindictiveness, though. I didn't think even he would destroy something just because he couldn't get his hands on it."

"You're wrong, Jessie, he'd do just that. And if it is Bowdre the trouble won't end now. You'll need all the help you can get."

"If there's going to be worse trouble, what I'll need is a gunfighter, not a gambler."

There was no contempt in her tone, so he didn't take exception. "I don't carry an Army revolver just for ornament, you know. I do know how to use it."

"But have you ever killed anyone?"

"Have you?"

Jessie didn't like the idea of his sticking around, not when she had it resolved in her mind that she wouldn't see him again. It had been hard enough, seeing him every day this week. She didn't understand the things he made her feel, and he had been at his charming best all week, which made it worse.

"You're in no condition to help anyone, Chase. And this isn't your fight anyway."

"Look," he said impatiently, "until the rest of your men get back, you can use my help and you know it. I'll be as good as new in a few days, and in the meantime, I wouldn't be overdoing it to stand guard over the herd, would I?"

"Why do you want to help me?"

He thought quickly. "Well, by winning that note, I figure I got you into this mess. It's only fair —"

She cut him short. "Bowdre never wanted the money, you know he wanted the ranch. If I'd paid him, he still would have turned vindictive." She sighed. "Oh, what the hell, suit yourself. But don't blame me if you have a relapse.'"

She left the room, and Chase grinned. He was ridiculously delighted.

Chapter 31

Chase woke to the sounds of pots clanging as someone put coffee on and started breakfast. He stared in vexation at the still-black sky. Three mornings ago, when he'd been awakened in a similar manner for the first time, he'd been angry enough to voice his objections, but had received only laughter and jesting from the others. They were used to rising before dawn for a day's hard work. He was not. They called him a greenhorn. Hell, he *was* a greenhorn.

But he'd gotten himself into this, had insisted on it, so it did no good to complain. He'd like to think he was only being gallant, coming to a lady's rescue and all that, but that was far from the truth.

Actually, he had seen less of Jessie in the three days since he'd followed her out to the range than he'd expected. He had been given the easy task of guarding the water hole where the cattle were being brought and seeing that the herd didn't wander too far off. He saw Jessie once, maybe twice, a day, when she brought in the stragglers from the hills. At night, she was so tired that they exchanged no more than a few words before she bedded down close to the fire with the others. He never saw her alone. In the mornings, no one saw her, not even the cook, who was the first to rise.

Chase sat up and shivered in the predawn cold. It must be thirty degrees or lower, he thought. His blanket was sodden and covered by a thin layer of frost. But it was only the first week in November.

Why would anyone want to start a ranch in such cold country? But Thomas Blair had, and the cattle had survived it. The men were used to working in freezing weather.

A cup of hot coffee would help, he decided, shivering at the prospect of having to get up to get it. He glanced over to where Jessie had bedded down last night, but the spot was empty. There was only the frostless outline where her blanket had been. Gone, the same as every other morning. Why? At least the sun was coming up by the time the men finished their breakfast and headed out, but Jessie took off while it was still pitch dark. He'd asked her where she went so early, but she had shrugged evasively.

He shook his head, his mind going back to what had happened the night before last. She had taken the new calamity better than most would, after her initial burst of outrage. The last thing she'd expected to hear from Mitch Faber when he rode into their small camp that night was that every single head of cattle he had taken north had been stolen, stolen the day before they were due to deliver the herd.

The men were set upon at night, while they slept, the man standing guard over the herd disappearing altogether.

"Knocked us clean out," Mitch said. "I didn't even know what hit me. We weren't hurt worse than that, though. They weren't out to kill us, just take the herd."

It hadn't been necessary to kill them, Jessie learned. By the time Mitch and the men with him reached the first mining town on their list, so they could report the theft to the sheriff, it was all pointless. The cattle thieves had their timing perfect. The thieves had every cow sold before Mitch and his men woke up. And the most galling part was that the herd would be sold to the very miners Jessie had contracted with. An agent had bought the whole herd and divided it and had the cattle ready to be driven on to the surrounding towns. He had a receipt. He'd paid in cash, dealing through the bank, which was his witness. There wasn't a damn think the sheriff could do.

There wasn't a damn thing Mitch could do, either. The agent could not be blamed for assuming the men who brought the herd into town were from the Rocky Valley Ranch. They sold him the contracts, which had been stolen from Mitch while he was knocked out. Jessie had never dealt with an agent before, so he didn't know her or Mitch.

"How could they know about the contracts?" Jessie had demanded.

She took the news hard, her face ashen, her eyes disbelieving. Chase understood. He knew of the outstanding loan she had at the bank. She would have no money coming in now to put toward the debt, and no money to pay her men with, either.

Jessie turned furious when she heard of the disappearance of the man who had been standing guard. Blue Parker. Mitch confessed that Blue had been acting strangely during the drive. Yes, Blue knew of the contracts. And he had been surly and discontent for a month before the drive. Chase realized that was about the time he'd arrived at the Rocky Valley. Jessie realized it, too, and gave him a withering look, as if it were all his fault. Chase didn't even know Blue Parker, but he found out later that he was the young man he had discovered with Jessie that first day. That was all Jessie told him, explaining who Blue was. But it was obvious she thought Parker was in with the cattle thieves, and it was obvious who they were.

She was too angry that night to explain any more to Chase, cursing Parker, cursing Laton Bowdre. By the time she had calmed down, Chase didn't have the heart to bring the subject up again. But he was damn well curious about Parker. Remembering that scene he had come upon, finding them together, gave him little sleep that night.

Chase finally braved the cold and put his bedding away. What a difference a month made! It hadn't been nearly so cold when he'd camped out under the stars on his search for Jessie, and that had been only late September.

He took a cup of coffee, clasping it tightly to warm his hands. The other two men who sat near the fire eating fried steak and eggs grinned at him as he stood there shaking.

"You'll get used to it, Summers, if you stick around long enough," Ramsey offered.

"Gonna get worse, friend," the middle-aged cowpuncher called Baldy told him, chuckling. "Looks like we'll be havin' us some snow any day now."

Chase grunted, and both men laughed. It was only the three of them, as it had been from the start, for they were the only two hands Jessie had besides Jeb and the two others who had gone on the drive with Mitch and Blue. Jessie had sent Mitch and one of the men to Ft. Laramie to try to sell some beef there, enough to pay her men. The second man had quit when she refused to give him time off for a little revelry. She had had to ride back to the ranch with him in order to scrape up enough money to pay him off. Chase had wanted to clobber the bastard, but it was Jessie's business, and he knew she wouldn't appreciate his interfering.

He wanted desperately to help her out of this new trouble. Hell, he would give her every cent he had if she would just take it.

"Either of you get a chance to talk to Jessie before she left this morning?" Chase asked casually as he took a plate and filled it.

Baldy shook his head without looking up from his breakfast. "Her ridin' out was what woke me. Didn't see nothin' but the tail end of her horse."

"Which way did she go?" Chase ventured.

Ramsey answered. "She told me last night she'd be riding west today, up into the foothills. Said not to expect her back for a few days."

Baldy shrugged. "If she's goin' that far afield, she's probably gonna stop by the supply shack. She should've said somethin' to me. I was by there yesterday and stocked up good. I could've saved her the trip."

Chase was feeling more and more miserable. The thought of not seeing her for several days

. . .

"Switch places with me today, Ramsey?" Chase said impulsively.

Ramsey looked at him in surprise. Both men knew that he had recently been wounded.

"You sure you're up to it?"

"Some of them older cows can get pretty testy about bein' herded in when they're used to roamin' free," Baldy added.

"I think I can manage," Chase said firmly.

"And I need the exercise. I've been resting up too long as it is."

"Sure thing then," Ramsey agreed.

Chapter 32

With the sky a solid sheet of clouds, it didn't look like the sun was going to do much warming. Without a clear dawn, there was only a hazy blue light over the land when Chase left camp. But it was light enough to define Jessie's tracks, distinctive as they were on the frost-covered ground.

In the mood he was in, he didn't care if the men noticed he was taking off in the same direction she had gone. They might wonder about his relationship with her, but what *was* his relationship with her, anyway? He certainly didn't know.

Chase rode on over the cold plain, the icy wind biting at his cheeks. He had his jacket fastened clear to the neck and wore his bandanna over his ears as Baldy had suggested. But even the old pair of woolly chaps he'd borrowed from Jeb weren't helping. Nothing was helping.

He cursed himself for leaving the camp fire to go chasing a woman it would probably take him all day to find.

It didn't, though. He had ridden no more than half a mile when he topped a low-lying hill and pulled up short, seeing Jessie's big-boned Appaloosa grazing on the next rise. On the level plain between the two hills, Jessie lay on the ground. Had she taken a fall from the horse?

Chase felt his stomach constrict. He raced down the hill, holding his breath. It was only when she turned her head at the sound of his horse that he let out that breath.

He got off his horse so quickly he nearly stumbled. He knelt beside her, taking in her ashen pallor.

"For God's sake, Jessie, what happened?"

"Nothing."

"Nothing?"

"Nothing," she repeated in a groaning voice. "What the hell are you doing here?"

He drew back, frowning. "Damn it, Jessie —"

"Will you go away!" She cut him off forcefully.

"Of course not. You're hurt."

"I'm not."

Jessie started to sit up but paled even more and lay back down, closing her eyes. God, why did he have to find her like this? She had been lucky so far, managing to get away by herself while she was plagued with the morning sickness. This wasn't the first time she'd curled up on the cold ground until the waves of nausea passed. She'd always managed to do it in secret.

"Jessie, please, tell me what's wrong."

There was genuine concern in his voice. That warmed her. She had to tell him something — not the truth, but something.

"I'm just not feeling too good, is all. I suppose I've been overdoing it."

"Well lying on this cold ground can't help. You'll catch your death."

"I tried to make it to the supply shack, but I couldn't this morning."

Too late, Jessie realized she'd said more than she should have.

"This morning? Is that where you've been going all these mornings? Why?"

She wanted to say, "'Cause it's warmer there for what I have to go through." But she couldn't very well say that, so she lied. "I've been riding the northern range. Why shouldn't I stop off there for a bite to eat? You got any more questions?"

"I'm getting you back to the ranch."

"No! Damn it, I just need to lie down for a while. If I could ride, do you think I'd be lying here?" she asked caustically.

"You're not staying here. I'll take you to the cabin. You can lie down there."

"No, Chase." He reached for her, and she panicked. "Don't touch me!"

He ignored her. But Jessie had known the

slightest movement would stir her stomach, and it did. She jerked away from him and turned just in time to lose every thing she hadn't lost already. As soon as she was finished, he gently picked her up and carried her to his horse, set her sideways in the saddle, then mounted behind her, gathered her against him, and went to collect Blackstar. She didn't protest anymore, but rested against him, snug in his arms all the way to the cabin. He carried her inside, putting her down on the cot closest to the fireplace. Immediately he got a fire going, then helped her remove her jacket, boots, and gun holster so she would be more comfortable.

"Can I get you something to eat, Jessie?" Chase offered.

"No!" she said quickly, but added in a softer tone, "But you can boil me some water if you would. I've got some wild mint in my saddlebag that's good for . . . settling the stomach."

Chase didn't question the home remedy but did as she asked and put some water on over the fire before he went out to get her saddlebags. While he was waiting for the water to boil so he could add the herbs, Jessie fell asleep. He didn't wake her. Sleep was probably the best thing for her, and the tonic could wait until she woke. He sat down to watch her, wondering if he should go for a doctor. But the nearest one would be at least a day's ride away, and he couldn't leave her alone that long.

The more he thought of it, the more he figured

it was probably just as Jessie said. She had been overdoing it. Getting up well before dawn and working till sunset — even she wasn't used to those hours. And she was worried, damn near wiped out by the theft of her cattle.

Chase went out to bed down the horses in the lean-to. When it started snowing, he cursed. Then he realized that if it continued, they might get snowed in. And they wouldn't have to worry about the cattle, either, because the weather would put a halt to Bowdre's activities as well. As soon as he saw the horses had plenty to eat, Chase hurried back inside the shack.

Chapter 33

Jessie woke snuggled in a warm cocoon of blankets, the fire crackling near her and a tantalizing aroma wafting through the air. She found she was ravenous and feeling just fine.

She sat up. Chase was by the fire. He had his back to her and was stirring whatever it was that had aroused her hunger so.

"Didn't know you could cook."

He turned and grinned at her. "Passably."

"It smells good."

"Thank you, ma'am." He came over to the bed. His expression turned more serious as he peered at her closely. "Can I get you your tonic now?"

"I don't need it right now, but I can sure use a plate of your grub."

"You're sure you're all right?"

"I'm fine, Chase, really. I just needed to lie

down for a while. Now I'm starving."

His lips split into a delighted smile. "You got it, sweetheart."

Jessie frowned. She wished he wouldn't call her that. She wished he hadn't shown so much concern for her. She didn't know what to make of him anymore.

As she moved to the table and sat down, her eyes remained on Chase. There was no stiffness in his movements, so his back must not have suffered from his exertions during the last few days. Her eyes traveled the breadth of his back, down to his hips, down his long legs, and back up to those lean buttocks. He looked like he was up to anything. Yes, anything . . .

Jessie blushed and looked away. Where had that thought come from? She might be having his baby, but ever since his bragging about being a womanizer, she'd known he didn't really care about her. Therefore, she didn't care about him. Remember that, Jessie, she told herself.

"Is it too hot in here for you?" Chase asked as he set a plate down before her.

Jessie blushed more, knowing he'd noticed the color in her cheeks. "A little," she said testily.

They ate in silence, Chase confused by her abrupt change in mood. He watched her covertly, while she kept her eyes lowered and devoured her food as if she hadn't had a meal in days. She seemed perfectly well, too well, back to her old high-tempered ways. It was hard to recall that she had been pale and sick just a few hours ago. A little sleep must have been all she needed. She'd better take it easy for a day or so, he thought, so there would be no further problem.

This silence continued. Perhaps she was more worried about Bowdre's attempts to ruin her than he realized.

Chase began hesitantly. "You know, Jessie, if you're just going to keep it bottled up and brood about it, it's going to fester."

"What?" She looked at him with wide eyes.

"You know what I'm talking about," Chase said flatly.

"I'm afraid I don't," she hedged.

"Laton Bowdre, of course. The theft of your cattle. It's not the end of the world, you know."

She sighed. "No."

"Well?" Chase prompted after a while.

"There isn't much to say." She shrugged. "I'm simply going to kill the bastard if I ever see him again."

Chase burst out laughing. "No, you're not, Jessie. Come on now, be serious."

"I'm dead serious."

"What will you do, challenge him?"

"Why not?" she countered.

"Because he can decline, and no one will think the worse of him for it. No man would face a woman in a gunfight, not even scum like

Bowdre."

"He's not going to get away with this, Chase. If I had proof, I'd leave it to the sheriff, but without proof, I have to take care of it myself. What else can I do?"

"Let me take care of it."

"You challenge Bowdre?"

"Yes."

"No."

Her flat refusal irritated him. "But he would accept a showdown with me, Jessie."

"I said no! That's not right."

"It's probably all over with, anyway," Chase said. "Bowdre undoubtedly got what your father's note was worth and more when he sold your cattle. He's probably satisfied and long gone from this area."

"I hope not," Jessie replied bitterly.

"Bloodlust never solved anything, Jessie. You're not ruined. Just scratch this loss. Forget it."

"That's easy for you to say, Chase Summers. It's not your life that's threatened. My ranch isn't big enough to absorb this loss. Thomas Blair never meant to be a cattle king. He just wanted to settle on the land where he'd spent his youth, and ranching offered the solution. Our herd was never very big. We lose a good portion of it every winter, anyhow. The blizzard of '66 wiped out seventy percent of our gain, and Thomas went into debt then, too, to replenish the stock. No sooner did he pay that debt off than he got the idea for the grand house. It seems we've always been in debt, selling just enough cattle each year to get by. I can't afford this loss."

Chase felt strangely affected by her speech. He was feeling her pain right along with her. "You know your mother would gladly help you out, Jessie."

"Forget it," she snarled.

After that, he knew he'd be wasting his time making his own offer. But then, you never knew. He had to offer.

"Would you consider taking a loan from me? I won a good sum in Cheyenne, more than I need."

Jessie sat back, shaking her head. "What is it with you, Chase? First you want to fight my battles, now you want to lend me money. Are you feeling *that* guilty over my ruination at your hands? Has Rachel gotten to you?"

She surprised him. She wasn't angry, just confused. Well, no more confused than he was!

"Well, Chase?" she prompted.

He scowled and replied gruffly, "All right. Let's just say I owe you."

"No. Let's be honest and agree you don't," she came back coolly.

Again she managed to surprise him.

"Facts are facts, Jessie. You were a virgin before I touched you."

"Oh, so what!" she cried in exasperation. "If you had forced me, then you would owe me.

But you didn't. Have you forgotten that I wanted you, too?"

Jessie could have bitten her tongue. Furious with herself, she added curtly, "It was purely physical."

"Far be it from me to assume anything else," he said just as curtly.

"You needn't be sarcastic."

"And you don't have to convince me that you feel nothing for me," he retorted coldly. "I am quite aware of that. But you've skirted the issue. You may feel now that the loss of your virginity doesn't matter one bit, but you'll feel differently when you marry someday and have to explain that loss to a husband."

Chase thought he had lost his senses when she burst into laughter, rich, musical laughter.

"I fail to see what's so amusing, Jessie."

"I bet you do," she laughed, barely able to get the words out.

She tried to stifle her laughter. How she would have liked to tell him what she found so ridiculously funny. If she ever did marry, her husband would be accepting her with a child in tow. Her virginity, or lack of it, would hardly be a question!

"I'm sorry," she said, calming herself.

"Not at all," he replied caustically. "Why should I expect you to feel like other girls? I keep forgetting you're not at all like other girls."

Jessie sobered. "I'm not so different."

"No?" he said rudely.

"No. It's just, being raised as I was, I see things in a different light. I see things like . . . how many men go to their wedding beds virgins? If it's acceptable for a man to have lovers before marriage, why can't a woman? As long as I'm faithful afterward, it shouldn't matter."

"Only *you* would think so, Jessie. Men aren't so open-minded."

"Well, then, it just goes to show the difference between the Indian's and the white man's viewpoint. Little Hawk didn't care that I wasn't a virgin."

Chase stiffened, and his eyes turned coal black. "And how did he know that, Jessie? Did you let him find out firsthand?"

Jessie stood up, placed her hands on the table, and leaned forward. "I'm not going to take exception to that." Her blazing eyes belied her words. "Little Hawk was entirely honorable except for one stolen kiss. *He* wanted me for his *wife*, not some passing fancy."

It struck home. Her eyes bored into his. Chase's anger shriveled. He was guilty as charged. He hadn't wanted her for his wife . . . but that didn't mean he didn't want Jessie.

Chase stood up slowly and leaned forward in the same manner as Jessie, their faces only a foot apart now. His voice was a deep whisper. "Do you have any idea how beautiful you are when you get like this?"

Jessie drew back warily. "That's a far way

262

off from the subject we were on."

"True. But when you look like this, I have a hard time thinking of any subject but one."

Jessie could scarcely meet his eyes. His voice was so husky when he got in this disarming mood. And that damned knowing smile of his . . .

She made a frantic dash for the door, but just as she opened it, he slammed it shut. "You don't want to go out there. The cattle are fine, and there's too much snow to get any work done. We'll stay right here." He turned her around and hooked his hands behind her back. "Isn't it nicer in here, and warmer? And you've got nothing better to do than let me love you."

He was kissing her before she could think. She wouldn't let herself feel anything this time — she wouldn't! He was no good, he was . . . he was setting her blood on fire, damn him, just like before. Her muscles relaxed, making her lean into him. Her legs felt useless.

He was doing it to her, making her want him with the feel and touch of his body, the persuasion of his lips. His belly was pressed against her, making hers flutter wildly. The moment she wrapped her arms around his neck, he crushed her to him even closer.

"You'll let me love you, Jessie?"

"Yes."

"All day?"

"Yes."

"And all night?"

"For God's sake, stop talking!" she whispered.

Chase laughed deeply and swept her into his arms. He carried her to the cots and, with his knee, shoved the two together before laying her down. He began to remove his clothes immediately, and Jessie did the same. She couldn't take her eyes away as one article of clothing followed another into a pile on the floor. She found that just the sight of his body had the power to excite her, and her own hands were clumsy because of it. He was done before she was half finished undressing.

Chase leaned over to help her, and impulsively Jessie caught his face between her hands and kissed him, not with passion, but tenderly.

When she released him, Chase was looking at her strangely. That kiss hadn't been a response to his own kisses, but something entirely different. He stood looking at her for a moment, then lay down beside her. They were both naked, and he enjoyed just lying there, bare skin against bare skin.

She was watching him, running her hands over his chest in a delightful way.

"Are you going to act this way with every man who wants you?" His voice was light and teasing, but he wanted to know.

"I haven't so far," Jessie replied.

"Which doesn't mean you won't."

"No, it doesn't."

He looked down at her, his features rapidly

turning solemn. "Jessie . . ."

She caught her fingers in his hair. "Shut up and love me, Chase."

Chapter 34

The next morning, Chase woke before Jessie. The sun was shining, the snow having given up sometime in the night. He didn't feel the slightest urge to get up and face the new day. He leaned on one elbow and stared at Jessie. She slept on her side, facing him, wrapped tightly in her cocoon of blankets. He wished they were in a large single bed so he could get closer to her and share her warmth.

He thought of her illness and wondered if she would be sore today. He supposed he had overdone it. He had made love to her no less than four times in the course of the late day and evening, and even then he didn't feel he'd had enough of her. He had taught her the benefits of patience where loving was concerned and had explored her body to his heart's delight.

She was incredible, ready every time he was ready. And she'd been just as passionate and giving the fourth time as the first.

He wished it had gone right on snowing. He wished like hell they didn't have to leave the cabin.

Jessie moaned softly, and her face screwed up in a frown.

"Jessie?"

She moaned again, and he shook her lightly in case it was a bad dream.

"Don't . . . shake . . . me!" she groaned.

"Wake up, Jessie."

But she didn't want to wake up, not with her stomach awakened to her morning complaint.

"I'm sorry, Jessie," she heard Chase say. "It might help some if you got up and walked the stiffness out of your muscles. The sun's up and shining this morning."

Morning. How early was it? How many dreadful hours did she have yet to contend with this infernal nausea? But even a short time in Chase's presence was too risky. She couldn't let him know she was sick again. He wouldn't understand, not after her perfect health of yesterday afternoon and night. Or he might understand all too well.

"I, ah, don't think I can move right now," Jessie managed.

"You're making me feel guilty as all hell, Jessie. It can't be that bad."

She finally opened her eyes. "It's not that bad," she offered. "I'm just going to lie here for a while yet. But you don't have to wait here. Go on and get to work. That's the privilege of being the boss, you know." She tried to grin. "Giving orders and taking it easy while others do all the work."

Chase didn't buy that for a second, not from Jessie. He got up and dressed, casting worried glances at her all the while. Perhaps she just wanted some time to herself, time to think. He wished she would simply say as much, instead of making him feel like a louse.

After he dressed he got the fire going for her, its warmth quickly filling the small room. But Jessie still hadn't moved.

"I'll head out then," Chase said reluctantly. "But the least I can do is offer some relief before I go. A massage is in order, I think."

"No!"

"Now, come on, Jessie. Quit being so modest. It can only help," he said as he pulled her blankets down and turned her onto her back.

"Don't . . . touch . . . me!"

Chase drew back as if burned and watched her curl slowly back onto her side. She had said exactly the same thing yesterday morning when she'd been so sick. The pale face was the same, too, and the way she kept her arms well away from her stomach.

"Jessie? Jessie, look at me."

"Go on to work, will you?"

He sat down on the side of the cot. She groaned as he did, and groaned worse when he touched her shoulder.

Chase felt so helpless, and his voice rose because of it. "What's wrong with you, damn it? How can you be sick again? You got a good night's sleep. We ate the same thing yesterday, and there's nothing wrong with me. Jessie?"

"I'm not sick." She wouldn't turn to face him. She was as still as a dead thing. "I'm just . . . just too . . . sore."

Chase scowled. What the hell was she trying to hide?

"I'm going to dress you, Jessie, and then I'm taking you to Cheyenne to see the doctor."

"For a little soreness? Don't be ridiculous."

She tried to make her voice light, but there was an unmistakable effort behind each word. He shifted his weight on the bed, and the movement made her face flush with heat. Not now! It's got to stay down! But her body wasn't listening. She felt the bile rising and clamped her hand to her mouth. She turned so quickly then that her legs slammed into Chase's hip. If he hadn't jumped to his feet she would have knocked him over.

Jessie was off the bed in a second and dashing for the tin pail in the corner. He watched her, dazed as she knelt over the pail, retching. Finally he got his thoughts together enough to grab a blanket from the bed and drape it over her shoulders. She was hardly aware of him.

Chase could think of nothing else to do at the moment, so he left the cabin, walking outside to give her some privacy. Jessie, hearing him go, cursed him for not going sooner, before he'd witnessed her illness. Assuming he was gone for the day, she stumbled back to the cot and fell asleep.

Chapter 35

When Jessie woke the second time that day, she stirred hesitantly, then relaxed. It was over. The awful nausea was gone for the day.

Her first thought was of food. Her second was of Chase. Had he gone on to work? Had he gone for a doctor? Oh, Lord, she hoped not. At least he wasn't there, so she had time to think. What could she tell him? That she had an illness that struck only in the mornings, or an allergy?

She sat up and stretched, then stared, unbelieving, at the table across the room.

"I thought . . . you had gone," she said uncomfortably.

"Did you?"

She didn't like his calm reply at all.

"Let's just say I stuck around out of curiosity," he said blandly. "I wanted to see if you would have another miraculous recovery, like yesterday."

Her eyes narrowed. "You could at least be a little sympathetic."

He got up from the table and came to stand by the side of her bed, gazing at her steadily. Jessie grew nervous under the look and couldn't meet his eyes for long.

"You're pregnant."

"I'm not!" She said it much too quickly and reiterated more calmly, "really, I'm not."

"Of course."

He sat down on the bed and drew her blanket away from her. "You've got beautiful breasts," he said casually, touching them gently. "Strange, but they're a lot fuller than they were the last time I touched them."

Jessie slapped his hands away. "Don't be absurd!"

"You're trying my patience, Jessie." He gripped her chin, forcing her to meet his eyes. "I've been around women most of my life. When I was a kid, before my mother married Ewing, half her clientele were pregnant women. It happens to be the only time in a woman's life when she has a legitimate excuse for a new wardrobe. Those women discussed their complaints freely, unaware that I was around. You think I can't figure that's why no one ever sees you in the mornings anymore?"

She shoved his hand aside, furious that he was more knowledgeable about the subject than she had been. "Leave me alone."

"You were going to let me take off without knowing, weren't you?" he continued relentlessly. "You were going to face this all alone?"

"It's my business, not yours."

"It most certainly is my business!"

"Oh, really?" She sat back. "What difference has been made, now that you know? Nothing has changed."

"We're getting married."

"No." She shook her head slowly. "I considered it when I first knew, but that was before I found you in bed with a whore."

"Nothing happened, Jessie. I was drunk."

"I know that. But the intention was there. When I do settle on a man, he will never even look at another woman. The one thing I will not tolerate is unfaithfulness. It would be like — never mind that." She wouldn't think of her parents now. *"You* — you have always had your pick of any woman you wanted. So you'll always be a philanderer."

"Don't sell yourself short, Jessie," Chase said softly. "You'd be quite enough to satisfy me."

She grew flustered under his steady gaze. "This discussion has reached an end."

"This discussion is about my child."

"My child!" she retorted. "I'm the one who's suffering for him. I'm the one who'll bear him. And I'm the one who'll raise him."

"You plan to raise him without a father? I know what that's like, Jessie, and no child of

273

mine is going to be raised that way."

"You have no say in it!"

"We'll see about that!"

They glared at each other for a long, tense moment. Jessie was furious. She hadn't expected him to be so bossy. Chase was just as furious. He realized that Jessie had done everything she could to keep the child's existence from him, and she'd nearly succeeded.

Chase got up abruptly. "Get dressed."

"With pleasure," she replied stonily, but it wasn't until she was fully dressed that she noticed what was missing. "Where's my gun?"

"In my saddlebag."

"What?"

"I have rendered you a woman at the mercy of a man's whims." He said it lightly, but he was deadly serious. "You're coming with me, Jessie, and for once you're powerless to say otherwise."

"Coming with you *where?*" she demanded.

"To Cheyenne. I told you, we're getting married."

"Chase." She kept her voice level, though she wanted to scream. "You can't force me to marry you. You'll only be wasting your time on such a long ride, not to mention my time."

"I don't think so, Jessie. Now, do you walk outside and mount up, or do I carry you?"

Jessie stalked past him and out the door, stiff with anger. But if she'd thought to dash for her horse and take off ahead of him, she had to

274

forget it, for Chase was right behind her. He took charge of Blackstar's reins from the start.

For the first several hours of that long ride to Cheyenne, Jessie simply fumed. But there were many more hours and she gave those to clear thinking. By the time they reached town, she had pretty much made her resolves.

Late though it was, Chase rode directly to the church. They dismounted together, and then Chase drew his gun on her. But Jessie had expected that. She was amused but managed to hide it. It was so ironic. Hadn't she considered getting him to the altar in the same way that night she had decided to marry him? And now here he was, ready to march her up the aisle with a gun in her back.

She stayed silent while he roused the preacher, while he positioned her in front of the altar, while the first words were said. She knew the preacher couldn't see the gun at her back. Her silence continued right up until it was time for her to respond.

Chase gritted his teeth, waiting to hear Jessie speak. But she was being stubborn. He pressed the gun against her spine, not really expecting it to do any good, but as he did, her answer came out clearly and loudly. Chase was so surprised, it took him a moment to make his own responses. They were married in no time, and Jessie even hastily scrawled her name across the marriage certificate before she walked out of the church without waiting for Chase.

He walked after her quickly. "I'm sorry I had to do it that way, Jessie."

"Don't kid yourself," she replied. "We both know you wouldn't have shot me. And you know I wouldn't have gone through with it if I weren't willing. But don't think you've accomplished anything for yourself, Chase Summers. I've let my baby have his legitimacy, that's all. Now you can go your way, off to Spain or wherever you like. I'll stay here. You'll be welcome to visit from time to time, but no more than that. I *won't* live with you — is that clear?"

She didn't wait for him to answer but mounted up and rode toward the hotel. Chase stared after her, a dark frown settling on his features. *We'll just see about that. Damned if we won't.*

Chapter 36

Chase woke to find Jessie dressing in an all-fired hurry. He didn't say anything, only watched her covertly. Her face told him what kind of mood she was in. She probably wasn't pleased to have awakened to find him in bed with her.

He hadn't followed her directly to the hotel, but had gone to the nearest saloon. He didn't recognize anyone there, and he let himself be drawn into a game of 7-up for the distraction it offered. But he was recognized after a while, and in the course of the evening he received a good deal of ribbing over what had happened in Silver Annie's room. He was a celebrity. During the evening, he heard an account of the part Jessie played that night. He was amazed. When he got to the hotel and found that Jessie had registered as Mr. and Mrs. Summers, he was further amazed. But his excitement ended when he got to the room and found some bedding and a pillow thrown on the floor for him. He put the bedding back where it belonged and took his place beside his wife.

"So 'no one messes with what's yours,' eh?"

Jessie swung around to face him, her mouth open in surprise. But she quickly recovered.

"So you heard about that?"

"An amusing tale."

"Don't go getting the wrong idea, Chase," she said airily. "I'd just found out about the baby that day and decided I'd marry you. It wasn't anything . . . personal."

"So that's why you came to the saloon to find me that night?"

"Yes. Of course, finding you the way I did put an end to all thoughts of marriage. But I was still angry that someone had nearly killed you. You *are* my baby's father, after all." She turned away, embarrassed. "I just said what I did to your lady love to make a point, nothing more."

Chase flinched. He should have known better than to bring it up.

"That's too bad," he said softly.

"Why?" She misunderstood. "I happen to think Silver Annie had more to do with your attack than she admitted. She needed a warning of some kind."

"Well, that episode is over and done with, and best forgotten."

Jessie gasped, her turquoise eyes rounding.

"You're kidding, aren't you? You can't mean you don't want to find out who put a knife in your back?"

"Not particularly," Chase replied, grinning at her indignant expression.

Chase had no thought for revenge. He was grateful to his assailant. If not for his wound, Jessie would never have taken him back to the ranch and he would have left Wyoming without knowing about the baby. Remembering that she hadn't intended for him to know, his warm mood fled.

"Were you planning on sneaking out of here this morning without waking me, Jessie?"

"It happens to be afternoon already. We both overslept."

"Answer my question."

"I wasn't going to just leave," she said sullenly.

"I doubt that."

"Doubt all you like, but the fact is I had something to ask you and couldn't very well leave without asking." She stopped, apparently at a loss for words.

"Well, go on. You have my rapt attention."

She hesitated, then blurted out, "I want you to come back to the ranch with me."

"I had planned to."

Her eyes narrowed. "At least until Rachel leaves."

"Ah, yes, I had forgotten all the benefits you will be getting out of this marriage."

279

"You don't have to be sarcastic, Chase."

"Oh? Forgive me if I'm wrong, but I'll wager you just can't wait to inform Rachel of our wedding. I'm right, aren't I?"

"Not this time, you're not. I want *you* to tell her. In fact, I had planned to ride directly back to the range. I don't want to see her at all."

"Not even to say good-bye?"

"I've got no reason to say good-bye to her," she replied stiffly. "I never invited her, and I'm not going to pretend I'm sorry she no longer has an excuse to stay." Her voice turned softly pleading. "Will you tell her for me?"

"And what happens when she finds out I'm expected to be an absentee husband?"

Jessie's eyes darkened. "You don't have to tell her that!"

"Why not? Afraid she might consider it her duty to stick around for a few more years?"

Jessie glared at him. Chase got up slowly and straightened out the clothes he had slept in. He let her stew for a while, his mood greatly improved.

"You know, Jessie, this new situation is really quite amusing."

"If you're considering blackmail, I would hardly call it amusing. That *is* what you're thinking, isn't it?" He grinned, and she snapped, "It would only work until Rachel left!"

"True. But when will she go? Are you going to go home and tell her to pack immediately?"

"If you won't, then I guess I'll have to! What

are you fighting me for, anyway?" she cried in exasperation. "You didn't want to settle down. You may have forced me to marry you, but we both know why. It was quite generous of you, and I do thank you. So why can't you thank me for allowing you the freedom you really want? You have your father to find, remember? Go to Spain, Chase. Find him. You can't do that with a wife in tow."

"Why not? You could come with me, you know, after the baby is born."

"I'll never leave the ranch, Chase."

She wouldn't soften up to save her soul. "Perhaps you haven't realized it yet, but that ranch now belongs to me as well," he said irritably.

Jessie's body stiffened. "What is that supposed to mean?"

"It means, dear, that if I want to stay, I'll stay."

"Suit yourself," Jessie said icily. "But you'll wish you hadn't."

Chapter 37

The ride back to the ranch was a tense, bitter journey, with both Chase and Jessie bristling silently over their stalemate. They reached the valley just before dusk, riding up to the ranch as sullen and uncommunicative as they had been all the way from Cheyenne.

Jessie was and wasn't looking forward to the confrontation with Rachel. She wanted Rachel gone, but she realized it would be the last time she would ever see her mother.

Seeing Rachel waiting by the kitchen door as she came from the stable didn't bolster Jessie's confidence that she could handle this meeting in a calm, unemotional way. She drew on past memories to strengthen her determination, memories of her father sitting at the kitchen table with a whiskey bottle, mumbling about the treachery of whores. Memories of him angrily explaining away the absence of her mother.

Memories of him shouting about finding Rachel with Will Phengle.

Rachel blocked the doorway, looking neat and clean in a flower-sprigged dress. Just once Jessie wanted to see that woman with a little dirt on her face, a little dust on her clothes, a few hairs out of place — anything to make her seem more human.

"Your coming in, does that mean the trouble is over?" Rachel asked as Jessie reached her. "You have the cattle all herded together finally?"

Jessie just kept walking, forcing Rachel to step back so she could enter the kitchen. She stopped at the kitchen table and took off her hat and gloves, dropping them there. She was tense and getting tenser. Thank God she had slept past her nausea that morning. Her stomach couldn't handle so much disturbance in one day.

Rachel was watching her carefully. "Will *he* be leaving now?"

Jessie met her gaze firmly. "The answer to all your questions is no, Rachel."

"Oh. Well. You did say you wouldn't be coming back from the range until everything was settled."

"We'll be going back out tomorrow. Actually, Chase and I just came from Cheyenne."

"Oh?" Rachel's brow knit in concern.

"What?"

"Well, Jeb took Billy out looking for you. You see, I'm sending Billy back to Chicago. I

can't let him continue to neglect his schooling,"
she explained. "But he did so want to say good-
bye to you first. I hope they don't hear you've
gone to Cheyenne and decide to follow you all
the way there!"

"You get anxious over nothing," Jessie said
impatiently. "Jeb has enough sense not to take
the boy that far."

"Take the boy where?" Chase asked, appear-
ing in the doorway.

Rachel wouldn't look his way, so Jessie had
to.

"To town to find me to say good-bye," Jessie
answered as pleasantly as possible. "She's sending Billy away for his schooling."

Chase raised a questioning brow at Jessie.
"You didn't tell her yet then?"

"Tell me what?" Rachel demanded.

"I'll let Jessie have the pleasure, lady," he
said. "I held up coming in here just so she
could. What's the holdup, Jessie? Having trouble finding the words?"

Jessie gave him a withering look.

"We went to Cheyenne yesterday to get
married, Rachel. Chase is my husband."

Rachel looked back and forth between them,
slowly appraising but not the tiniest bit surprised.

"I see," she said at last. She was smiling.
"When you left, Chase, I wondered whether
you'd come to your senses. Oh, well, as long
as it's all worked out." She beamed at them,

delighted.

Jessie was incredulous. "Just what the hell does that mean?"

"Why, that I knew this would happen, of course," Rachel said calmly.

Jessie's eyes flashed. "That's impossible!"

"Is it? Any two people who affect each other the way you two do are destined for each other. I can't tell you how delighted I am that you realized it."

There was a moment of shocked silence. "How can you say that? You turned against him, remember?"

"Yes." Rachel smiled. "And when I did, you defended him. You might call it . . . a bit of strategy."

"I call it a crock!" Jessie snapped. "Strategy!"

Chase chuckled. "Did you really defend me, sweetheart?"

Jessie glared at him furiously, then glared at Rachel. No words would come that could adequately express her anger, so she swung around and left them.

Chase was still amused and grinning when his eyes met Rachel's. "You sure had me fooled, lady. You had Jessie fooled, too. You know that's why her temper's up, don't you? She had you figured for a different reaction altogether."

"I know." Rachel smiled. "I shouldn't have tried trickery with her. It's not that I wasn't upset over what you did to begin with, mind you, Chase Summers."

"Naturally," Chase agreed, solemn-faced.

"But I felt so sure you were right for each other," she went on.

Chase was chagrined. If only she knew the truth about why they were married.

"Don't worry," he offered. "She'll calm down."

"Will she? Before I leave?"

"When are you leaving?"

"I was going to put Billy on the train tomorrow. There's no point in my not going with him now, is there?"

"That soon?"

"Yes. So I'd better talk to Jessica now, before she has a chance to stew too long. I can't leave here with her angry."

"Well, if you're going to talk to her, Rachel, don't you think it's time you cleared the air about some other things as well? It may be the last chance you'll have to make her see your side of the past."

Rachel's smile faded. "I suppose I should try — again. Maybe if she knows I'm leaving, she'll hear me out this time." Rachel didn't wait for Jessie to answer her knock, but opened the door to her room and stepped determinedly inside. One look at Jessie's cold face and she nearly faltered. She had no idea how to begin.

"Ah . . . Kate started a roast, and it's almost

done. Will you be joining us for dinner, Jessica?"

"No."

"I wish you would reconsider," Rachel said evenly. "It will be the last time we can dine as a family. I will be leaving with Billy in the morning."

There was a pause. "I never considered us a *family,* Rachel. And I can't say I'm sorry you're going. You won't mind if I'm not around to see you off? I do have work to do, you know."

Rachel felt the sting of those words like a slap. She wanted to run, but she couldn't leave like that. She knew she would never forgive herself if she didn't make a full effort this one last time.

"Why would you never listen to my side of it?" Rachel said abruptly.

Jessie turned away and stared out the window. "Why? So you could malign Thomas and make him out to be a liar? He was a hard man to love, even to like, but he was all I had. If I thought the hell of these last ten years had been for nothing, I would dig up his grave and put a few more bullets into his carcass. But when a man tells the same story, drunk or sober, it usually tends to be the truth."

"The truth *as he believes it,* yes. But what if the truth as he saw it wasn't the truth at all?"

Jessie turned around slowly. Her eyes were as hard as turquoise stones. "All right. You've been dying to say it ever since you got here, so say it and then get out."

"I was never unfaithful to your father, Jessica."

"Of course. And next you'll be telling me Billy is Thomas Blair's son."

"He is."

The words were barely audible, but Jessie heard them.

"Damn you, if that's the truth, why didn't you tell him before you left? You know that all he ever wanted was a son!"

"It was too late to tell him anything, even if I could have."

"A nice try, Rachel," Jessie sneered. "I'm not buying it. He saw you with his own eyes in bed with Will Phengle — in your bed. He'd been gone a month, a month you no doubt took advantage of to be with your lover the whole time. If Billy is anyone's son, he's Phengle's."

"My God!" Rachel turned quite pale. She sat down on Jessie's bed. "That night . . . Thomas mentioned Will, but he never said exactly what set him off into such a blind rage. In my own bed!"

"That's good, Rachel," Jessie said dryly. "That's really excellent. You have truly missed your calling."

Jessie's sarcasm sparked Rachel's usually placid temper. "If your father saw Will Phengle making love to a woman in my bed, then that woman had to be Kate, because it wasn't me, Jessica. I wasn't at the ranch that whole day."

She stopped, then went on. "A homesteader had come by to ask for my help that morning because his wife was in labor. The wife and baby both died. I came home that night sick with exhaustion and anxiety. You had been a difficult birth, you see, and I knew I was pregnant again. There was no doctor even remotely near here, not back then."

"It was a miracle Thomas didn't kill Billy, he beat me so badly the moment I walked into the house. He never gave me a chance to say *anything*, Jessica, *anything*. After he was finished, I couldn't speak. My jaw was broken, and I was barely conscious.

"Ask Kate. She was the only other woman here, Jessica, so it had to be her with Will. Ask her."

Jessie said nothing. Her expression didn't change, and when she finally spoke her voice was hard. "You've had ten years to perfect that story. Who's here to deny it? Phengle isn't. Thomas isn't. Kate will naturally deny it, but she's just an Indian, and who would believe her over you, right?"

"Ask her, Jessica," Rachel pleaded quietly.

"I wouldn't demean her by asking her such a thing. My God, do you realize what you're implying?" Jessie's voice rose. "You're saying Kate held her tongue all these years, that she never stepped forward to right a terrible wrong! Why would she keep silent? What for? This place was hell with Thomas's hate. There was never any warmth here. Why would she let that go on?"

"I don't know why, Jessica, but she did."

"No!"

Jessie turned away again. Rachel sat there unmoving. "And what if I'm speaking the truth, Jessica?" she whispered before she got up to leave. "Does that make me a villain — or a victim? You think about it."

Chapter 38

"Mother, I can't find the Indian feathers Jeb gave me last night!"

Rachel shook her head. She looked sideways at Chase, then at her overflowing trunk open on the bed. She sighed. The morning had been more hectic than she had dreamed it could be.

"Would you mind closing this up for me and bringing it out to the porch? I imagine that son of mine will discover a few other missing items before we get his trunk closed. If we don't leave soon, we'll end up spending the night in Cheyenne. I'd rather not."

Chase nodded without saying anything. He knew Rachel was putting up a good front. She had told him about her conversation with Jessie. He knew the lady had to be hurting.

And Jessie? Was she really so heartless, or was she certain Rachel was lying? He had gone to question Kate himself when he'd heard the whole story, but the Indian woman could not be found. There had been no breakfast ready that morning, either. Was Kate gone for good? Didn't that prove anything?

Chase sighed and set about closing Rachel's large trunk. Would Jessie be around for a last good-bye? Billy worshiped her. It would break his heart if she didn't show up.

The trunk wouldn't close even after the third try, and Chase swore as he threw it open to find the obstruction. A slim book that had fallen out of the lining in the top of the trunk now stood on end to keep it from closing. Was that the problem? Chase tossed it back in and tried once again to get the damn thing closed. Why women had to travel with so many clothes was a mystery to him. It was just as well Jessie was determined not to travel with him, he grumbled to himself. He couldn't see himself going through this trunk-closing business every time they went someplace. Now, if he were rich and had servants to handle such things — oh, hell.

The trunk still wouldn't close. That book again. He hadn't tossed it far enough into the center. A corner was sticking out of the trunk. He tried shoving it in without opening the lid all the way, but the clothes were too tightly packed. He was tempted to take the book out and let Rachel have a fine time wondering what had happened to it when she got to Chicago.

Chase looked back at the door to be sure he wouldn't be caught in the act, dropped the book on the floor, and was about to kick it under the bed when the word *journal* caught his eye. He stared hard at it for several seconds. He couldn't. Not a journal. That was something Rachel couldn't replace. He'd thought it was a novel. Funny, but he wouldn't have figured Rachel for the kind of woman to keep a diary, not Rachel.

Chase closed the trunk at last and carried it out to the front porch, where Jeb was waiting with a wagon.

"Any more like this one coming?" Jeb grumbled as he shoved the trunk onto the back of the wagon.

Chase grinned. "I doubt Billy's will be quite so heavy. You be sure and get someone to help you unload them when you get to town."

"Humph. Show-off is what you are. As if I could heft that thing by myself! If that woman don't get a move on, it'll be night 'fore we get there."

"Have you seen Jessie by any chance?" Chase asked him.

"Are you blind, young feller? You just passed her in that fancy parlor."

Chase whirled around, delighted for Rachel and Billy's sake that Jessie was going to put in an appearance.

Halfway through the door, Chase stopped short. The girl sitting demurely in a chair by the crackling fire was only barely recognizable. It was Jessie all right, but a Jessie he'd never thought he'd see. She wore a dress of rose velvet and lace. Her hair was swept off her neck and entwined with white ribbons, striking against her rich jet tresses. He was speechless. She was the most beautiful woman he had ever seen.

Rachel entered the room just then with Billy. Both were stunned.

"Boy, oh boy!" Billy grinned from ear to ear. "You would put all the girls back East to shame, Jessie." He rushed over to Jessie, and she stood up. His arms slipped around her waist. Jessie wanted to pull Billy closer and squeeze him like she'd never squeezed anyone before, but she was looking at Rachel over Billy's head, and her arms wouldn't move. She felt choked. She shouldn't have come. She should have stayed shut up in her room till they were gone.

Billy didn't even notice that she wasn't returning his embrace. "I'm going to miss you something awful, Jessie. Can I come to see you again?"

A sound escaped her, but no one heard except Billy. She bent down and whispered, "If you don't I'll never forgive you, kid."

Her lips grazed his cheek as she straightened up. Billy stepped back with a beaming smile and let out a whoop of delight before he ran out of the parlor, nearly knocking Chase over.

Rachel came forward, hopeful. "Jessica, I —"

"Good-bye, Rachel."

Jessie's features were set. She had lost control, but now that Billy was out of the room, she had her control back.

Rachel let her eyes travel over this daughter who was lovelier than she ever dreamed she would be, and so entirely removed from her.

"Thank you for that," Rachel said, indicating Jessie's dress.

Jessie only nodded before she turned away.

Rachel stared at her unyielding back for several seconds. "Whatever else you may believe, Jessica, I love you."

The sound of Rachel's footsteps crossing the room, the closing of the door, reverberated in her head. Breathing was difficult. She groped for the edge of the chair, and when she found it, eased herself down. Jeb was shouting at the wagon team, and the wagon was rolling out of the yard. She could still hear it, still hear it, still hear it . . . she heard it no more.

"You're something else, Jessie."

How long had he been there? How long had she been sitting there since the wagon left?

"What?"

"You heard me," Chase said as he came forward to stand next to her. "You can show the kid you care, when you don't even believe he's your brother, but not your mother — your own mother!"

"Because I don't care," Jessie said softly.

"Liar!"

She shot out of the chair, but he caught her arm, pulling her back to face him. "You can't stand it that you're wrong, that you've been wrong all these years."

"You don't know anything."

"Don't I? Kate is gone, you know. Or didn't you know?"

"Gone?" Jessie repeated.

"It kind of confirms what Rachel said, doesn't it? Kate probably heard you shouting at your mother last night about her."

"What if she did?" Jessie retorted. "That doesn't mean she's left. She's around somewhere."

Chase forced himself not to shout at her. He dragged her to the sofa and shoved her down onto it.

"Stay put," he commanded sharply. "I've got something I want you to see."

He was back in a moment, and tossed a slim book down beside her on the sofa.

"I have no idea what's in that," Chase said. "I took it out of your mother's trunk after she left the room, and I forgot to give it to her. It may just be nonsense — or it may not. Look through it, Jessie. See for yourself what a woman like Rachel would have to write about."

Chase walked out of the room, leaving Jessie alone. She picked up the book, then angrily tossed it away. She didn't care. It would be nothing but lies, anyway. No, Rachel wouldn't write lies, not to herself, not in a diary. The book was meant for her eyes only.

Jessie stared at the book, then quickly picked it up.

Dec. 12, 1863. I never dreamed my fingers would heal as well as they did. When Dr. Harrison suggested writing as an exercise for them, I laughed. I have no one to write to. It was good to find I could still laugh, though. My jaw doesn't hurt anymore. And Dr. Harrison assures me that since my pregnancy was only two months along, the baby shouldn't be affected. I won't believe that until I feel it kicking.

Dec. 13, 1863. I still can't write about what happened at the Rocky Valley. I don't think I ever will be able to. Dr. Harrison said a journal was an excellent idea, and he thinks I should write about what Thomas did to me. I can't.

Dec. 23, 1863. I have forgotten what it's like to have a full belly. I never should have left Dr. Harrison's care and moved on with the little money he gave me. God bless him for trusting me to pay him somehow. But I can't find work. My body is still too tender for hard labor.

Dec. 27, 1863. I got a job finally. I'm in a little town I'd never even heard of. It was as far as Dr. Harrison's money would take me. Waiting on tables would be a lot easier if the hours weren't so long. With every penny I can save, it will still be another three weeks before I have enough to get me to Jessica.

Dec. 30, 1863. How can I write about this? But why not? What is being raped by a drunken old man compared to being beaten nearly to death by the man I love? This man was one of the customers, at least I think he was. He was waiting for me outside the restaurant. Thank God it was over so quickly. Am I becoming immune to pain?

Jan. 18, 1864. It is taking longer to leave here than I'd anticipated. The baby's first kick startled me so that I dropped a stack of dishes. I have to pay for them. But the baby kicked! Thank God Thomas didn't kill his son!

Jan. 26, 1864. God help me, but I'm beginning to hate Thomas. It wasn't enough that he beat me and kicked me out for no reason, not caring whether I lived or died. But now he's taken Jessica from me. The only thing waiting for me at her school was a letter from Thomas that he's divorcing me and he'll kill me if I try to see Jessica, ever. He took her out of school more than three months ago. Jeb must have told him I survived the beating. He would have left Jessica in school otherwise. What can I do now?

Feb. 8, 1864. I think Jonathan Ewing may have saved my life. I've never met such a kind man. With no work available for a woman in my condition, I had resorted to begging. Thomas had made sure that the few friends I had left would not help me. What happened to the man I loved? Will I ever understand why Thomas turned against me? Did he lose his mind?

Jessie ran from the room with the journal clasped to her breast.

Chapter 39

The Union Pacific was late. Otherwise, Rachel and Billy would have missed the train. Their trunks were loaded, and boarding had begun. Rachel was waiting on the platform while Billy had a few last words with Jeb. She was trying not to think about leaving the ranch, leaving the Rocky Valley again.

"Mother!"

Rachel froze. That wasn't Billy's voice. She saw the Appaloosa halting at the end of the platform, and recognized the rider. Jessie sat on her horse and stared at Rachel for a moment before jumping down from Blackstar.

She was aware of nothing around her except Rachel, getting to Rachel as fast as she could. She ran. There was a whirlwind of emotion running through her.

Rachel held her breath as her daughter came toward her. Jessie's eyes reflected feelings she had never seen in them — misery, desperation. She saw the book Jessie was holding out to her, and she flushed hotly with the realization of what she'd read. What did it mean for Jessie to be there with it? That silly book had accomplished what nothing else could!

"Jessica?" Rachel held out a hand tentatively, but the moment their fingers touched, Jessie's control shattered, and she threw herself into Rachel's arms. "Mother! Oh, Mother, I'm so sorry! I've been so cruel to you," Jessie cried. "But I couldn't let you see that I love you, that I've always loved you."

"I know, dearest. It doesn't matter now." Rachel could barely get the words out, she was so choked. "Oh, Jessica, don't cry."

"When I think of what I put you through, what Thomas did, oh, Mother, you've been so wronged!"

"Jessica — Jessie, look at me." Rachel clasped her face in her hands. "Dearest, none of it was your fault. And none of it matters now that I have you back."

Jessie looked into her mother's eyes. She cried all the harder. "Hold me, Mother. If you only knew how often I have dreamed of being held in your arms again."

The train whistle blew. Rachel stiffened. Jessie looked up, panic in her face.

"You can't go now — not now!"

Rachel smiled gently. "Our trunks are already on board."

"Then we'll take them off!"

Rachel laughed at the stubborn note that came so quickly to her daughter. "Dearest, you need some time alone with your new husband."

"Damn, don't use that excuse. You wouldn't be leaving if I hadn't married him."

"But you did."

"I'll divorce him!"

"No, you won't, Jessica. Your baby needs him, even if you think you don't."

Jessie lowered her eyes, her cheeks reddening. "He told you about that, I suppose?"

"Yes."

"Well, I still don't need time alone with him."

"Yes, you do. All newlyweds need time to themselves. But I'll be back as soon as I get Billy settled in school and attend to some business matters I've neglected. It won't be long, Jessica. All right?"

"You promise to come back, Mother?"

There was such pleading in Jessie's voice that Rachel nearly decided to stay. But she felt strongly about not intruding on the first weeks of the new marriage. Chase and Jessie needed time. All was not happy between them.

"I promise to come back. But I want you to promise you'll give Chase a chance. He's a good man."

Jessie sighed. "We can talk about that when you come back."

Rachel grinned. "Stubborn to the end, my

darling."

Jessie handed Rachel the diary.

"You didn't read all of it, did you?" Rachel asked, remembering the heartache she had poured into it recently.

"No, but I'd like to."

Rachel patted Jessie's cheek, then gathered her in her arms again for a last hug. "I don't think either of us needs to read this book again."

"I love you, Mother."

"Oh, Jessica, I've waited so long to hear you say that." The tears began again. "I love you, too, and I'll be back soon, darling."

Long after the train was out of sight, Jessie stood on the empty platform. Jeb had wandered off to the saloon once he saw Jessie and Rachel embrace. He knew Jessie would need to be alone awhile.

Chase found Jessie at the depot later. "She's gone?" he asked hesitantly.

Jessie wouldn't look at him. "Yes." She continued to stare down the empty track.

"Why the long face?" He asked hesitantly.

Jessie raised her eyes slowly. "She wouldn't stay — because of you."

"Now just a damn minute, Jessie. How did I get into this?"

"She thought I should be alone with you."

"Oh, well." Chase grinned. "The idea has merit."

"It does not!" Jessie retorted before she swung around and headed for Blackstar.

Chase followed quickly. "Where are you going?"

"Home."

"You can't, Jessie. It's too late to ride all that way."

"I can ride by moonlight."

"You'll freeze," he pointed out.

"I'll be riding too fast to feel the cold."

He grabbed her shoulder. "What's your hurry? You've never ridden home at night before."

"I want familiar surroundings. I want to sleep in my own bed, in my own room, with my own things around me." She shook away, angry that she had said that much. She was feeling bereft, as if she had lost her mother all over again. "I'm not asking you to ride with me if that's what you're worried about. You can ride back with Jeb in the morning."

Without waiting for him to answer, she mounted and rode off without looking back.

Chapter 40

Jessie didn't know what first alerted her to the other three riders. They were too far away for their horses to be heard, but she sensed them somehow. A little later, she saw them. The hairs on the back of her neck tingled as she realized how close she was to home and that the three riders were racing away from her ranch.

It was the fact that they weren't on the main track to town that worried Jessie, as if they didn't want to run into anyone. She didn't think twice about veering Blackstar off the path to follow them. She didn't stop to wonder if Chase would miss her, either. He had been following pretty far behind her nearly all the way. She knew he was there, but she didn't care. This was Jessica Blair's business, and she would see to her own interests without any help from an interfering husband.

With her urgency affecting Blackstar, Jessie

closed the distance between her and the three riders in no time at all. They heard her. The first shot whistled past her ear and brought her own gun to hand. She got off two returning shots, still galloping furiously, before Blackstar's reins slipped out of her other hand and she had to fight like mad to get the reins back. The men fired another shot at her, but they were running for their lives by then, and the aim was wild.

Jessie continued the chase undaunted. She saw who they were. The moonlight was bright enough for that. She was so furious, she wasn't going to stop until she had all three dead in the dust at her feet. Thank God she had changed out of her dress and was wearing her gun. But then there was a horse behind her, and Chase was yanking her reins away.

"Are you crazy?" she shouted at him. "They're getting away!"

"I don't fancy seeing my wife with a broken neck," he said as he pulled Blackstar to a stop. "You know you can't race across terrain like this at night. Think of your horse if not yourself."

He was right. A hole in the ground could kill a man as easily as a bullet, because it left his horse with a broken leg. But that didn't lessen her fury. She was watching her quarry get farther and farther away.

"Damn you! It's too late now!" she screamed at Chase.

"Tell me what happened, Jessie."

"They shot at me. I shot back."

"And?"

She shrugged. "I probably wounded what I aimed at."

"Jessie, who —?"

"Bowdre's hirelings. I saw them riding away from the ranch. By the time I got close enough to recognize them, they were shooting at me."

"Clee and Charlie? Was Bowdre the third man?"

"I wish it were Bowdre, but it was Blue Parker! That no-good bastard!"

"Are you sure?"

"He looked right at me before he dug his spurs into his horse. I've known him too long to mistake him for someone else."

"So Parker really has thrown in with them," Chase said thoughtfully. "They must have offered him a lot of money."

"It's more likely spite. He was interested in me, wanted to marry me," she explained. "After you came, he thought I was avoiding him because of you. He didn't know I'd left the ranch those two times to go north. When I ran into him one day, he accused me of throwing him over for you. I told him it wasn't true, but he didn't believe me. He's just like my father, a man who feels he's got to avenge himself for any wrong."

"What do you think they were up to?" Chase asked.

Jessie caught her breath. Her anger had overcome her fears.

"Let's get to the ranch," she cried, turning

Blackstar around. "I'm almost afraid to guess what they've done."

Baldy found them just as they got back to the trail leading to the valley. He had been on his way to town to look for them. When he finished talking, Jessie felt numb. She had thought herding the cattle together had been the answer, but all she had done was make it easy for them to be shot. Nearly half the herd lay dead or dying around the campsite. Ramsey was still unconscious from a blow to the head, and the rest of the herd had been stampeded right toward the poisoned waterhole. Baldy had gotten back to camp in time to see the three men riding off and to assess the damage. A man who had worked with cattle all his life, he was in tears from the waste he had seen.

No sooner had Baldy finished talking than Jessie saw the orange glow over the rise that shielded the valley. Chase saw it a second later. A deep animal sound escaped from Jessie. She spurred Blackstar on, and Chase followed, afraid.

Jessie rode no farther than the top of the rise that looked down on the ranch house. The glow from the fire lit her face, revealing such a depth of anguish it tore Chase's heart.

Every building on the ranch was consumed by flames.

Chapter 41

Two weeks had come and gone since the fire, two weeks Jessie couldn't remember. She was in Chicago at her mother's mansion. She didn't remember anything of the trip there, didn't remember anything at all.

But Jessie was no longer sleepwalking. She swung around to face her mother, her eyes alive for the first time in two weeks. "How dare he leave me? I'm not an old piece of baggage he can throw away and forget about!"

"Jessica, you haven't been listening," Rachel said calmly.

Jessie continued to pace the richly carpeted floor of her mother's room. "I've been listening. I couldn't believe it when I woke today and it dawned on me what you'd told me yesterday. It *was* yesterday, wasn't it?" She didn't wait for an answer. "Well, I won't stand for it. He can't just dump me on your doorstep.

I'm his responsibility, not yours."

"In the first place, Jessica, Chase didn't dump you here. You've been here a week, and he's been by your side night and day. In the second place, he's not deserting you. He'll be back before the baby is born, I'm sure."

"I don't believe it. He won't come back. He'll find his father and decide to stay in Spain. Why should he come back? He didn't want to marry me. He only did it so the baby wouldn't be a bastard."

"There were other reasons, Jessica, and you know it."

"Then why isn't he here? How could he leave me the way I was?"

"You didn't even know he was here, darling," Rachel explained gently. "You have only responded to me, to my voice, in all this time. You weren't aware of anything. And there was no telling how long you would be that way. Your apathy could have gone on for months, but you were in no danger. So since Chase couldn't do anything for you, anyway, he thought it best to get the trip to Spain over with now. Why, if he hadn't left, you would probably still be living in your cocoon. Hearing that he left is what brought you out of that state."

"That is beside the point," Jessie said stubbornly. "He has still left me here for you to support. Now that I have nothing — nothing of my own." She choked up for a moment, but then her eyes lit up again. "That's why he left me! Because I'm penniless! He won't get away with it!''

"Honestly, Jessica, you're not being at all sensible. Chase didn't marry you for your money. And you're certainly no burden to me. Frankly, I'm delighted you'll be with me during your pregnancy. I'll be able to help you. Would you deny me this chance to mother you?''

"I don't need mothering, Mother.'' Jessie smiled. "I'm glad to see it's taken me less time to call you Mother again than —'' She wouldn't get into that. "Understand, it's not that I wouldn't like to stay here with you. I'd like nothing better. It's just that I can't be dependent on you. Chase isn't going to return.''

"You don't know that,'' Rachel insisted.

"Yes, I do. You see, I made it clear when we married that I wouldn't live with him. I had the ranch then. I felt . . . I didn't want . . . he's a philanderer, Mother,'' she blurted out angrily. "I knew I couldn't live with that. If he was going to have other women, I felt it would be better if he did his whoring far away from me, where I wouldn't know about it.''

"I see,'' Rachel said quietly.

"Do you?'' Jessie asked hopefully. "Then you can understand why I have to go after him.''

"Wait a minute, Jessica.'' Rachel became alarmed. "Go after him?''

"I have to,'' Jessie said firmly. "He knows everything has changed for me since I told him

311

he could live his own life. He knows I can't support myself, not yet, anyway. If he could force me to marry him, then he can damn well take care of me now that I need him."

"Is that the only reason you want to follow him, Jessica?" Rachel asked softly.

"Of course," Jessie said plainly. "What other reason could there be?"

"Because you love him."

Because you love him. The words haunted Jessie on the train ride to New York, on the terrifying nights she spent cramped in the small cabin of the ship, on the even more frightening journey alone across Spain's foreign landscape. Those words gave her no comfort. They caused her nothing but despair. She couldn't love a man like Chase Summers, a man she couldn't trust, a man who didn't feel anything remotely resembling love. She couldn't.

She wouldn't think about it. She pushed the words away with thoughts, remembering how her mother had conceded at last and insisted on paying all the expenses of the trip, the frantic time they had had packing all the clothes Rachel had ordered made for her, the tearful farewell and admonishments that she was to return immediately if she couldn't find Chase in New York before he sailed. But he had sailed the morning she arrived, and she hadn't returned. She had bought passage on the next available ship, frightened, yet determined.

But all the books she had read and all the stories she had heard had not prepared her for the awesomeness of the ocean and travel across it. When she wasn't frightened out of her wits, she was bored. She spent many of the endlessly lonely hours examining her vague memories of the two weeks after the fire.

There was scant recollection of a room unfamiliar to her and Chase bringing Kate before her. It seemed more like a dream, hearing Kate beg forgiveness for never telling Thomas it was she he had found with Will Phengle, hearing her confess to loving Thomas all those years, being his mistress for the year after Rachel was gone, being discarded for another because she hadn't been able to give him the son he wanted. Kate had still loved Thomas, even after that. She had kept silent about Rachel in terror of what Thomas would do to her if he learned the truth. That was one excuse. In the end, she admitted, she hadn't confessed because Thomas might have brought Rachel back.

Jessie didn't know what she'd said to Kate, if anything. She couldn't even be sure she hadn't dreamed it all. It was something she would have to ask Chase about, among other things. There was something he had told her about Jeb, and something about Rachel having paid off her debt at the bank, and something about his making arrangements with the sheriff. But none of it was clear.

Arriving in Cádiz, with her feet on firm

ground again, she felt more like her old self. It was not difficult to find out that Chase's ship had not docked there. It was not even difficult to learn that there was a rich man by the name of Carlos Silvela who lived near Ronda. In fact, information of any kind was easily obtainable, for Jessie found the Spaniards almost aggressively hospitable, willing always to go out of their way to help a stranger. It made her glad, because the more she saw of Spain, the more alien she felt. The newly settled Wyoming territory had not prepared her for a country alive with history. Cádiz in fact claimed to be the oldest continuously inhabited settlement in western Europe. Jessie was perhaps more amazed by her first glimpse of palm trees.

After a day in the southern port, Jessie faced a dilemma. She couldn't just wait there for Chase, for his ship might dock anywhere along the busy seacoast, not necessarily at Cádiz.

There really was no choice. The odds were that Chase would find his way to Ronda and the Silvela family there, so she made arrangements for the trip. She was awed by the splendid land with its castles and ancient churches and magnificent scenery. The winding roads were bumpy, and the coach she hired old and creaky, but Jessie was thrilled by the journey.

She was still wondering what to say to the family when she arrived just after dark, three days later, at the huge white house of the Silvela estate, on the outskirts of Ronda. If Chase hadn't gotten there, how would she explain herself? The maid who answered the door was courteous but not helpful. To Jessie's relief, a young man came to the door, dismissing the servant. He was of medium height, with blond hair cut short, and golden eyes so sensuous that Jessie caught her breath as they looked her over with obvious interest.

"May I be of service, *señorita?*"

"It is Señora Jessica Summers, and yes, you may indeed be of service. I have come from Cádiz — actually, all the way from America — to find Carlos Silvela."

The man's golden eyes turned quite curious. "You come from America and speak Spanish very well, yet your skin is so fair —"

"I am not Spanish." Jessie realized his confusion and explained, "I learned the language as part of my schooling. English is my first language."

"Ah, I see."

"About Señor Silvela?" she asked, wondering how long she must stand in the doorway.

"Forgive me," the man said. "What must you think of me, to keep you standing like this?"

"That's quite all right," Jessie said politely.

"You are as gracious as you are beautiful, *señora*. However, my Uncle Carlos is not allowed visitors. He is quite ill, you see."

"He is not dying, is he?" Jessie knew that was rude, but how would Chase feel if he never

315

got to see him?

The man lingered in the large foyer, wondering what to do with her. "It is a shame you have come at this time, and such a long way. Perhaps I can be of help to you. My uncle . . . cannot see anyone."

Jessie was thinking wildly. What was she to do? If she couldn't see him, how could she find out if he was the right man?

"California!" Jessie blurted. "Do you know if your uncle was there, many years ago?"

"I believe so, before the family sold the land we owned there. But that was so long ago, about twenty-four years. You do not seem old enough —"

"No, Señor Silvela, I did not mean to imply that I knew your uncle."

"Ah, I see my manners are lacking again, *señora*. I have not introduced myself. I am Rodrigo Suárez. Uncle Carlos has only sisters, my mother one of them. He is the only Silvela left."

"He . . . has no children?"

He did not seem to mind the personal question. "There was a daughter, but she died in infancy. His wife could have no other children. But he did not divorce her, or even marry again after she died."

"He must have loved her very much."

Rodrigo smiled. "Who is to say? He seemed more disinterested than devoted. But it is more romantic to think he loved her, yes."

His smile deepened. Jessie got the impression that he was a romantic, a man in love with love. He was a charmer, too. But she was embarrassed to have touched on this intimate subject, and it showed in her hesitant manner. She lowered her eyes.

"Rodrigo, do you intend to keep me waiting all evening?" They both turned as the young woman appeared from one of the side rooms off the foyer. "We have a game to finish — but who is this?"

"I am not at all certain, Nita," Rodrigo replied, smiling. "She has come from America and believes she has business with Uncle Carlos."

Jessie's guard went up as the somberly clad Nita narrowed dark brown eyes at her. She was not much older than Jessie, and incredibly lovely, even in mourning clothes. Her dark blonde hair was severely knotted at her neck. The bones of her face were sharp, her features aristocratic. She was very beautiful. And most disdainful.

"An American friend? A relation?" Nita sneered. "A bastard daughter perhaps, hoping to claim part of my inheritance?"

Jessie's temper flared. "No, wife to a bastard son," she said coldly. Well, there it was, out in the open.

Nita turned ashen. "You lie, *señora,*" Nita hissed. "Uncle Carlos has no son. Where is he, this son? Why are you here? I will tell you why. Because you are a fortune hunter. You hope to delude a sick man into thinking he has a son. You hope to trick him."

"I don't —" Jessie began, but Nita said, "Throw her out, Rodrigo!"

"Nita, please," Rodrigo intervened. "If what she says is true —"

"Exactly," Jessie cut in pleasantly. "You wouldn't want your uncle to know you had not been hospitable to his daughter-in-law, especially when I happen to be expecting his first grandchild. Would you? Of course not. So why don't you run along, Nita, and see about a room for me."

"Vaya Ud. al paseo!" Nita hissed. She stalked down the hall.

"Well, I have no intention of going *there.*" Jessie grinned at the embarrassed Rodrigo.

His smile disarmed her, it so reminded her of Chase's smile.

"Oh, *señor,* so you know and don't send him away, my husband's name is Chase Summers. He should show up any day now."

Chapter 42

The weather in mid-January was extremely pleasant. The atmosphere in the Silvela household was not. For three days Jessie tried to see Don Carlos, but he was never left alone, and each time she tried to enter his room, she was ushered right back out.

It gave her no peace to realize that the man could die at any time. So wouldn't he want to know he had a son? Wouldn't that give him some pleasure? Chase would never forgive her if Don Carlos died without knowing he had a son, not when she was right here in the house with him. There was no telling when Chase would get there, so there was no point in waiting for him before talking to Don Carlos.

Jessie quickly learned quite a bit about Don Carlos's family. Emilia, the little maid Rodrigo had sent to tend her, was a veritable fountain of information. Jessie learned why Nita was so furious at her arrival and her announcement about Don Carlos's son. The girl's parents had died penniless, and Don Carlos was her only provider. She had been living under his roof for two years, refusing to marry so that she could take care of him. Quite noble, if her motives weren't so obvious.

Rodrigo on the other hand was there out of genuine concern for his uncle. He was wealthy in his own right, his mother having married much more wisely than her sister. She was a social butterfly, traveling through Europe just then. News of her brother's condition had not reached her yet.

It was disquieting to learn that Don Carlos's health had been failing him for many years. He had always been an active man, but a bad case of pneumonia had left him so weak as to turn him nearly sedentary. That had led to other ailments.

Her third night in that strange household, Jessie waited until she heard Nita leave Don Carlos's room and Rodrigo take her place. She left her own spacious room and tiptoed down the hall. It was early. There was plenty of time before ten o'clock, the ridiculous hour when dinner was served. She had yet to adjust to the unusual eating hours caused by the three-hour *siestas* in the afternoon that the whole country observed.

No sound came from Don Carlos's room. The old man was probably sleeping, with Rodrigo sitting by his bedside. The last time she had tried to get in, a harridan of a servant had been there, and Jessie had been unable to get a word in, the old woman rattling off a stream of "hushes" and "be quiets."

She could only hope Rodrigo was alone. She could handle Rodrigo. She had found that out her first day.

The door opened silently and Jessie had moved to the foot of the great four-poster bed before Rodrigo, standing at the window overlooking the courtyard, turned and saw her. The bed was curtained with fine gossamer, but there was only one light, across the room, and it was impossible to see inside the curtains.

"Why do you keep him smothered like that? Has he something contagious?"

"Of course not," Rodrigo whispered, coming forward. "His doctor recommends no disturbance, and we follow his instructions."

"But the man should have air and light. He shouldn't be enshrouded like that."

"I would agree, but I am not a medical man, and I cannot say what is best for my uncle."

"Common sense — oh, never mind," Jessie said irritably. She hated feeling like an intruder, but she was an intruder.

"You must leave, Jessica," Rodrigo said gently but firmly.

Jessie's brows narrowed. "He hasn't been told about me, has he? Was that the doctor's idea, too, or Nita's?"

"You are being unfair. Can you not see how upsetting it would be for him to think about something that may not be true?"

"Your uncle would know the truth."

"But have you considered that the shock could kill him?" asked Rodrigo.

"I'm sorry," Jessie conceded, "but I believe it's worth the risk."

"Rodrigo, who is that you have with you?"

Jessie started at the soft voice. Rodrigo gave her silent warning with his eyes.

"There is no one, Uncle." His voice was no longer a whisper.

"Lying to me, my boy?" the voice scolded. "My eyes have not failed me. I can see out of this mausoleum even if you can't see in."

"I only meant to save you disturbance, Uncle," Rodrigo said contritely. "You need your rest."

"I rest entirely too much. What I need is diversion. Now, who is this?"

Long, tapered fingers drew back the thin curtain, and Jessie gasped. "You're so young!"

"Not as young as I used to be, my dear."

"But I had another image of you," she blurted without thinking. "Gray-haired, wrinkled . . . damn, I didn't mean —"

Don Carlos chuckled. "What a delight you are, young woman. Come closer so I can see if you are as pretty as you appear. My eyes may not be failing me, but the light in here is deplorable."

Jessie moved to the side of the bed, amazement growing. She had not once considered that resemblance would bear out the truth, but it did. The man lying in the enormous bed was so like Chase it was uncanny. Older of course, but not nearly as old as she had thought. It had not occurred to her that he could have been so young when he knew Mary. He was only forty-six or -seven now, gaunt and pale and quite underweight, but that did not hide the fact that he was much too young to be dying. His hair was as black as her own, with only a single thin streak of gray running above his forehead. His eyes were dark and inquisitive. His lips turned up at her perusal, just the same way Chase's always did.

"You seem even more surprised by my appearance than you were before," Don Carlos said.

"Señor," Jessie replied disconcertedly, "it is just that you look like someone I know."

"Jessica," Rodrigo's voice warned her.

"It is true, Rodrigo." He caught her double meaning, and she nodded at him. "But I have not forgotten our talk."

"Talking about me, eh?" Don Carlos sighed. "A disagreeable subject for young people to be discussing. You should be talking of gay things, of parties and — hasn't my nephew confessed his skills as a matador?"

"Ah, no, *señor,* he has not."

"Really, Rodrigo? You usually charm all your

new ladies with tales of your bravery."

Jessie reddened at the assumption.

"You are mistaken about Rodrigo and me. We have only just met."

"You are Nita's friend then?"

"No, I . . . my name is Jessica Summers. I was traveling —"

Jessie couldn't finish. How could she lie to him?"

"Traveling?" Don Carlos repeated. "On a tour through Europe perhaps? And now you are my guest? But this is wonderful. I am glad to know the hospitality of my house has been extended even though I could not extend it myself. And where is your home, *señorita?*"

"It is *señora,* and my home is in America."

"America. How delightful. You will have to visit me often, and we will speak English together. Mine has grown rusty, and I would like to test it."

"I will be glad to, *señor.*"

"*Señor, señor* — you must call me Carlos. And where is this lucky man who is your husband?"

"We, ah, became separated during our travels."

"But will he find you here?"

"I am certain of it, Don Carlos."

"Good, good. You must bring him up to meet me as soon as he arrives. And no nonsense from you, Rodrigo, about my being too ill to have visitors. I need the stimulation. Why, this lady's

324

company has done me a world of good."

Rodrigo smiled. "That is wonderful, Uncle, but you really should rest now."

"You are not listening to me, Rodrigo. Why don't you run along and leave me to converse with my guest? Have you not told her of my trips to America? She and I have much to talk about."

"Trips, Uncle? But you have only been to America once, when you were even younger than I am now."

"Nonsense," Don Carlos announced. "I returned ten years ago. But of course you wouldn't know that. It was after Francisco's funeral, and your mother immediately took you off with her to France."

"You sailed to America? Why?" Rodrigo asked.

"To search for someone."

"You didn't find her, did you?" Jessie asked quickly, before Rodrigo could stop her.

"No. That country of yours is much too big, my dear," Don Carlos replied sadly. He looked at her strangely.

Jessie saw the startled look that came over him and realized she had blundered. She'd assumed he had gone back to look for Mary, and she'd said "find her."

"I . . . I really should be going now, Don Carlos," Jessie said uncomfortably. "I couldn't forgive myself if I overtaxed you."

"You haven't, I assure you," he replied in

an unusually quiet voice. "But you will come again?"

"Yes, of course."

"Then I suppose I must let you go."

She took his hand, and he brought her fingers to his lips. All the while his eyes locked with hers so penetratingly that she felt he could read her every thought.

Don Carlos stopped her as she reached the door. And his English words, the first he had spoken and which she knew Rodrigo could not understand, made her catch her breath.

"One more thing, Jessica Summers. This man that I remind you of and my overcautious nephew would rather you not speak of, who is he?"

Jessie looked back at him. She thought she heard hope in his voice. Impossible. He couldn't have guessed, not by the little she had said. But she had come so far, and he had to know.

"He is my husband, Don Carlos."

"My God," he whispered brokenly. "Thank you."

Chapter 43

The sun was at its highest, and heavenly scents drifted through her open window with the heat from the garden. But Jessie did not appreciate the lovely day. She had spent a restless night thinking about Don Carlos. She suspected that she had done what she'd set out to do, she couldn't be sure. Oh, where was Chase?

As if she didn't have enough worries, she had felt the first stirrings of her baby last night, just the faintest flutterings, but enough to set her wondering about the next few months. Damn Chase, when would he get here?

Chase couldn't believe his luck. It had gone sour for a while after they'd had that bad storm at sea and been blown so far off course that they were nearly a week behind schedule. He'd made port in Málaga and found an interpreter who could also act as guide. Most promising was that the name Carlos Silvela was well known, through his shipping and banking concerns. It proved easy to find him, and now here he was.

But he was afraid his luck was about to turn again, for the beautiful blonde who had opened the door was looking at him as if he had two heads. Her mouth was open, but no words came out. He was about to call his guide when the lady finally spoke.

"So it's true!"

"I beg your pardon?" Chase replied. "I don't speak Spanish."

"*Dispense*. I . . . I speak English, but not so well. You come for . . . to see . . ."

"Carlos Silvela," Chase supplied. "My guide assured me this is the place. Is he here?"

"Slower, *señor*. Too fast for me."

"I'm sorry. I'm looking for Carlos —"

"*Sí, sí,*" she interrupted. "This I know. Your wife, she say you would come. I did not believe her story."

"My wife?" Chase frowned. "Ah, I think you are mistaking . . . let me get my guide."

"You are not Chase Summers?"

He had turned away, but he spun around again. "How could you know that?"

"It is as I say, *señor,* your wife is here."

"Impossible!"

Jessie had let it go on long enough. She stepped out from her hiding place just off the foyer.

"Not impossible, Chase."

Nita looked from Jessie to Chase, confusion overcoming her. "You see, *señor,* your wife. Now I leave you to her. Understanding your English has given me the aching head."

Jessie watched Nita leave the foyer. A thoroughly sour expression clouded the Spanish woman's lovely features. But she gave Nita no further thought, turning back to Chase and wondering why he was just standing there looking shocked.

"Have you a perfectly reasonable explanation for being here, or do I turn you over my knee and beat the living tar out of you for being the most irresponsible —"

"Don't you take that tone with me, Chase Summers!"

He started toward her, but she backed away.

"How dare you travel in your condition? Have you no thought for yourself or the child? What if something had gone wrong?" Then his tone changed. "Did something happen? Are you all right?"

"Do you really care?"

"Jessie!"

"I'm fine."

"What the hell are you doing here? I leave you safely with your mother —"

"Let's be more specific," Jessie fumed, always more comfortable attacking instead of defending. "You dumped me on my mother and then deserted me!"

"Deserted? Didn't Rachel tell you I'd be back before the baby was born?"

"She told me," Jessie said stiffly. "I didn't believe it, and I still don't. I haven't forgotten I told you you could go your own way. Damn you, you sure didn't waste any time leaving, did you?"

"Jessie, I'm this close to wringing your neck!"

"And I'm this close to socking you in the nose," she retorted. "But I doubt it would solve anything."

They glared at each other for several seconds. Then Chase's eyes softened and turned a velvety brown.

"Oh, Lord, I'm glad you're here," he said. "I've missed you, Jessie."

She was crushed in his arms, his lips molded to hers. He kissed her as if he were starving and she were his first taste of food. It didn't take a second for Jessie to return his kiss with equal fervor. She clung to him, digging her fingers into his back. How she had missed the taste of him, the feel of his arms! She had almost forgotten the way he could make her feel, how he could make her want him to the exclusion of everything else.

"You've missed me, too, sweetheart."

The words came from somewhere far away, muffled. He was nibbling at her neck.

"I haven't missed you," Jessie answered automatically.

Chase straightened, his eyes happy.

"If you'll recall, Jessie, one of the last times you said anything to me at all was in Cheyenne. You were nearly in tears because your mother wouldn't stay with you. So I thought you'd be delighted to spend some time with her. It was the perfect opportunity for me to get this part of my life settled. You couldn't travel, anyway. Or you shouldn't have."

"I'm not quarreling with your motives, Chase," Jessie said levelly. "I won't even say you could have waited until after the baby was born. You left me without telling me. You didn't discuss it with me."

"How could I, the way you were? There was no telling how long you would be in shock." He looked suspicious then. "When did you recover — as soon as I left?"

"As a matter of fact, yes."

"Thanks," he grumbled. "I suppose you'll be telling me my presence was what was keeping you in shock?"

"No, your leaving was what snapped me out of it," she admitted.

"So you missed me! You weren't pleased to find me gone?"

"Well . . . no," she admitted again.

"Then I feel sorry for Rachel. She must have had a hell of a time coping with your tantrums." He shook his head mournfully.

"Stop teasing me, Chase. I don't think it's at all funny. You had no right leaving me with my

331

mother. I'm not her responsibility, I'm yours. You wanted to marry me, and now you're stuck with me."

"You mean it, Jessie?"

His soft voice caught her off guard. "Of course I do."

"Well, I'm not complaining, sweetheart."

"You're not?"

He was grinning at her. "I like the idea of being stuck with you. Now, why don't you show me where our room is? We never did get around to sealing our marriage vows."

Jessie blushed.

"It's the third door down the hall," she said. "I can't tell you about your — about Don Carlos until we're alone."

Chapter 44

Jessie caught a lock of his hair and twirled it about her fingers, sighing in utter contentment. Chase lay on top of her, so still he might have been sleeping. But he wasn't.

Jessie giggled, remembering that time in the wagon. "I thought you never slept on your stomach."

"I'm not." Chase didn't move. "I'm sleeping on you."

"I know you're holding your weight back. You can't relax —"

"I'm doing just fine," he murmured.

"Come on, you can't sleep now, anyway. *Siesta* isn't for another hour or so. There's lunch first, and you have to meet your cousins and —"

He looked up at her, grinning. "You mean we get to come back up here today and no one will think anything of it?"

"Chase, you're terrible!"

"Am I? It's been forever since I've seen you."

"It's only been —"

"Forever." He kissed her to shut her up. Then he sat up, and his mood changed. She knew he'd been dying to ask, yet afraid to. She decided to help him.

"Aren't you going to ask about Don Carlos?"

He wouldn't look up. An interminable time passed without a response.

Finally he mumbled, "There's no hurry."

"I don't believe —"

"Leave it alone."

"But you've come so far!"

He looked at her, then looked away. "Jessie, it's been twenty years since my mother first told me about the man. That's a hell of a long time to wonder about someone. It's a long time to —" He paused. "Call me a coward, but I'd rather not hear it."

She couldn't let him falter, not after all this time.

"Chase," Jessie said gently. "Don Carlos has been ill for a long time, and now . . . now he's worse. They wouldn't even let me see him, afraid I would upset him."

"But he *is* alive? You're sure, Jessie?" He was gripping her shoulders.

"Yes, I'm sure. I got in to see him in spite of them."

"*Is* he dying, Jessie?"

"I don't know," she sighed. "They haven't actually said, but they treat him as if he were. Nita wears mourning clothes already. She's your cousin by the way, the one who answered the door."

"Never mind. Tell me."

"Well, he didn't seem to me like a man who was dying. His voice was strong. He's alert. He's just weak, and, well, maybe he just doesn't have any reason to live."

"Leave it to a woman to come up with a diagnosis like that," Chase said disagreeably.

"Well, it's possible. Anyway, I intended to tell him all about you, but Rodrigo —"

"Rodrigo?"

"Don Carlos had two sisters. Nita's mother is dead. Rodrigo is the child of the other sister. She's still alive, traveling now. Anyway, Rodrigo was with Don Carlos last night. He made me realize that such shocking news could do Don Carlos more harm than good."

"Has he so many children that one more would be too much of a burden to acknowledge?"

"Chase, he has no children. That's why I had to be so determined. I thought knowing about you would please him. But I couldn't tell him if the shock would make him worse."

"So he doesn't know? And now you're telling me I've come all this way for nothing because I shouldn't try to see him, either?"

She gave him a second, then announced, "If

he saw you, he would understand instantly. Why do you think Nita was so surprised when she saw you? You look just like him, Chase."

She watched his face as he took in the realization. If he looked just like Don Carlos, then Don Carlos truly was his father. He stood stock-still, staring into space. "So, one look at me and he drops dead from shock, eh?"

Jessie supposed it wouldn't hurt to tell him about her fanciful notion.

"Actually," she began hesitantly, "I mean, well . . . I can't be sure —"

"Damn it, when did this problem expressing yourself start? You've never had any trouble before."

"Don't go taking your temper out on me, Chase Summers! If you don't want to hear what I have to say, then I won't say any more."

He sat down on the bed again. "I'm sorry, Jessie. You have to understand —"

"I do," she interrupted. "And what I wanted to tell you was that your father might just have realized for himself what I couldn't bring myself to tell him. I can't be sure, mind you."

"How?" He was so bewildered, it hurt her to look at him.

"Well, I was amazed at the resemblance between you, and he saw my surprise. I admitted that he reminded me of someone I know. But" — she made herself recall all of it — "it wasn't only that. We were talking about America, and he mentioned that he had gone back

there ten years ago, looking for someone. I
don't know why I assumed it was your mother
he was looking for, but I did. I also assumed
he hadn't found her, and I said so. He looked
at me so strangely when I said 'her.' And then,
when I was about to leave, he asked me right
out who it was he reminded me of. I didn't
think it would hurt to admit it was my husband,
so I did. I think he thanked me then, but of
course I could easily have misunderstood. I was
across the room and could barely hear him."

"But it's possible he knows and *wasn't*
shocked at all!"

"Yes."

There was silence, and then Chase said,
"Let's go. Let's go see . . . my father."

Chapter 45

They hurried along for nothing. Don Carlos was sleeping. They got no more than a foot into his room before the old servant sitting guard just inside his door stopped them. Chase had no choice but to wait a little longer.

They joined their young hosts for lunch. Introductions were strained. Rather than use Jessie as interpreter, the two men chose to ignore each other. Nita, contrarily, wouldn't leave Chase alone. She fawned all over him, and what her halting English wouldn't convey, her eyes did. Jessie was disgusted.

She would have made nothing of it if Chase had been only politely tolerant, but he seemed to be basking in the blonde's overexuberance. No doubt he thought he'd made another conquest. And right before his wife's eyes.

Before the second course was served, Jessie left the table, mumbling some excuse. Chase caught up with her at the bottom of the stairs, an amused expression on his face.

"Not hungry anymore?"

"I've had my fill!"

He grinned. "I thought my little performance wouldn't escape your notice."

"Liar!" Jessie hissed. "If you expect me to believe that disgusting exhibition was for my benefit —"

"But of course it was. It's lunchtime, Jessie, and they have to feed Don Carlos. He'll be awake now."

"Oh, sure. You can't tell me you didn't enjoy Nita dribbling all over you. She'd like nothing better than to win you from me because she knows who you are. She's after your father's fortune, and you're a threat to the inheritance."

"Jealous, sweetheart?"

"Of that . . . that Spanish hussy? Don't flatter yourself. I was simply disgusted."

"Come on, Jessie. She's my cousin."

"That doesn't matter to her. But I warn you, Chase —"

"I know, I know," He cut her off with a teasing grin. "If I so much as look at another woman, you will shoot off some part of my anatomy. One that's quite dear to me. Correct?"

"Make light of it," she replied stiffly. "But that happens to be the reason I didn't want to marry you in the first place. You can't be *trusted* to be faithful."

"Give me a little more credit than that,

Jessie," he said seriously. "I never had reason to be faithful before. But I married you. I made the decision. And I happen to take this marriage seriously, even if you don't. It wasn't my idea to live separate lives. That was your idea. I was ready to settle down the moment we walked out of the church. Why do you think I stuck around after I was well enough to leave the ranch? I —"

"Señora Summers, Don Carlos is asking for you."

They both looked up. The old servant was at the top of the stairs, looking at them sternly.

Don Carlos was sitting in bed, a mountain of pillows propping him up. A half-empty tray of food was beside the bed. The servant came in only long enough to take out the tray. The curtains were open, Jessie was glad to see, and the room was flooded with light. She was glad Chase was waiting outside in the hallway. Seeing Chase without any warning might have shocked Don Carlos badly.

Jessie stepped to the foot of the bed, but Don Carlos motioned her closer. "I feared I had overtaxed you last night," she began.

"Nonsense." He smiled, putting her at ease. "I have not felt so good in months."

"I'm so glad."

"Your husband has come."

"They told you?"

"No one had to tell me, my dear. You have a glow about you."

Jessie was embarrassed. She was more likely glowing because she and Chase had been arguing. But she couldn't very well tell Don Carlos that.

"I, ah, suppose I am glad to see him," she hedged.

"You do not have to be shy with me. It is well that you love your husband. That is as it should be. What kind of man is he? I suppose I should not ask. Is he . . .?"

He let the sentence trail away and Jessie could see how nervous he was.

"So you know?" Jessie said simply.

"I have searched for my child for many years, Jessica. With no luck. I could only hope that the child would find me. Every stranger I meet, I hope. It was easy to hear what I wanted to hear in your words. I even thought it was you at first — until you said I reminded you of someone. You see, resemblance is strong in the male line of my family. I look like my father, my grandfather, and it has been the same for centuries. Eye and hair coloring change, but Silvela features remarkably appear in every generation."

Jessie smiled. "Now you've found your son — and you will also be a grandfather soon."

His eyes widened, and he reached for Jessie's hand. "Thank you, my dear. You have breathed life into me."

"Good, because you must recover, Don Carlos. I never knew my grandparents, and I want

341

my child to know his. But right now, Chase is waiting."

"It seems I have waited a lifetime to meet him. Bring him to me, please."

Jessie had only to smile at Chase, and he knew it was all right. Yet his feet dragged as he entered the room. He was afraid. It was the end of such a long road.

Jessie felt like an intruder as she watched them staring at each other, stupefied. "I will leave you two alone now."

"No!" Don Carlos stopped her. "It will be easier for us if you stay, please."

Jessie thanked heaven that Don Carlos spoke English so well. How awkward things would be otherwise.

"Don Carlos, this is my husband, Chase Summers. Chase —"

"That's not necessary, Jessie," Chase cut in nervously.

Don Carlos came straight to the point. "Your mother, she told you about me?" His voice quavered.

"Very little," Chase said coldly.

Jessie could have kicked him. What was wrong with him? He had been dying to get to Spain to meet the man, and now this cold attitude.

Don Carlos didn't know how to proceed. Did the young man hate him?

"I think perhaps we would do well to get questions out of the way," Don Carlos suggested gently. "You must have much you wish to ask me, and I have many questions of my own."

"You mean you're actually interested in me?"

"Chase!" Jessie gasped.

His sarcasm was ignored by Don Carlos. "This man Summers. Was he good to you?"

"Her married name was Ewing actually. There was no Summers. She didn't marry Ewing until I was ten. She called herself the widow Summers for the first ten years of my life because she had to hide her shame. She wasn't a woman who could deal with shame very well."

"No, Mary Beckett wouldn't have," Don Carlos said sadly.

"Was that her name?" Chase cried.

"You mean she never told you her name?"

"The most she would tell me about herself was that she came from New York. She never talked of her past. She was very bitter."

"And so are you, I see," Don Carlos replied softly. "I cannot fault you for this. I have been filled with bitterness myself these many years since my uncle died and I learned all of what he kept from me."

"You're saying you didn't know she was pregnant?" Chase asked, disbelief clear in his manner.

"My boy, it is much worse than that. For seventeen years I thought your mother had only toyed with my affections to amuse herself. I did not know of my Uncle Francisco's machinations

343

until ten years ago when he lay dying and was determined to confess the wrong he had done me.

"You see, I had every intention of marrying Mary Beckett, but I had not asked her because I felt it was my duty to explain my intentions to my uncle first. He was my guardian while I was in America, so that was proper."

"And he refused?"

"No. He was not happy about it, but he did not refuse. What he did do, that I was unaware of, was keep me from seeing Mary. He kept me busy at the hacienda with one thing after another so I could not go to see her. And when she came to see me, he told her I was unavailable and he never told me she had been there. He thought that I was too young to know what was good for me. He believed that simply keeping us apart was all that was necessary, that the young quickly forget."

"But he was told about her condition. She told me that she and her father went to see him, that her father demanded you marry her."

"Yes, that is true. And my uncle was so surprised and shaken by the news that he told them the first thing that came to mind, that I had already returned to Spain, that marriage with an *americana* was unsuitable at any rate, that I was already promised to another and was returning to Spain to marry this fictitious *novia*."

"But surely you tried to see her?"

"I thought it would be weeks before she sailed. All this took place in only a matter of days, you see. I was not worried about the loss of a few days helping my uncle. I would have the rest of my life with Mary. But in fact her father was so furious with my uncle that he sailed that very night after their meeting. When I learned that their ship had gone, I did not understand. I was ready to follow her to New York on the next ship.

"Then my uncle furthered his lies by telling me he had seen Mary with another man and had confronted her for my sake. He had let it slip that I meant to marry her. And here he used the same lie he told her father, telling me that she laughed at him, saying she would never marry a foreigner, that she was already engaged and just having some fun before she had to settle down. The ship was gone, and I made the mistake of believing my uncle. He was my father's brother, and I had always been close to him since he had no children of his own. I never dreamed he would lie to me. It never occurred to me. I was so despondent after that, he made arrangements to send me home, not knowing what else to do with me. Once I got home, I let my mother marry me to the first girl she found suitable. I just didn't care."

"But why did your uncle interfere, for God's sake?"

"Uncle Francisco took his guardianship too seriously. He felt that he was doing the right thing, that I really was too young to make such an important decision. He also feared that my mother would not approve. He had written her about it to ask her guidance, but of course everything happened so quickly. He panicked when he was confronted with Mary's pregnancy. He resorted to lies because he didn't really know what to do."

"You defend him?" Chase asked angrily.

"No," Don Carlos replied. "I damned him myself when he told me and could not give him the forgiveness he begged for before he died. But I do understand better now. And he did try to make amends. You see, his great guilt was that my marriage had produced no children, none that lived. Yet he knew I must have a child somewhere in America. So he left his entire fortune at my disposal to find that child. I have spent nearly half of it doing just that, but with no luck. Now that you are found, his last instructions can be fulfilled. The rest of his wealth was to be given to you. It is yours."

"No it's not," Chase said automatically. "I'll be damned if I'll take any of his money."

"But you must take it," Don Carlos said. "It was left to the child of Mary Beckett. There is still a considerable amount left, and I also have much to make up for."

"No! I didn't come here looking for money from you and certainly not from your uncle."

"You've made that quite clear, Chase," Jessie interjected, angry at his obstinacy. "But

346

we'll take the money, Don Carlos."

"Like hell we will!"

"*I* certainly will. I'm not pigheaded enough to throw away money."

"I can support you, Jessie."

"Yes, well, we can talk about that later," she said evasively, sorry she'd opened her mouth. "I think I'll take my leave now, Chase, since you've broken the ice so nicely."

Jessie couldn't get out of that room fast enough. She regretted her sarcasm but wondered why Chase couldn't be a little bit gracious. Remembering how she'd treated her mother, she pushed the thought aside. She returned to her own room and paced the floor nervously.

The knock at the door startled Jessie, but she sighed when she saw it was Rodrigo. "I thought you were my husband."

"And you do not wish to see him?"

"How did —? It's just that we had a little argument."

Rodrigo stepped forward into the room. "You do not have to explain. I could not help but overhear you on the stairs."

"Oh." She had forgotten about *that* argument already.

"I did not understand the words, but the tone was unmistakable."

Jessie flushed. "Did Nita overhear, too?"

"No, I don't think so. But you must not be embarrassed that I know. I could not be more delighted."

He reached for her hand, but Jessie stepped back, frowning. "Delighted? I think we are having a problem with translation here. And I thought my Spanish was so good."

Rodrigo shook his head, smiling at her. "You may think me callous, but I am glad to know all is not well between you and your husband. I wish I had confessed my feelings to you before now. I would not have had to hide them these last few days."

"Rodrigo, what exactly do you mean?"

He smiled. "I knew I loved you from the first day I saw you."

Jessie gasped. "But you can't love me. I just got here, and you barely know me."

"What does time mean where the heart is concerned?"

Jessie very nearly laughed, but stopped herself in time.

"Rodrigo, you are very sweet, but I cannot take this seriously. I'm sure you don't, either."

"You doubt me?" He did not appear wounded, only determined. "I have dreamed of being able to bare my soul to you. I have dreamed . . ."

He gathered her into his arms. His kiss was startling, neither welcome nor unpleasant. Jessie's only thought was, I'm married now — no one can kiss me but Chase. It was disquieting that she should think only of Chase when another man was kissing her, quite a handsome man, too.

She turned her head to the side, ready to

admonish Rodrigo. The words stuck in her throat. She faced the door, and Chase was standing there. She had never seen him looking so forbidding.

"That is what I have dreamed of doing, my love," Rodrigo was saying, blissfully unaware of Chase. "This and so much more. When we are married."

"Rodrigo, stop it!" Jessie shoved him back and looked away from Chase to glare at Rodrigo. "You assumed far too much from overhearing a little argument. I have a husband. And now I have to explain this to him."

"You will tell him? But that is wonderful!"

"I have no intention of leaving him," Jessie said curtly, "but I will have to explain your actions. You see, he happens to be standing behind you right now."

Rodrigo whirled around. His color rose. Jessie was grateful that Chase didn't understand Spanish. She could make light of the situation because he hadn't understood Rodrigo's declaration.

"Just go, Rodrigo," Jessie sighed. "I believe there is going to be another argument here."

Rodrigo reluctantly did as she asked. But he could not look Chase in the eyes and cautiously moved around him. What could he say to him? A fine meeting for cousins!

"Why don't you close the door?" Jessie suggested nervously when after an intolerable lapse of time, Chase had not moved an inch.

He closed the door very slowly, then walked into the room. "Correct me if I'm wrong, but didn't you give me some dire warnings earlier about improper behavior?"

"You don't understand, Chase," she said hurriedly.

"Yes, I understand. It's quite clear. I am the only one forbidden the slightest indiscretion. You on the other hand are free to make a mockery of our wedding vows whenever it suits you."

"I am not," she replied indignantly. "And I haven't. Damn it, will you let me explain?"

"By all means," he said tightly. "This ought to be interesting."

Jessie raised her chin stubbornly. "If you're going to take that attitude —"

"Jessie, if you'd rather I let loose what I'm really feeling —"

"No! I mean, you haven't got a single reason to be angry." Her hand went nervously to her throat. "It's not as if I welcomed Rodrigo's embrace. He just got carried away."

"And of course you didn't encourage him."

"Damn it, he thinks he loves me. I was as surprised as you are."

"Surprised isn't what I am, Jessie," Chase returned coldly.

"What was I supposed to do?" she demanded angrily. "He heard us arguing and assumed all was not well. He wouldn't have spoken other- wise. He had only just declared his feelings and kissed me to prove his sincerity when you walked in. I didn't take him seriously. But I did explain to him that he was mistaken in his assumption about us, Chase."

"Did you? What would you have fold him if I hadn't walked in, Jessie?"

"How dare you!"

"How?" Chase exploded then. "I'll tell you how! Every damn time I turn my head you've got another lovesick gallant falling at your feet. First a cowpoke who takes revenge on you for your rejection. Then a Sioux warrior who would happily kill for you. A Cheyenne brave who would die to protect you. Now my cousin falls under your spell. How long was this going on before I arrived, Jessie?"

"You bastard!" Jessie stormed. "If you're angry over what happened in Don Carlos's room then say so, but don't use this as an excuse to pick a fight with me."

"I'll get to that another time."

"No, you won't," Jessie said icily. "I don't need this kind of treatment, not in my condition. Get out of here. Find yourself another room," she added stiffly. "This one is taken."

Chapter 46

Rodrigo drew up the carriage and unhitched the horses they had brought with them for the rest of the journey. Jessie had the gentlest mare in Don Carlos's stable, while Rodrigo mounted one of Don Carlos's magnificent white Spanish-Arabians. How Jessie missed her beloved Blackstar, waiting for her with Goldenrod back in Chicago. But she wasn't put out over having been given a tame horse. She knew she shouldn't be sitting a horse at all, even side-saddle and heavily cushioned as she was. She shouldn't even have left the house, for that matter, but the way things had been between her and Chase meant she needed time away from him.

So she was on her way to Ronda to watch Rodrigo dazzle a large audience with his bull-fighting skills. It wouldn't have been so bad if the only road to Ronda hadn't been an old mule path, inaccessible by carriage. It must have been fine for the legendary Andalusian bandits who made Ronda their final stronghold in the last great rising of the Moors against Ferdinand and Isabella. One narrow path was easy to guard. But it was a damnably difficult crossing for a heavily pregnant woman.

Jessie had been to Ronda several times already with Rodrigo and Nita over the last months, but she was just as awed as she'd been the first time she saw the town perched high above a rocky cleft that plunged three hundred feet deep. The cleft was spanned by three bridges. She had been terrified crossing the Puente Nuevo, the highest bridge, looking down at the gorge dividing the town. Far below were the other two bridges, both built on ancient Roman foundations.

In the older section of the town one could see gypsies in the streets and watch them dance the fiery and passionate flamenco. Nita proudly claimed that she could dance better than the gypsies did.

Don Carlos's dying was never mentioned anymore. He had improved with each day since Chase's arrival, and he left his room once or twice every day, swearing to become his old self again very soon. There was already talk of traveling, even of his returning to America with Chase and Jessie.

Chase was delighted. He was getting closer and closer to his father. In fact, the only time Jessie saw Chase act like his old self was when he was with Don Carlos. At all other times, he was coldly unapproachable.

She was beginning to think Chase never would forgive her for what had happened between her and Rodrigo. He paid no attention to her explanation. They were strangers now, it seemed. She had opened the subject several times, but he always left the room when she did. He plainly wanted nothing more to do with her.

These last months had been intolerable. In her loneliness, she'd spent more and more time with Rodrigo and even Nita. Rodrigo had never confessed his love again, but he was always attentive, always eager to please her.

So there she was in Ronda. She knew she had no business traveling, not that close to her delivery. Rodrigo thought it was perfectly safe, of course, because he was with her.

The heavy perfume of orange blossoms assailed them as they passed the gardens of Paseo de la Merced in Mercadillo, the newer section of Ronda — newer by only a few centuries. The bullring was in that part of town. Truth to tell, Jessie would rather have been in bed resting. But Rodrigo had told her so much about bullfighting and about his own skill that she'd had no heart to refuse him.

She recalled the three elements critics looked for in judging bullfighters. The style of the matador was one. It meant standing straight, firmly planted, unyielding, and bringing the bull past him with a grace that gave no ground. Mastery of the bull, controlling the animal's every move and spinning him around at will, was the second element. The third was performing the maneuvers as slowly as possible, for the longer the time of dangerous closeness lasted, the more opportunities the bull had to change his tactics and test the matador.

Rodrigo left her alone in the stands and went to dress. She did not see him again until the opening parade across the ring, which involved all the participants in the spectacle. There were two matadors besides Rodrigo, and they all looked grand in their tight-fitting silken hose, knee-length pants, and brilliantly jeweled jackets. Most of the crowd was gaily dressed as well, the exceptionally warm weather allowing the women to wear sleeveless blouses. They wore flounced, colorful skirts, and their hair was rolled up under high combs and mantillas. But the Moorish influence was not entirely lost. Some women covered their heads and the lower half of their faces with embroidered linen, and their dresses were much more somber.

After the parade, the first bull was released and the maneuvers around him began. Then Rodrigo came out, the first matador to demonstrate his skill with the cape, and the tension increased palpably. For a while Jessie forgot her nagging backache and the overall discomfort the last week had brought her. She watched as he went through a series of passes, playing with the bull, testing the huge animal and she joined in the roar of "olé!" as the crowd cheered Rodrigo.

On her fourth "olé," a sharp cramp made Jessie double over. There was so much more to see, the entrance of the picadors with their lances, more passes by the matador, the planting of the banderillas in the bull's shoulders, then the final playing of the bull and the killing. But Jessie was going to miss all of it. She hoped she was mistaken but another cramp dispelled that hope.

She had to get out of here before the crowd dispersed and knocked against her. It wasn't easy going, having to stop every few minutes to let a cramp pass then continue slowly. She felt like a huge cow.

She didn't know where the hell she was going or what she was going to do when she got there. Why wasn't Chase there to help her? He should have offered to come along. This was his baby, damn it. He should be there to take charge, to scold, to say he had told her not to make the journey, to tell her she would be all right. Where was he? Did he really hate her?"

"Señora Summers!

Jessie turned slowly, relief washing over her at the sight of Magdalena Carrasco, a woman she had met in Ronda, an old friend of Don Carlos's. Magdalena had only to look once at Jessie's pale, cramped expression to know what was happening.

"Where is your husband, Jessica?"

"He didn't come today," Jessie panted.

"And you should not have come either, *¡Por Dios!*"

Jessie nodded guiltily. "How will I get home?" She asked meekly.

"Home? Nonsense! It is too late for that. You will come with me, and I will see you settled in my house."

"But . . . my husband?"

"He will be sent for," Magdalena assured her firmly. "You have nothing more to concern yourself with."

Jessie was more than glad to let Magdalena take charge. She had enough to worry about.

Chapter 47

Jessie was losing track of time. The pain was so bad she could hardly keep from crying out. The constant waiting and hurting was taking a terrible toll. She couldn't remember ever being so exhausted, yet Magdalena kept saying, "Relax, it will not be for some time yet."

And then she thought she was dreaming. Chase was there. "I could wring your neck, you know?" His soft tone belied the words.

"I've heard that before."

"This time you've gone too far, Jessie." Anxiety marked his face.

"How was I supposed to know?" she retorted guiltily. "If you've come just to holler at me, you can —"

She had to stop. This time, just to spite him, when the pain was at its peak she let out a scream. She was satisfied to see Chase lose every bit of his coloring. Maybe now he wouldn't snap at her for being such a fool. *She knew she'd been a fool.*

"Jessie, for God's sake, you need a doctor!" he whispered urgently.

"I've seen a doctor," Jessie said tiredly, "and Magdalena is in the next room."

"Where is the doctor?"

"He'll be back."

"But he should be here now!"

"To do what? He can't help me, not until later. I have a long wait yet, they tell me."

"Christ!"

"I don't see what you're getting upset about. I thought you knew more about this than I did."

"Not about the actual — are you all right? Can I get you something?"

She wanted to laugh.

"Well . . . there is something I —"

"Anything, Jessie, anything."

"There is something you can clarify for me." She had to wait for another pain to pass before continuing. "I . . . have such vague memories of everything that happened after the ranch burned. Did you . . . did you bring Kate to me somewhere?"

"Yes, at the hotel the morning before we left Cheyenne. I found her in one of the saloons. She didn't want to face you, but I thought seeing her might bring you out of your shock. It didn't."

"Did I forgive Kate? What did we talk about? Were you right?"

He nodded. "If the woman felt no remorse all these years, I think she does now. If you ask me, that's very little price she's paying for what her silence did to you and Rachel. And you didn't talk to her at all, just stared at her, then turned away."

Jessie groaned. The pains were getting closer and more intense.

"What happened to Jeb and my men?"

"Jeb said he'd see to letting the others go, but he'd stick around and round up whatever cattle remained. I told him to keep whatever he found. Rachel paid off your debt as a wedding gift, so you owed no one. I didn't think you'd mind letting Jeb do whatever he liked with the strays."

"No, of course not. I'm glad. That was very thoughtful of you."

"He earned it, Jessie."

"Yes, he sure did. Oh! What about the sheriff?"

"I left descriptions and reward money for Clee, Charlie, and Blue Parker."

"What about Laton Bowdre?"

"I couldn't charge him with anything."

"What?"

"Jessie, Bowdre left town the day before the fire, so he couldn't be implicated. The man is smart. But maybe not quite smart enough."

"Chase, tell me what —"

"Your recognizing his hirelings could be his downfall. I talked it out with the sheriff, and he agreed that if he caught any of the three, he would let them go if they volunteered the name of the man who hired them. Clee and Charlie may think loyalty comes first, but I doubt Parker will feel that way. It's just a matter of finding at least one of them."

"Do you think there's any hope of finding them?" she asked anxiously.

"We can always up the reward later," Chase said.

"With what?" she said sharply. "You're not exactly rich, you know. And I'm wiped out."

"Well," he reminded her, "I did inherit a sizable sum when we found my father."

"You're going to keep it?" she asked, surprised.

"I'd be three kinds of a fool to let a bad mood decide the matter. Besides —"

Jessie had tried to hold it in, but this time she couldn't. The scream sounded horrible even to her. Chase panicked, thinking something had gone wrong. He gripped her hand.

"Jessie, you can't die, you can't! I love you! If you die, so help me —"

"You'll wring my neck?" Jessie said weakly. She looked at him for a long time. "Love me?" she said softly. "You have a fine way of showing it, the way you've treated me lately."

"I was jealous," he said simply. "Damn it, I've never been jealous of anything or anybody before in my life, and now all of a sudden . . . I didn't know how to handle it, Jessie. I wanted to scream at you, but I wanted to love you, too. I wanted to fight for you, but I held all the feelings in, afraid I might upset you too much. Believe me, Jessie, if you weren't pregnant, we would have had this out long ago. I've never been more miserable in my life than these last months, being near you but unable to touch you, and afraid to speak my mind. And you kept encouraging Rodrigo —"

"I did not," she interrupted tartly. Then her voice softened. "Rodrigo is sweet and entertaining, but he . . . he's not you, Chase. I felt nothing at all when he kissed me that one time. I guess just any man won't do for me."

Before Chase could reply, Jessie cried out again. Magdalena came in to say that she'd sent for the doctor. She tried to get Chase to leave, but he wouldn't budge. It wasn't proper, and she left shaking her head.

Jessie relaxed and gave Chase a reassuring smile. "She's right. You'd better leave. It's bad enough that I have to listen to myself yell, but you shouldn't have to."

"Don't be absurd."

"No, I really would feel better if I didn't have to worry about you fainting."

"It's nothing to joke about, Jessie!"

"I'm sorry, Chase. Would you wait outside, please? I just don't want you to see me like this."

He couldn't refuse such an earnest request, but he left very slowly, his face a mask of worry, looking back at the bed with every step.

"Chase." Jessie caught him as he was going out the door. "I love you, too."

Chapter 48

"Pedro?" Jessie exclaimed. "Did she really name you Pedro?"

"Surprised?" Chase grinned.

"But I would have thought she'd scorn anything Spanish."

"Actually, I think my mother enjoyed feeling sorry for herself."

"But why did you change the name?"

"With my dark hair and a name like that, I was marked a foreigner in Chicago. Kids can be pretty tough on foreigners. I was fighting every damn day, it seemed. So I changed the name — and dared anyone to remember the name Pedro."

"But it's a nice name, Pedro." She grinned.

"You start calling me Pedro, and I'll start calling you Kenneth."

"That's not funny!" Jessie cried.

"I didn't think so, either."

They laughed together and snuggled closer on the divan. In the next room, two-month-old Charles slept. A son who looked like his father and his grandfather. Both men were bursting with pride. Jessie liked to think it wasn't only pride that lit up Chase's eyes when he looked at his son. Perhaps it was happiness, too. Contentment. Certainly love. He did love that boy. And in the last two months, she had felt as secure in his love as Charles did.

Love wasn't the fairy tale she'd once thought it was. Love was real and wonderful, and she gloried in it. Love was the heart of happiness, and Jessie had found her happiness in her husband and child.

Jessie kissed Chase on the cheek, and he turned his head, capturing her lips. She sighed as his hand caressed her back. She had learned to control her impetuous passion some of the time, for there was much to be said for anticipation. But a fiery union also had its merits. She looked over at the bed and sighed. It was still early.

"Have you given any more thought to what we're going to do when we get back to America?" Jessie asked.

"I thought maybe we'd visit your mother for a while. I think Rachel will like my father."

"Matchmaking, are you?"

"I have no intention of messing with anyone's life except my own."

"You've done a pretty good job there." Jessie

smiled. "We can't stay with my mother forever, though."

"Do you have something in mind?" he asked.

"I would like to start my ranch again. If you're willing," she said.

"But, Jessie, we can buy a house somewhere and raise our son. You don't have to work."

"And I can get lazy and fat and die of boredom, too," Jessie came back saucily. "I want a ranch, Chase. Don't dismiss the idea."

"Dismiss it?" He laughed. "As if you'd let me. Oh, Lord, I never dreamed I'd end up a rancher."

"You mean it?" she asked excitedly.

"Yes," he sighed. "But if it's to be ranching, then we'll do it right this time. Never mind the nonsense about just making ends meet. And I hope you don't have your heart set on settling in Wyoming. Wouldn't you rather start a new ranch someplace where it's a little warmer? Texas or Arizona?"

"No," she said firmly. "Winter might be a little cold in Wyoming —"

"A little!"

She grinned. "There are ways to get warm, ways that can be fun."

"Will you teach me all of them?"

"If you ask me nicely."

"Tease."

"Charmer."

"I love you, sweetheart."

167282

DATE DUE

SS-167282   L-T

Lindsey, Johanna
Brave the Wild Wind

DEMCO